THE CURSED TREASURE

The Adventures of Captain Hunt

Gabriel Rabanales

CONTENTS

Title Page
1. Cibola — 1
2. New York — 31
3. Little Italy — 52
4. Mount Sinai Hospital — 72
5. Bowery — 94
6. Manhattan — 117
7. New Mexico — 136
8. Under the cliff — 161
9. California Limited — 183
10. Sangre de Cristo — 203
11. Great house — 226
12. The camp — 246
13. Waldorf-Astoria — 262
14. Public library — 287
15. Manhattan Bridge — 307
16. British Consulate — 328

17. Woolworth Building	344
18. Top of the world	364

1. CIBOLA

The conquistador Don Rodrigo González de Salamanca y Armas took off his morion, wiped with his hands the blood that had splattered on his doublet and then plunged his sword into that hard and parched earth. Under the inclement sun that shone brightly on the plain, he knelt in front of the sword to raise a prayer for victory over those barbarous Indians. He thanked Almighty God for having enabled him to reach his destination at last, for having defeated the fierce defenders of the village, and for having survived to find at last that coveted goal, in the pursuit of which hundreds of brave and determined men had perished.

The terrain around him was barren and desolate. Only a few cacti and a few parched shrubs interrupted the monotonous and stony landscape. The heat was suffocating. Salamanca wiped away the sweat that bathed his face and continued praying. Fray Antonio, who was blessing the men and giving the last rites to the dying, approached the conquistador. The hilt of the sword cast a cross-shaped shadow on Salamanca's face. Fray Antonio shuddered with emotion. He raised his right hand and with a gesture crossed the conquistador.

"Our Lord has blessed you, captain."

"Amen," Salamanca said.

He rose and girded his sword to his belt again.

"Did you find the treasure, Father Antonio?"

The Franciscan friar nodded solemnly. He was a middle-aged man, with a lean appearance and a stern face, sweating profusely under his thick brown cassock.

"By the grace of God, my son." He pointed a finger at the village. "The treasure is located in that circular chamber that juts out there, in the middle of the other structures."

About twenty paces further on stood a complex of structures made of rock and mud brick, several stories high. They were located in a hollow in the land that hid them from the view of any traveler who approached the village, until it was almost above the houses. The complex had a semicircular configuration and stretched from one end to the other about one hundred and fifty paces. In the center of the housing complex there was an open square and next to it, half-sunk in the earth, was a circular chamber about fifteen paces in diameter.

"Ramírez!" Salamanca called.

His lieutenant, a vigorous young man of

twenty-five, came running. His clothes and his sword, which he still held in his hand, were covered in dried blood and sand. Ramírez had personally killed more than ten Indians, including men, women, and children.

"Organize the men to get the treasure out of that chamber immediately," Salamanca ordered. "It should be all loaded on the horses before nightfall."

"Yes, my captain!"

While his men got down to work, Salamanca looked around. He told himself that he would never have found that place by himself. Now that he was there, he understood perfectly well that Coronado's expedition, carried out twenty years before, had failed in the same objective. Although the accounts of Fray Marcos de Niza had been inaccurate, and his findings very exaggerated, the truth was that Coronado had been quite close to finding the cities of gold. However, the Indians had hidden them well and knew how to confuse the Spanish explorers so that they would not find them.

Salamanca, on the other hand, had had unexpected help. A few weeks before he had passed through another of those rocky villages, where he had set up camp to rest and replenish his provisions. There they had shown him the way to reach the mythical Cibola. The cost of that information had been high. He was about to reject the offer. However, his ambition and courage made him change his mind at the last minute. Once his transaction was completed, he immediately embarked on the last stage of his journey. He was still unclear about what exactly had made him reconsider, but he had certainly been right. No doubt God himself had led him there through his mysterious paths.

He made his way through the corpses of the Indians strewn on the ground, swollen in the sun, and covered with flies, until he reached the thick perimeter wall of the town. Once again he was surprised by the advanced architecture of that place. Further south, the Indians lived in tent camps or in simple adobe huts. In this place, on the other hand, the houses were solid and efficiently designed. The various levels of the structures were connected through wooden stairs and stone ramps. Those circular chambers, of which there were several scattered around the village, had skylights and ventilation systems.

Salamanca went in through one of the entrances to the village. He crossed several rooms with high ceilings, connected to each other by perfectly aligned portals that allowed the entire extension of the complex to be seen, from one end to the other. It was not surprising that such a place was considered special, or even magical, by those people. The natives' utensils were made of precious metals and all of them wore jewel-studded ornaments. Or, rather, they had been worn. Salamanca's men had stripped all the fallen bodies as soon as the brief, but intense, battle ended. None of the natives had survived, and now their jewels adorned the necks and clothes of the soldiers in lots.

In the central square there were a handful of men who were accumulating the loot of what they had plundered in the village. The pile of objects was taller than the men standing next to it. Salamanca observed as he passed by that the vessels, ornaments, and even the weapons of those Indians were made of gold and precious stones. The conquistador felt a shudder as he made his way toward the great central chamber. There was what he had come to look for in that remote land. The treasure of the city of gold. The treasure of Cibola.

The roof of the chamber protruded about four feet above ground level. Near the edge of the roof, a wooden staircase peeked out of a square entrance whose sides were a little more than two feet long. Trembling with emotion, Salamanca entered through the narrow opening, descending the thick steps until he reached the floor of the chamber. The interior was dimly lit by oblique rays of light that entered through the small windows at the top of the circular wall. Below the windows, a stone bench ran along the entire edge of the wall.

In the center of the room rose two columns that supported the roof, separated by about ten steps. Next to one of the columns was a small pit dug into the ground, in which burning logs were rapidly consuming. Smoke from the fire escaped through an opening in the ceiling, located just above the well. On either side of the bonfire, two soldiers stood guard with their spears firmly resting on the ground in front of them. They hardly noticed the presence of Salamanca. His eyes were fixed on a vault that was embedded in the floor between the two columns. The receptacle, which was more than five paces long and two wide, was overflowing with all manner of gold objects that glittered brightly under the rays of light that converged in the center of the room.

The pieces were piled up in any way inside the vault, as if they had been thrown in there a short time ago. Which was probably what had happened when the town's sentinels spotted the invaders approaching at a gallop on those animals they called "giant deer." The mound of objects stood about three feet above the edge of the vault. It was composed of hundreds of bracelets, necklaces, vessels, ornaments, jewelry, and other utensils that the natives used in their daily lives.

In the other villages inhabited by those Indians that Salamanca had visited, he only saw clay utensils and wooden tools. In Cibola, on the other hand, everything seemed to be made of gold encrusted with precious stones. What had been revealed to him in the previous village had turned out to be true. Until that moment, Salamanca had serious doubts about what he had been told. It was too fabulous to be true. But there was the greatest treasure in northern Mexico. The conquistador stared at that fortune for what seemed to him an eternity.

Rodrigo de Salamanca had come to the New World as part of the entourage of the new viceroy, Don Luis de Velasco, of whom he was a distant relative. From the beginning he had stood out in the service of the new ruler. Thanks to his loyalty and cunning, he rose rapidly under the command of the viceroy. Soon after, Velasco appointed him in charge of several provinces in the north of the extensive colony, in the region that the Spaniards called Nueva Vizcaya. While the new position allowed him to prosper, he was still an employee of the governor's office. His fortune was small compared to the large landowners and nobles who were getting rich in the new colony.

Salamanca had always been fascinated by the story of his predecessor in that adventure, Francisco Vásquez de Coronado. Two decades ago, and for two years, Coronado led a large expedition to the lands located north of Nueva España, attracted by the legends of the Seven Cities of Gold, settlements of fabulous wealth that supposedly were located in the mountains of the unexplored region. During the time that the expedition lasted, Coronado traveled through a large part of that territory and visited dozens of native towns. However, the trip turned out to be an absolute failure that led to his ruin. He never managed to find gold or any city of legend and had to face the attack of countless parties of savages, whom he ferociously exterminated. To make matters worse, on his return to Nueva España the accounts of his atrocities had preceded him and the Audiencia tried him for war crimes. Although he was acquitted, he ended his days in poverty.

Salamanca had read several chronicles and accounts of that expedition. He was convinced that the legends were true, but he believed that Coronado had made several mistakes. Eventually, he decided to set out on his own quest for the city of gold. After months of preparation gathering supplies and followers, in which he spent a good part of his patrimony, he managed to get the viceroy to grant him authorization to travel to the lands that Coronado had visited. But Salamanca was not willing to repeat the mistakes of its predecessor. This time he would bring a smaller group of followers, better prepared and equipped. In addition, the expedition would head directly towards the most likely place where the mythical Cibola was located.

And there he was now, after six months of travel. Several men had perished on the way, as a result of diseases and skirmishes with the

Indians, but the group still had about forty brave and well-armed men. And each of them had a horse, as well as several pack mules. Salamanca planned to take all the treasure hidden in the village. He had not gone so far or spent so much money as to abandon even the smallest piece of the find. But now he doubted whether the saddlebags of the horses would be sufficient to carry such a vast fortune.

While his soldiers were moving the pieces outside the town, to fill the saddlebags and some cloth sacks, the conquistador imagined entering Mexico City on the back of a magnificent steed, dressed in exquisite newly made clothes, at the head of several carriages loaded with gold articles. The viceroy himself, Don Luis de Velasco, would receive him in the main square and then the archbishop would bless him in the cathedral. The noble and wealthy colonists would receive him as an equal. His family would be welcomed in the most luxurious salons in the city. If one day he returned to the Motherland, even the king and queen themselves would grant him an audience.

Engrossed, the conquistador left the village and approached his horse to drink water from a leather boot. The heat was getting hotter. Over the houses, vultures circled and squawked menacingly. The stench of the corpses was unbearable.

"Ramirez!" The lieutenant approached

immediately. "Pile the bodies of the savages about fifty paces from the village and set them on fire."

Ramirez recruited some men to do the unpleasant work. All the others were busy filling their saddlebags with shiny golden pieces. Suddenly, two soldiers began to shout and immediately faced each other with pushes and blows. Salamanca had expressly forbidden the theft of the most insignificant object found in the village. He would be the one to distribute the booty, according to rank and privileges. Of course, he did not intend to give the soldiers more than some trinkets of little value. That treasure would be his and no one else's. Even the king's fifth, the percentage of tax charged by the Crown for any find, he planned to hide by reducing the inventory of what was found.

Fray Antonio tried to separate the two men, who were already engaged in a tough fight. But none of them paid attention to him and they continued to throw punches and kicks at each other. Salamanca cursed in a low voice and went towards them to put an end to this foolishness. He imposed iron discipline among his men and would not tolerate any insubordination.

"What the hell is going on here!"

"He's a thief!" one of the men shouted, still struggling with the other.

"It's mine!" The second man replied.

Salamanca remembered their names. He

didn't know many of them before embarking on the trip, but after six months he was able to identify them.

"Sánchez! Pérez! Stop it!"

The soldiers were enraged. At every moment the fight became bloodier. Salamanca watched them in amazement. How could they not obey him? It was intolerable. He took a step towards them, but they still didn't stop. Both muttered 'it's mine!' while still hitting each other. Only then did Salamanca discover that they were disputing an object that they were both furiously holding. None of them tried to let it go, which prevented them from greater freedom of movement. Such was the greed that these men showed that the conquistador understood that, if one of them managed to keep the object, the other would kill him instantly.

"Give me the piece right now, damn it!"

A crowd of soldiers had gathered to watch the brawl, forming a circle around the fighters. Salamanca could not allow the matter to slip out of his hands. He drew his sword from his belt, lunged at the men, and slashed between them. Sánchez got the worst of it. The sharp blade cleanly cut through his abdomen. A stream of blood splashed Pérez. The injured man fell to the ground, holding his guts with both hands. He let out a few death rattles and then died. Pérez laughed as a madman.

"It's mine! It's mine!"

He lifted the object with a raised fist. He looked at his companion's corpse and spat it out. The sword whistled in the air. The soldier's head separated from his body and rolled away. Several of the spectators turned away, disgusted. Salamanca took the object from the lifeless fist and showed it to his men.

"The treasure has only one owner, sons of bitches! Get back to work!"

While the men dispersed in terror, Salamanca carefully observed the cause of so much fury. It was a simple-looking, but strangely captivating, medallion. Like the other artifacts in the treasure, it was made of solid gold. It was round, half a palm in diameter, and had a turquoise embedded in the center. Around the precious stone was engraved inscriptions that the conquistador could not decipher. A thick chain, also made of gold, held the medallion by a ring fastened to the edge. Despite its rustic and unelaborate appearance, Salamanca could not take his eyes off the object.

Without realizing it, he stood there, with the medallion in front of his eyes, for several hours. His men loaded the treasure into the saddlebags, burned the corpses of the Indians and the insurrectionary soldiers, and finally stood by the horses to await further orders. Lieutenant Ramírez approached his boss and cleared his throat. Salamanca felt that he was slowly waking up from a long sleep.

"We are ready to go, my captain."

The conquistador hung the medallion around his neck and felt a shudder. An electric shock ran through his body. Somehow, the jewel was now part of him. He would never take it off.

"My captain?"

Salamanca glanced at Ramírez sideways. The lieutenant shrank at the cold gaze.

"Let's go," ordered the conquistador.

Ramirez swallowed hard and turned to gesture to the men. He wanted to get away from that place as soon as possible. The smell of death and blood permeated the air. Besides, Ramírez told himself, somehow his boss had... *changed*.

The sunset dyed the arid landscape with yellowish tones. The huge mesas that stood on the horizon were silhouetted against the bright disk of light that was rapidly descending. In the middle of the plain, small steep mountains rose like islands, casting long shadows on the prairie. Overhead, a flock of vultures circled over the group of travelers. The horses stirred nervously as they moved across the hard terrain.

"We'll go straight south," Salamanca said.

"But the town we came from is over there," Ramírez replied, pointing in a southeast direction.

"We will not return to that place," added the conquistador, in a cold tone. "A long journey back to Nueva Vizcaya awaits us."

"But we promised that..." Ramirez's whisper

was cut off with a single glance from his boss.

The lieutenant had known Salamanca for many years. He had always thought of him as a tough man, but now his expression had become sterner, and his voice made blood run cold. Ramirez gently tugged on the reins to move his horse away from the captain's steed. Salamanca motioned for Fray Antonio to come closer. The friar hurried his old mount to catch up with the conquistador.

"I hope your chronicle is a faithful record of our expedition, father," Salamanca said. The friar nodded solemnly. "However, you don't need to go into so many... *details*. The important thing is the feat that this trip means for the Motherland. And for our reputation, of course. Including yours."

Fray Antonio immediately understood the veiled threat.

"Of course, Don Rodrigo. But I doubt whether my modest chronicle will be able to do justice to the achievements of your worship.

Salamanca smiled pleased. However, his eyes looked dull.

"I'll keep that in mind when we have to divide the booty, Fray Antonio. *Very* much in mind."

The friar murmured a few thanks and went away immediately. He shared a look of fear with Ramirez, but none of them dared to say anything. They just rode in silence and with their eyes down.

For an hour, the explorers continued their advance, guided by the moonlight. Until the terrain became too uneven for the horses. Salamanca ordered in a dry tone that they set up camp for the night. At first he forbade making fires, but the cold intensified and he had to allow his men to light some campfires. At the same time, he arranged several sentries next to the saddlebags with the gold and deployed several soldiers to form a perimeter around the camp.

The men ate the squalid provisions they had left. The next day they would have to hunt some animals; that is, if the captain would allow it. There was a rumor among the soldiers that Salamanca wanted to return to Nueva España as soon as possible. Ramírez had informed them that they would only stop in Durango for a few hours. There they would divide the booty and the men would be released from their levy. Salamanca and his main entourage would then continue on their way directly to Mexico City.

Only the most battle- and expedition-hardened men managed to sleep that night. A sense of uneasiness fell over the camp. Most of the soldiers were too restless to fall asleep. They were mostly young men born in the New World, after the Conquest. They had no greater experience in fighting with the Indians, nor had they participated in the European battles fought by their fathers or older brothers. The howling of wolves came down from the mountains and other nocturnal animals could be heard in the bushes. Some of the soldiers prayed and others drank *pulque* in secret, trying to make the liquor lull them to sleep.

Salamanca, for his part, seemed oblivious to the fears of his subordinates. He was sitting by a campfire, staring at the medallion. He spun it around in his hands, without removing it from his neck. The fire drew gleams from the jewel, and the inscriptions engraved on the edge seemed to dance on the burnished metal surface. Salamanca had not even eaten. He felt a powerful call from the center of the medallion. He couldn't stop paying attention to it.

Fray Antonio, who was watching him from a prudent distance, approached Ramírez and spoke to him in whispers:

"Why so much fixation with that junk?"

"I don't know, father. But since he took it, the captain is like... *possessed*."

"Jesus, Mary, and Joseph!" exclaimed the friar, making the gesture of the cross several times. "What nonsense you say, Ramírez."

"Those men, Sánchez and Pérez, found the medallion in the underground chamber and immediately began to fight for it," the lieutenant insisted. "I think the jewel is cursed, father."

Fray Antonio turned pale. It was true that the behavior of the men who had made the find changed abruptly after they found the piece. Perhaps that was why the Indians kept the treasure hidden and defended its secret to the death. The friar knew that the Indians of the last town they were in had revealed the location of the treasure to Don Rodrigo, but who knew the hidden intentions they had had to give him that information.

"I think they set a trap for us," Fray Antonio murmured.

"Who?" Ramírez asked. "Do you mean..."

Then he suddenly fell silent. The friar stared at him.

"You were there, in that hut," the friar insisted. "What happened?"

"I'm sorry, father, but I can't say."

"You can tell me in confession, my son. You know that everything you tell me is secret."

Ramírez stretched himself out on some blankets and turned his back on the friar.

"Go to asleep, father."

Salamanca ordered a departure shortly after dawn. When he was already mounted on his horse, waiting for the men to pick up their belongings, Ramírez approached him with a disgruntled expression.

"We lost a couple of men during the night, my captain. Two of the sentries that we posted on the edge of the camp."

The conquistador remained undaunted.

"Were they attacked?"

"There are no traces of struggle. They just disappeared."

"They must have fled, the damn cowards."

He spurred the horse on and set off. The lieutenant shrugged his shoulders and ran to get his mount. It was impossible for two men to have left the expedition in the middle of the night, in unfamiliar terrain. Ramírez was convinced that something had happened to them, but he could not say what. He would have liked to send a party of soldiers to survey the surroundings, but it was not even possible to determine the direction the sentries had taken. The other men murmured about the sudden disappearance of their companions. An air of uneasiness came over the group.

At noon, the expedition members came across a large herd of bison grazing on a meadow next to a river. The soldiers were amazed by the size and corpulence of the animals, whose names they did not know. However, they resembled cows in their quiet wandering and in the way they grazed. After a few moments, some men volunteered to go hunt some of the specimens. With just one of those beasts, the expedition members would have meat for several days. However, Salamanca estimated that the hunt would take too long and ordered them to continue.

"We'll find other game later," he said. "Or we will take the food from some barbarian villages."

The men reluctantly moved away from the appetizing herd. Ramírez understood that his boss wanted to get away from Cibola as soon as possible, but he did not know the reason for such a hasty march. Perhaps it was a matter of protecting the treasure from the attack of the savages, but Ramírez knew that the Indians did not usually face such large groups of invaders. It could only be the unfulfilled promise. Salamanca had sworn to return to the town with the treasure, but now that he possessed that fortune, he had simply decided to undertake the return trip directly to Nueva España.

Was he afraid that those Indians would follow him or that they would try to take the treasure by force? No, that was impossible. If the villagers had been strong enough, they would have simply attacked Cibola much sooner, without using the pale-skinned foreigners to obtain the treasure. Or perhaps Salamanca feared that what had happened in that hut would turn against him? Ramírez had not witnessed everything that had happened inside, but he had heard those strange noises coming from inside.

The group made a brief stop to eat and gather water downstream in the same river where they had seen the bison. Then they remounted and continued their way south, advancing through ravines and mountains parched by the sun. Only a few bushes streaked the ochre landscape with green, interrupting the monotony of the grand canyon. Fray Antonio had announced that they were crossing a great plateau, but none of the men cared about the geography of that vast and unexplored land. Everyone was fed up with the trip and not even the distribution of the loot seemed to encourage them.

In the afternoon, a strong wind began to blow. Clouds piled up in the sky and turned gray. The day suddenly darkened and immediately the coyotes and wolves began to howl. It seemed that a storm was going to break out at any moment, but the rain did not come. Electrical discharges swept through the clouds, casting bluish rays on the mesas that rose in the distance. The horses reared with each flash of lightning and the soldiers were increasingly nervous. Salamanca decided to camp when darkness became total.

Food was already running low. The rations became smaller, and the men cursed in low voices. *Pulque* circulated this time in a more evident way. Not even Fray Antonio refused a good sip of the milky liquor. The bonfires were barely burning. No one dared to sleep. The wind was blowing with a roar and the clouds seemed lower and more threatening. The blue flashes did not stop. Each electric shock resounded over the cannon, twitching the nerves of the men who were squeezed between the blankets.

"What was that?" asked one of the soldiers who stood guard at the edge of the camp.

"What's wrong, Álvar?" One of his companions asked uneasily.

"I saw something there, under the lightning."

The other man approached the sentry and peered into the darkness. There was another discharge of bluish light and they both saw it. A silhouette against the lightning. It looked like a man, but the light passed through its body as if it were made of glass. A second flash of lightning showed that it was carrying a spear.

Álvar gave a shout of terror. His closest companions suddenly stood up and groped for their weapons. The blue flashes showed more and more translucent figures slowly approaching the camp. Alarm-laden shouts spread through the camp. At the other end, Rodrigo de Salamanca looked up from the medallion and asked what was happening.

"They are the spirits," answered a voice in the darkness.

Salamanca recognized the voice of a mestizo who served as their guide. He was an old man, with weathered features and long black hair. Everyone called him Red, because of the color of his skin.

"What do you say, Red? Don't talk nonsense!" The conquistador rebuked him.

"They are the spirits of the Indians we killed in Cibola," insisted the mestizo. "They come to punish us for our sins."

"All of you, take up your weapons!" Salamanca ordered. "Defensive positions!"

The wraiths attacked from all angles. Lightning illuminated their translucent bodies, showing their skeletons under the thin skin. Their features were darkened and deformed. Although their eye sockets appeared to be empty, the attackers had no trouble finding their way perfectly among the horrified Spanish soldiers. Their weapons, on the other hand, were solid and very real. Several scouts were immediately skewered by sharp spears and torn apart by the great battle-axes. But that was not what terrified the explorers the most. During their raids, the Indians would let out fierce howls to instill fear in their enemies. These attackers, on the other hand, did not produce any sound.

The only noises that could be heard under the thunder were produced by the Spanish side. Men shrieked in terror, bodies creaked as their limbs were torn apart, and horses snorted trying to free themselves from their tethers. The soldiers fled in disarray in the face of the phantasmagorical attack. Salamanca took a burning log from a campfire and waved it against one of the wraiths that was thrown at him. The figure immediately recoiled. The conqueror chased it with the fire in front of him until he saw it disappear behind some bushes.

"The fire!" Salamanca shouted to his men, still waving his own torch. "Use the logs to scare them away!"

The most resolute soldiers were the first to

follow the captain's example. Each picked up a log and began to swing it like a mace at the figures that still roamed the camp. The attackers must have understood that they had lost the element of surprise, for they immediately retreated, all at once, and disappeared into the darkness. Soon after, the soldiers managed to calm the frightened horses. Slowly, a certain calm settled in the air. An hour later, only the faint groan of the wounded could be heard among the loud lightning bolts that still lingered among the clouds.

It seemed to the explorers that dawn would never come, but finally the sun appeared on the plateau. The clouds had dissolved as quickly as they had appeared. The sky was radiant, and the air got hot immediately. In the daylight, the panorama in the camp was bleak. According to Ramírez's report, they had lost half of the men, between dead and seriously wounded, and almost a dozen horses. Some of these had fled in terror to the plain and others fell in the midst of the onslaught of the wraiths.

"They weren't ghosts," Salamanca muttered. "Only some Indians painted to instill fear."

Neither the lieutenant, nor the friar, nor the soldiers who were nearby, believed this foolish explanation. The remaining explorers fell into a restless silence and remained crestfallen. Except for one man who was on his knees a little further away.

"We must return the treasure," he murmured. "They won't stop hunting us until we return it."

Salamanca made his way through the bodies of the fallen until he was in front of that soldier. He discovered that it was the mestizo guide. His expression was crooked, and his gaze was lost.

"What the hell are you saying, Red?"

"We must return..."

"The treasure is mine, damn!"

Rojo hugged the conquistador's leg. His body trembled noticeably.

"Please, my captain, you must listen to me." Salamanca waved his leg furiously to get rid of the man's embrace. It was obvious that he had gone mad. "The treasure is doomed."

At last the conquistador managed to free himself.

"Follies," Salamanca snapped.

"Do you not see it? The treasure is doomed!" Red shouted, at the top of his lungs. "Damn..."

The sword flashed in the morning sun. The head of the mestizo separated cleanly from the torso and fell to the side of the decapitated body. Salamanca kicked the corpse, which was still kneeling, and knocked it to the side. More than a dozen soldiers watched the scene, dumbfounded.

"Break camp, damn it!" Salamanca ordered them in a furious tone.

Much to his regret, Ramírez approached the

conquistador.

"He was our only guide," he said, pointing to the mestizo's body.

"We will be guided by the sun and the stars," Salamanca said. "How many saddlebags did we lose during the fight?"

"Only four. Most of the horses were unloaded to rest overnight."

Salamanca turned sharply to his lieutenant and took him by the doublet to bring him close to his own face.

"Four saddlebags?!" The conquistador's eyes were on fire. "That's thousands of escudos! From now on I hold you personally responsible for the treasure, Ramírez. We can't lose a single piece on the return trip."

He pushed him and turned to mount his steed. Ramírez approached the friar, who had seen the outburst with a sorrowful expression.

"He doesn't care about men," said the lieutenant. "He only cares about his damn treasure."

"God protect us!" Fray Antonio exclaimed.

The twenty surviving explorers mounted on their horses, spears at the ready and with their morions well capped. Salamanca ordered that the saddles carrying the treasure be placed in the center of the group. In the face of any attack, the soldiers had to protect the horses at all costs. Though exhausted from the long night and the struggle with the wraiths, the men silently obeyed orders. Salamanca had confiscated the remaining *pulque* and emptied all its contents on the arid ground. If any of the men were caught with a bottle of the liquor, they would be executed immediately.

In a somber mood, the group set off. They advanced at horse walk for much of the day, under the inclement sun and closely followed by the flocks of vultures that did not stop fluttering over the exhausted group of explorers. The only one that seemed oblivious to the inclement landscape, and the atmosphere of tension that reigned among the men, was Salamanca. He was at the head of the group, his face haughty and his medallion shining on his chest. It seemed that a supernatural force was guiding him.

At dusk, the explorers crossed a grove that relieved them for a while from the oppressive heat. On the other side of the grove they found themselves on the edge of a curved horseshoe-shaped cliff. At the deepest part of the curve, the cliff face sank inwards forming a high and deep cavern. A village of houses several stories high, stone towers and the characteristic circular chambers, occupied the entire interior of the cavity. The complex was made of sandstone, whose yellowish color blended into the cliff face. The curvature of the cliff made it practically invisible and could only be seen completely from the opposite end of the cliff top, where the group of explorers was located.

The village was abandoned. There were no signs of life and some of the structures had begun to crumble. Due to the size of the complex, Salamanca calculated that a hundred people could have lived there. After gazing in captivation at the impressive village, he turned smiling to his men.

"God has led us here. We will settle in this village for a few days," he announced. "We will be able to heal our wounds and regain our strength."

The soldiers smiled in relief. More than one shouted for joy. They immediately skirted the cliff until they found a slope that led them to the bottom of the canyon. In front of the complex there was a narrow esplanade that completely bordered it. From there, stairs carved into the rock and ramps communicated with the towers and circular chambers. The rest of the space was occupied by square rooms connected to each other by narrow interior openings.

Salamanca installed his men in the rooms at the back of the village and he went to the upper level of the main tower, a square-shaped structure that rose almost to the ceiling of the cave. Its four levels were connected on the inside by a long wooden staircase that went through aligned openings arranged on the floor of each of the levels. Ramírez ascended first. The stair rungs, made of cut logs, creaked under his weight and some splintered. The lieutenant reached the upper level and from there shouted to his boss that it was safe to go up. The conquistador climbed carefully and finally found himself in a narrow room with a very low ceiling.

"These damn Indians were dwarfs," he murmured.

Through the single, narrow window you could get a good panoramic view of the canyon. Outside, the sun was setting. Because of the sharp angle of the cliff, the village was quickly plunged into darkness. Salamanca had to recognize that these savages had built a well-designed complex with good defenses. No one could approach the village without being seen from afar. In addition, the ground adjacent to the cavern was clear. Even at night any movement in that direction could be noticed.

When it was already dark a strong wind arose again. The sky was covered with clouds and the moon disappeared. The darkness became absolute. The tranquility of the Spanish soldiers had been short-lived. If they were already restless, a salvo of bluish lightning made them shudder.

"It's the wraiths!" They shouted. "They're back!"

Salamanca stood guard at the top of the tower. He looked out of the narrow window and found that several figures were approaching through the canyon. Each burst of lightning illuminated their translucent bodies for a few seconds, but then they were hidden in the shadows again. With each apparition they were closer to the complex. Now Salamanca could see the weapons they were wielding.

"Beware!" The conquistador shouted to the men who were stationed on the roofs of the chambers. There they awaited the enemy, trembling with terror, but at the same time unable to flee under the watchful eye of their leader. "They are armed with bows!"

A volley of arrows fell like rain on the village. The screams of the men hit by the projectiles ricocheted off the cavern wall. The soldiers disbanded and sought refuge inside the stone rooms. The wraiths ascended the stairs and ramps and launched themselves into the village. The rooms were filled with screams of terror, prayers for mercy, and frightful creaks of bodies being crushed by maces and torn apart by axes.

At the top of the tower, Salamanca shrank in a corner, with his sword raised. An instant later, the wooden staircase shook, as if someone were climbing it. It could not have been a soldier, for the traversed steps did not creak. The conquistador realized that the wraiths were after him. The staircase kept moving, but no sound came out of the opening in the floor. Nor were there any noises coming from the village. Through the window, the lightning flashed bluish into the narrow room. Salamanca took off the medallion and locked it in a fist. A voice in his

head told him that he must protect it at all costs.
The wraiths rushed up the stairwell.

    Salamanca gave himself to God.

2. NEW YORK

Dozens of pedestrians crowded the corner, waiting tightly for the traffic officer to indicate that they could cross the street. When the policeman gave the stop sign, hundreds of cars, buses, and trucks stopped their accelerated march in both directions. The large group of people hurriedly crossed to the opposite sidewalk, as if a dam had been overflowed by the human tide. On the other side of the street, the group joined dozens of other hurried passers-by who were already filling the sidewalk. Other people crossed in the middle of the block, skillfully dodging the cars and the fast tram that passed just then in the middle of the road.

Huge billboards, hanging from buildings above the crowds, advertised a myriad of consumer products, car brands, household appliances, and the latest Broadway theater productions. Higher still, the rooftops of the skyscrapers seemed to come together to form a concrete horizon that was lost of sight in every direction one looked. It was a breathtaking cityscape for the newly arrived traveler, but the inhabitants of the city no longer noticed it. They just seemed to be in a hurry to get from one place to another.

Peter Hunt watched the hectic scene standing next to a newsstand. Dozens of newspapers and magazines covered the stall from end to end. Signs indicated that the kiosk also sold milkshakes, ice cream cones and something called a 'sundae'. Hunt went through the headlines for a moment. Most of them referred to the recent inauguration of Calvin Coolidge, the former vice president who had assumed the presidency just over a year earlier, in the face of the sudden death of Warren Harding. He had then run, and won, for the next election to the highest office.

A man coming down the sidewalk approached Hunt as he glanced at the magazines. There were publications for all subjects. It was almost overwhelming. The man tapped his shoulder to get his attention.

"Excuse me, sir. Which tram line I have to get to go to..."

"Oh, I'm sorry!" Hunt interrupted him. "I'm not from the city."

"Like everyone else!" muttered the man, who went on his way immediately.

Hunt smiled. So that was the hectic life of New York. He looked at the trench watch on his wrist and realized that he was running late for his appointment. He joined the hundreds of pedestrians who lined the sidewalks and headed back to his hotel. On the way he was accompanied by the noise of car horns, the voices of passers-by in many languages, and the tobacco smoke of the many smokers who walked on the street.

Sir John Connelly was standing at the entrance to the Biltmore Hotel on Vanderbilt Avenue. He wore an elegant dark gray striped suit and covered his head with an elegant light gray Homburg hat. His appearance was unmistakably British. Hunt wore a similar suit, but navy blue. His hat was black. Sunset was approaching and it was already getting cool. Hunt wondered if it would be necessary to go and get a coat from his room.

"I hope you enjoyed your stroll, captain."

His boss and mentor was in his early sixties, but his haughty and elegant bearing gave him a younger appearance. Only the bushy white beard, which he wore well-trimmed, evidenced his true age. Between his lips he held his permanent briar pipe, which he never lit.

"This place is impressive. Full of people and constantly growing," said the captain. "They're building more skyscrapers on every empty lot!"

"Nearly six million inhabitants," added Sir John. "More than two million in Manhattan alone."

They had settled in the hotel that same

morning. After resting and eating a light lunch, Hunt had insisted on taking a short reconnaissance walk around. Anticipating that he would return at the time of his appointment, he had dressed for his meeting before leaving. That city was huge! He only managed to tour part of the Terminal City sector, a commercial and office real estate project that had been developing since before the Great War around the new Grand Central railway station. But it was enough for him to understand that New York would soon surpass London as the most populous city in the world.

A sleek Packard Twin Six pulled up to the curb in front of the hotel. A uniformed chauffeur descended from the front seat and approached the two British visitors.

"Good afternoon, gentlemen. Sir John Connelly? Captain Hunt?" They both nodded. "Professor Lester sent me to pick you up."

They settled into the back seat of the car and left immediately towards the north of the city. They headed down Madison Avenue and then skirted the magnificent Central Park on its south side. At Columbus Circle they took Broadway, on a northwest route that then continued parallel to the Hudson River. Unlike Midtown, with its skyscrapers, hotels, and theaters, the Upper West Side was a residential district that abounded in elegant apartment buildings and stately mansions.

Hunt and Sir John's voyage from Southampton had taken nine days aboard the Cunard Line's steamer RMS Berengaria. Sir John Connelly headed a discreet department in the British Museum tasked with studying the occult sciences and obtaining mystical artifacts. Because of its secretive nature, it was known simply as Department X. Peter Hunt was the unit's lead investigator. Both he and his boss had been invited to the United States to collaborate in the examination of certain archaeological pieces related to occultism, recently found in the mountains of the American West. The trip and all its expenses were borne by the American Geographical Society.

Sir John and Hunt spent most of the boat trip studying about the culture and mythology of the indigenous peoples of North America. In the evenings, when the director of Department X came to the first-class lounge to play bridge with other passengers, Hunt took advantage of swimming in the magnificent steam pool. Then they had dinner, had a drink, and returned to their cabins escaping the balls that were held every night.

Hunt was enthusiastic about getting to know New York City. He had read many times about its dynamism, its impressive architecture and its famous nightlife. It all sounded fascinating. He probably wouldn't have time to see every corner of the city or enjoy its countless pleasures, but he counted on at least visiting a few attractions. He even hoped that Sir John would accompany him to some places of his interest. After all, the study of those artifacts was not going to occupy all their time each day.

After leaving the campus of Columbia University behind, the Packard ventured into a district where pedestrians were very different from those in midtown Manhattan. Most of them appeared to be immigrants and black people abounded in the streets. Hunt deduced that it must be Harlem. He had read that the district had lively nightclubs, dance halls, and theaters. However, the Italian mafia and gangs of different ethnicities had a significant presence among the local population. Harlem was the land of jazz and nightlife, but also of crime and poverty.

Beyond Harlem was the Washington Heights district, a developing area located on the northern edge of Manhattan. Dozens of apartment buildings were being built there to attract middle-class European immigrants. Arriving at West 155th Street, the Packard found a complex of imposing buildings built in the architectural style that in the United States was properly called the American Renaissance. The driver stopped the car in front of the building that occupied the corner of Broadway and 155th Street. He jumped out and opened the back door so that his passengers could get out.

The building, with its serious and elegant appearance, was the headquarters of the American Geographical Society. The institution, founded in the middle of the previous century in New York City, enjoyed great academic prestige. During the recent war, the society had advised President Wilson to prepare the peace agreements that would be signed once the Allies won the conflict, which ended up materializing in the Paris Peace Conference. The society's board of directors included wealthy philanthropists, prominent publishers, academics from various universities and, of course, the country's most renowned geographers.

A receptionist led the guests directly to the spacious office of the society's president, Professor Robert Lester. He was waiting for them standing next to a globe more than a meter in diameter, arranged on a wooden pedestal.

"My dear Sir John! It is a pleasure to see you again. I hope the trip was smooth."

Lester, a professor at Princeton, had a vivacious appearance and a polite tone. He was the same age as his British friend, but he was thicker in build and still had dark hair. He wore a stern black three-piece suit, somewhat old-fashioned but elegant. He held out his hand to both of them and smiled when he met Hunt.

"I've heard fascinating stories about you, captain. I hope you can tell me about some of your adventures during your stay."

"No doubt the stories have been exaggerated, Professor," said Hunt modestly.

"Your escape from that island in the Pacific was much talked about in our circle, Captain. And please call me Robert."

In November of the previous year, Hunt had travelled to Australia on behalf of Department X. A well-known financier of archaeological expeditions required his help. After being stalked by danger in much of the continent, the captain's mission finally led him to a volcanic island that did not appear on any map, located in the most remote reaches of the Pacific. The volcano erupted shortly after Hunt arrived. Although he managed to flee with a handful of locals, he first had to thwart the plans of a group of pirates who intended to conquer an underwater continent hidden under the island.

"I assure you, Robert," Hunt insisted, "it was not as exciting as you must have been told."

"At least not as much as the three weeks he spent in Tahiti afterwards," murmured Sir John.

The memory of the beautiful Mareva immediately came to the captain's mind. The girl had accompanied him for much of his adventure and they had also escaped from the phantom island together. After the deadly odyssey they had gone through, Mareva decided to return to her native Tahiti, from which she had left many years earlier. Hunt agreed to accompany her. They lived an intense idyll in that tropical paradise, but finally the captain had to return to his duties in the cold English capital. Sir John was glad to see him return safely, though he could scarcely conceal his exasperation at his lead investigator's long vacation.

Professor Lester invited them to sit in soft wing chairs. Hunt observed that the globe had several signatures traced in pencil on its face. Lester explained that he was collecting the signatures of several land and sea explorers, travelers, and pioneers of international aviation. With enthusiasm, he showed the various signatures to his guests. There were the names of the greatest adventurers of that time.

"Do you want a coffee, gentlemen? As you may know, the law prevents me from offering you something stronger," he added in a tone of unease.

"Coffee is all right," said Sir John.

During the boat trip, the bartenders had poured copious amounts of liquor, reminding their passengers that it would be the last drinks they would have until they left the United States again. For almost five years, a constitutional amendment had been in force throughout the country that absolutely prohibited the production, importation, and sale of all types of alcoholic beverages.

An assistant brought them coffee. Lester asked not to be disturbed.

"Again, I am grateful that you have come

from England to assist in the investigation, Sir John," said the professor. "This discovery is extraordinary in itself, but when we found the gems among the pieces, we realized that it was something... *fantastic*."

"You mentioned it in your letter, Robert. But I would appreciate it if you could give us more details."

"Certainly. As I explained in my invitation letter, three months ago, four leather saddlebags were discovered, by mere chance, buried in a remote corner of the mountains in New Mexico. Erosion affected them a lot, but at the same time it slowly dug them up over time. However, the contents of the saddlebags were intact."

Lester took a file from his desk. From inside the folder he extracted several photographs that he showed to his visitors.

"The saddlebags contained a total of nearly twenty pounds of solid gold pieces," Lester explained, pointing to the photographs. "Evidently, these were very ancient indigenous artifacts."

"But the natives of that region did not work with gold or other precious metals," said Sir John.

"Indeed! Fortunately, the pieces were found by honest people who promptly sent them to the authorities. At first, the discovery wandered through some local institutions, until it reached the hands of our society. After the war our prestige has been very recognized."

"I know. What happened then?"

"We did several preliminary studies of the pieces, about their composition, engravings and origin. Everything points to the fact that the objects were created by the Anasazi, a native people who lived in that region until the thirteenth century. Then their culture died out and probably the secret of the gold deposits was also lost. It is likely that their descendants used the artifacts, but they certainly did not continue to work gold.

"You say the pieces were in leather saddlebags," Hunt remarked.

The saddlebags are much later and alien to that culture. The manufacturing work and embroidery of the material show that they would be of Spanish origin. From the sixteenth century.

Hunt's face lit up immediately.

"The Seven Cities of Gold!" exclaimed the captain.

Lester smiled and nodded.

"So you are familiar with the legend."

"In the middle of the sixteenth century," Hunt said, "a Spanish conquistador named Coronado made a great expedition from Mexico in search of some supposed indigenous cities located hundreds of kilometers to the north, in the middle of the desert. According to rumors, the cities contained unimaginable riches."

"That's right, captain. Francisco de Coronado

was looking for the mythical city of Cibola. After many hardships, he arrived at the place indicated by his guides, in the year 1540. But he found nothing but adobe villages. He returned humiliated to the Viceroyalty of New Spain, where he was declared bankrupt and put on trial for war crimes against the natives. He was acquitted but died in obscurity."

"One moment," said the captain. "If Coronado failed in his search, how do you explain the Spanish saddlebags that contained the treasure?"

"Twenty years later there was a second Spanish expedition that set out in search of the cities of gold," Lester said. "This expedition did manage to find the mythical Cibola."

Sir John and Hunt looked at each other in surprise. The director of Department X was the first to speak.

"There is no reference to this second expedition in the books on the subject."

Lester nodded. He had a funny twinkle in his eye.

"Because no chronicle of that trip was ever written," explained the professor. "The expedition disappeared in the remote lands north of New Spain and there were no survivors."

"But so..."

Lester interrupted the captain's question by raising a hand.

"There are only a few archives that give an

account of the expedition. Some were found in Mexico City's National Palace, which was the former viceregal palace. A few mentions were also found in the historical archives of the Royal Audience."

"It is only known that the expedition was led by the conquistador Rodrigo de Salamanca, who had only fifty men and a Franciscan monk who served as chronicler. The journey departed in 1560, but none of its members ever returned. The fate of the expedition members remains a mystery. History could only be partially reconstructed much later, when the Spanish conquered what is now New Mexico."

"The saddlebags found were those carried by Salamanca's men," Hunt deduced. Lester confirmed it with a nod. "I suppose the expedition suffered some kind of accident and all the men perished in the mountains."

"Yes, it is possible. Or maybe they were attacked by Indians. Coronado, in the first expedition, fought against several native peoples. Perhaps Salamanca did not have the same luck."

"Do you know where the gold came from?" Sir John asked.

Lester shook his head.

"In that area there are several ruins of villages built in adobe and rock by the Anasazi. But in none of them are there gold artifacts or clues that lead to any nearby deposit. The

Anasazi took the secret to the grave."

"Then why do you think the treasure comes from Cibola?" Hunt insisted.

For all response, Professor Lester went to his desk and took a small object from a drawer. He sat back down in the wing chair and held the object in the outstretched palm of his hand so that his guests could get a good look at it. It was a rectangular box, somewhat smaller and thicker than a cigarette box. It was made of solid gold. He handed it to Hunt, who watched it fascinated for a moment. On the shiny surface it had several engravings and primitive drawings. Hunt tried to remove the lid, but it wouldn't budge. He tried pulling it and sliding it, but without results.

"You must turn the lid and lift it when those small notches are aligned," explained the professor.

"A puzzle box! I didn't know that ancient peoples knew about these techniques."

"Neither do we. It took us a couple of days to figure out the mechanism."

Inside the box were seven glassy-looking blue-green gems, veined in a darker color, the size of marbles.

"Turquoise?" asked the captain.

Lester nodded.

"Look at this," said the professor.

Hunt handed him the gems. Lester turned on a radio receiver that rested on a side table next to the wing chairs. He tuned in to a classical music station and let it play for a few moments. The two Englishmen looked at each other intrigued. Lester held the gems in front of the device's speaker. Interference immediately occurred. He then brought the gems closer to the receiver and the interference increased.

"They're magnetic!" Captain Hunt exclaimed.

"Wait," Lester said.

He took one of the gems from his palm and the interference soon ceased. He ran the turquoise individually over the receiver's speaker, but there was no squeaking.

"We discovered it by chance," explained the professor. "The spheres only produce electromagnetism if they are together. Each gem, on its own, is not magnetic."

"Incredible!" murmured Sir John. "It must not be something natural, then. It is likely that someone has manufactured them that way. Whether by technological means... or *magical*."

A silence of amazement settled in the office. After a moment, Lester turned off the radio receiver and turned to his guests.

"As I told you in my letter, Sir John, your presence would be of great help to us. This matter has us all perplexed."

The director of Department X asked to examine the gems. All were irregular in shape, although they seemed to be carved from the same original ore.

"I will send a telegram to London so that

the Department can investigate the references to Rodrigo de Salamanca in the museum," he said. "I will also ask them to check about spells related to Native Americans and the turquoise stone."

"How did the discovery of saddlebags come about?" Captain Hunt wanted to know.

Professor Lester unfolded a map of the state of New Mexico on his desk. With his finger he marked a point near the Arizona border, about two hundred and thirty kilometers from the city of Albuquerque.

"Some amateur miners were looking for turquoise deposits in this area," he explained. "They camped for several days in the mountains and searched several cliffs and canyons. In one of the test excavations they found the saddlebags by chance. The relics and antiquities are protected by federal law, so the men turned the treasure over to the authorities as soon as they returned to the city."

"Did the Society explore the area of the discovery?" Hunt asked.

"We sent a group of geographers, geologists, and archaeologists to the area, but they were unable to find other relics or vestiges of the second Spanish expedition. If Salamanca was really there, he disappeared into thin air."

"I suppose the Spaniards did not discover what was in the box," said Sir John. "Otherwise, they would have stolen the gems or, at the very least, separated them."

"Yes, it is quite possible," Lester agreed. "Nor must they have noticed its magnetic effect."

"These gems must have been magnetized for a purpose," Sir John reasoned. "Especially if the effect was achieved by mystical means. In those times, electromagnetism must have had no practical use in daily life. No, it can only obey some ritual practice. From what I have read, most Native American peoples had healers in addition to their leaders."

"The texts on indigenous rituals that I read on the ship did not delve into these subjects," Hunt recalled. "For the natives it is taboo to talk about their beliefs with people outside their tribes."

"I know an anthropologist who works at the Museum of Natural History," Lester said. "I will consult him about it."

"Can I keep the gems for a while?" Sir John asked. "I would like to examine them in more detail and compare them with some images that appear in my books."

"Of course, my dear friend! I know that they will be safe in your hands."

The director of Department X put the gems in the puzzle box and slipped the artifact into a pocket of his jacket. He motioned to get up from the chair, but Robert Lester stopped him with a gesture.

"Oh, please, don't go! You are my guests, and I would like to take you to dinner."

"It will be a pleasure, Robert," replied Sir John.

"We're going to a lively establishment called the Cotton Club," the professor explained. "It's located near here in Harlem. They serve excellent dinner and present a musical revue throughout the evening. It's a real New York show, gentlemen!"

Sir John Connelly no longer seemed so keen at the prospect, but he managed to give a polite smile. Hunt had read some brochures on the ship about the city and knew that the club was a renowned establishment in the city. He longed to get to know the place. Lester called his assistant and asked him to tell the driver to get the car ready to leave. The three men made their way to the main entrance of the Society's building.

Outside it was already dark and cold. Hunt regretted not having brought a coat. He was thinking about that when he heard a loud screech of tires a short distance away. He looked up at the American Geographical Society's Packard, but it was stopped at the curb ahead. The driver had gotten out of the car and was waiting for them with the back door open. An instant later, a huge black Hudson sedan pulled up onto the curb ahead of the Packard and came to a screeching halt, blocking the other vehicle's path.

Two men jumped down from the Hudson. Captain Hunt had already activated his internal danger alarms. He reached under his jacket to draw his revolver from the holster under his arm. To his astonishment, he saw that the attackers were carrying Thompson submachine guns. They opened fire immediately. Two bursts swept the sidewalk in the direction of the entrance to the Society's building. The roar of gunfire broke the stillness of the night, and the flashes of the barrels illuminated the impassive faces of the attackers.

The driver was shot several times almost at point-blank range. His body shuddered from the impact of the rounds, and he was thrown into his own car. He collided with the bodywork and then bounced off the ground. Sir John Connelly and Robert Lester crouched and ran to take cover in the back of the Packard. A second burst of shots swept the sidewalk, in an attempt to cut them off. Hunt, who was further back, dropped one knee to the ground and raised his Webley Mk VI revolver in firing position. Both attackers were standing in the middle of the sidewalk, their machine guns raised at waist height.

Hunt aimed at one of them and fired twice in quick succession. He hit the man in the chest and knocked him down on his back. The other attacker turned towards him and shot another burst in his direction. But Hunt had already thrown himself to the ground and the rounds passed over him. From his new position, the captain fired two more times. The attacker shuddered and gave a few rattles. He tried to aim with the Thompson, but the submachine gun fell to the ground and bounced off the sidewalk. Then the man fell on his face and remained motionless.

The Hudson kept the engine running. Hunt got up and ran towards the car. The driver watched him with wide eyes as he put the reverse gear and sped back into the street. Hunt emptied the revolver on the Hudson but failed to hit the driver. With a loud screeching sound, the vehicle managed to turn in reverse and then was thrown forward. It was immediately out of sight in the night.

Hunt returned to the Packard but stopped short when he reached the car. Sir John was sitting on the floor, with his back against the bodywork. His head was down and with one hand he was holding his belly. Professor Lester was lying on his back on the sidewalk, a few yards away. Hunt approached his boss, but he shook his head.

"Help him!"

Hunt crouched down next to Lester. He was bleeding from several wounds and was barely breathing.

"Hang in there, Robert. I'm going to take you to the car."

"No... No..."

"A hospital! Is there a hospital nearby?"

Lester complained and coughed. After a few

anguished moments, he murmured:

"Mount Sinai... Fifth and 100..."

Hunt tried to catch him, but the poor man gave one last gasp and died. The captain looked at Sir John from where he stood and shook his head. Sir John cast an unaccustomed curse.

"How are you?" Hunt asked, in a desperate tone.

"I was shot in the belly. But I think that... argghh... Survive."

Hunt helped his boss get into the Packard. He laid him on the back seat and then jumped behind the wheel. As he started the car, Sir John asked in a weak voice:

"Why... did they attack us?"

"They wanted the gems, obviously." Hunt hurried the car toward Broadway.

Sir John gave a groan of pain. Then he said:

"But the most important question is another, Peter. How did they know we had them?"

3. LITTLE ITALY

Daniele Monreale was the king of the neighborhood. And like all kings, he let himself be seen among his subjects so that they would pay him homage. Like every morning, after eating a hearty breakfast prepared by his daughter, he left his apartment in a pleasant, inconspicuous building on Lafayette Street and walked toward Mulberry Street. It was a walk of few streets. He had no bodyguards, for he did not need them there. No one would have dared to raise his hand against his sovereign, even though everyone knew that every morning he walked across the neighborhood to his offices.

Arriving in the heart of Little Italy, he was greeted splendidly by the merchants of Mulberry Street. The open-air market carts filled the street with the smells of fruits and vegetables. The vendors offered their products at the top of their voices, competing with each other and filling the air with a cacophony of various Italian dialects. Hundreds of people filled the commercial premises that flanked both sidewalks. Some only wandered along the picturesque street to find out the news and gossip of the neighbors. Word soon spread that the king had arrived. No one wanted to be left out of the signs of affection they showed to their benefactor.

A hairdresser ran out of his premises, leaving his client with half-cut hair, to offer Monreale a shave at the house's expense. A mature woman placed her daughter well in sight of the king so that he could see how grown up she was. After all, the king had been a widower for several years and it was about time he married again. A tailor showed him his fabrics that had just arrived from the Motherland so that he could choose one, although not before praising the wonderful quality of the suit he wore. A well-known lady of the night called to him from a balcony and waved her long eyelashes, reminding him with a wink that he had not visited her for several weeks. Immediately, the woman who promoted her daughter shouted at her: '*Putana!*' Several shopkeepers laughed.

To all these signs of veneration, Monreale responded with a smile and a wave of his hand, but without stopping to talk to anyone. He couldn't neglect his daily routine, but that morning he was in a hurry. He had no time to entertain himself with his countrymen. He made only a brief stop at a fruit cart at the end of the street, on which some glistening and aromatic oranges stood out. The shopkeeper hurriedly filled a paper bag with his fruits.

"*Buongiorno, Don Daniele,*" the man greeted as he handed him the bag.

"*Good morning, Giuseppe.* How much do I owe you?"

"Oh, nothing! It's a gift from me."

"*Non posso accettare, Giuseppe.* It's your job and I don't want to take advantage of you."

"*Piacere mio, Don Daniele.* My family and I are grateful for your attentions."

"*Bene, bene.* Just for this once. If you have any problems, come to see me."

The man touched his cap and nodded vigorously. That kind of exchange was frequent for Monreale. He pretended that he wanted to pay for what he received, the merchants pretended to give it to him, and then he feigned a show of surprise. In the end, everyone was happy. With his bag of oranges under his arm, he moved away from Mulberry to hurry his steps in the final part of his journey.

Monreale had been born fifty-five years ago into a poor family in Sicily. Like many of his friends, he joined from a young age a gang of thieves and highway robbers who, in turn, paid tribute to the local mafia boss. But young Daniele was smarter and more ambitious than his companions. He soon discovered that he would never get rich having to share his winnings, first with the rest of the gang and then with the local town *Don*.

For a while he managed to keep his solo criminal activities hidden, until someone reported him. His former colleagues and, to make matters worse, the mafia, put an immediate price on his head. His parents disowned him, to avoid the wrath of the *Don*, and their own death sentence. Without refuge or friends, the young delinquent spent his savings on a third-class ticket on the next steamer that set sail from Palermo and emigrated to the mythical city of New York.

During his long and miserable quarantine stay at the Castle Clinton immigration center, Monreale met other boys who were in the same situation. Most came from Sicily, like him, and almost all of them had fled for criminal reasons. Monreale soon formed a new gang destined to operate in the city. Of course, there were already criminal organizations operating in the various neighborhoods of New York: Little Italy, Italian Harlem, the Bronx, and Brooklyn. Monreale was not daunted. Thanks to their cunning and determination, the gang soon transformed into a real clan. Its criminal activities grew and expanded and then surpassed rival gangs. By the turn of the century, Don Daniele was already running a small criminal empire.

Although he had no formal education, he was good at numbers, planning, and social skills.

He bought politicians, bribed the authorities, and eliminated the competition. At present, Monreale was one of the Big Five of organized crime in New York. From his fiefdom in Little Italy, he controlled gambling, extortion, narcotics, and prostitution. Since the entry into force of Prohibition, he was also engaged in alcohol smuggling, a lucrative business that would make him as millionaire as the Vanderbilts or the Rockefellers.

Unlike his countrymen in Sicily, chubby criminals who barely spoke English, Monreale had related to American society, spoke the language perfectly and dressed in the latest fashions. In addition, he remained slender and in good shape. With the operation he was working on, he would soon be not only the king of the neighborhood, but of all New York. Or perhaps of the country. Not even the Chicago Outfit could oppose his plans. He smiled as he peeled an orange with his razor knife and ate it along the way.

On reaching Bowery he passed under the elevated line of the Third Avenue Railroad and entered the doorway of an anonymous-looking building. Immediately the lieutenant of his gang, Franco Gagliano, came out to meet him. He was a man of the same age, but somewhat dull and gray. The two had met at Clinton Castle and since then Gagliano was his trusted man.

"Has Roselli arrived yet?" Monreale asked.

His lieutenant shook his head.

"No one's seen him since last night, Danny."

Monreale cursed in Italian.

"The success of the meeting depends on Roselli having done his job," he complained. "Who was with him?"

"Rocco and D'Amato. Nor have they appeared."

"Damn! Get our people to look for them, Franco. Have you already prepared everything for the meeting?"

"It's all set, Danny."

"I hope Roselli doesn't mess things up. Let me know as soon as one of those three *stronzi* appears."

Monreale walked away, muttering obscenities, toward the building's backyard. Six men were loading two trucks with boxes full of liquor bottles. The shipment had just arrived from Atlantic City and would be distributed in all the illegal gambling dens in New York. A group of soldiers from the gang waited in a corner of the courtyard, smoking, and holding their Thompson submachine guns in one hand. Rival gangs frequently attacked trucks to impose their own alcohol trade on nightclubs. Monreale hoped to obtain a monopoly on smuggling soon.

All that illicit activity was done in broad daylight because Monreale was the owner of the entire building. In addition to using it for alcohol smuggling, there were the offices of several of his front companies: a printing press, a couple of legal law firms, an olive oil importer and his main business, Monreale Transport. All the trucks belonged to the latter company. None of them were inspected in New York State. Monreale had on his payroll most of the police chiefs and several state politicians.

His operation to be promoted to *capo di tutti i capi* was already underway. That night, however, would begin the most important stage of the plan. Monreale had everything ready for several days, but Roselli's sudden disappearance could ruin everything. Monreale had assigned him the job because he was one of his most loyal and efficient captains. In fact, it was a fairly simple mission. And yet, the damn *stronzo* didn't report that morning. Monreale had no alternative but to think the worst. Roselli had betrayed him or was dead. In any of these cases, the operation was in serious danger.

Don Daniele had a hard time concentrating on his work all day. He delegated most of the functions to Gagliano and locked himself in his office to prepare for any contingency that might occur at that night's meeting. He smoked several cigarettes, drank a lot of alcohol, and ate little. At the end of the day his throat was dry, and he was in a foul mood. When Gagliano told him that the attendees of the meeting had already arrived, Monreale mumbled some orders and got up heavily from his chair. The moment of truth had arrived.

Monreale Transport operated on the upper floor of the building. The *capo* had set up a conference room in a large hall which he rarely occupied. The wide windows overlooked a panoramic view of the Bowery over the railway line. That night, however, the curtains were closed for security reasons. Armed guards guarded all the entrances to the building. None of those attending the meeting were allowed to come with firearms or knives.

When Monreale entered the room, he discovered a group of nine men chattering animatedly in the Sicilian dialect of Italian. Their ages ranged from forty to fifty years. They wore expensive clothes, but their manners and appearance betrayed them for what they were: criminals. Like the host, they had all been born on the island, had begun their criminal careers in the Motherland, and then had immigrated to the United States. They were fleeing from the police, from other gangs, or simply wished to continue their operations in the land of opportunity.

Those men were Monreale's captains, those in charge of controlling the various sections of his criminal empire. Some handled extortion, others clandestine gambling and betting, a couple were in charge of narcotics and so on. In addition, each group controlled a neighborhood or street where the gang operated. And they were all accountable to the boss, who took most of the profits. This is how Don Daniele's kingdom worked.

"Dan the man!" shouted the men when they saw their leader.

Each of them kissed him on both cheeks and then hugged him. Monrelae took a few minutes to ask each of them about their families. He remembered in detail the names of the wives and children of all his captains. He even knew the mistresses of several of them, but he refrained from mentioning them. After this ritual, he asked his men to take a seat. In the center of the room was a conference table with ten chairs. On the table there were only a few jugs of water and glasses. The men understood that the meeting would be about serious business. Monreale occupied the head of the table. Franco Gagliano sat behind his boss, in a chair leaning against the wall.

"Gentlemen," the *capo* began. "I called you tonight to talk to you about a plan that will take us to the top of all the bands operating in New York. Soon, our clan will have exclusive control over all criminal activities in the city."

The men whistled, clapped their hands, and banged on the table in joy. They were all ambitious and dreamed of being the kings of their own territories. Many were not even friends with each other, or outright rivals, but they were willing to work together under the leadership of the *capo* to share the profits of the business.

"This plan requires your maximum commitment and the availability of many of your men will be necessary. Everyone will have to contribute to achieve success."

"Including Roselli?" asked one of the captains.

The absence of the last captain had not gone unnoticed.

"Roselli is already doing his part of the job," Monreale said.

Or at least I hope so, he thought.

"What will it be, chief?" asked another. "Will we attack the other gangs? If we organize ourselves well, we can eliminate everyone else."

Don Daniele shook his head vigorously.

"An open war will destroy us all. You can see how Masseria and D'Aquila have been fighting for several years. None of them have won anything and they have only left a trail of corpses."

Violent fights between rival gangs were frequent in New York. The bosses were victims of attacks and gambling and alcohol dens suffered fires or sudden raids by the police. In the past five years, several chiefs and lieutenants had been killed in factional wars. Almost every week there was a shooting in the streets of Little Italy and Harlem. For that reason, Monreale always remained in his neighborhood and never summoned all his captains at the same time.

That meeting had taken several days to prepare and to notify all the attendees.

"Is it alcohol, boss?" asked another captain. "Are we finally going to have a monopoly on speakeasies?"

"It's a robbery, gentlemen," Monreale clarified. "The biggest robbery of the century. The greatest ever!"

"The Assay Office?" The same man insisted.

Several of his teammates cheered excitedly.

In the Financial District of Lower Manhattan was located the headquarters of the federal office in charge of assaying the purity of precious metals and keeping part of the national gold reserve in deposit. It was a coveted target for many, but an assault had never been attempted. The building was impregnable.

"No," said Monreale. "We'll steal this."

He took a newspaper from a side table and threw it into the center of the table. The men passed it around among themselves after reading the headline of the page on which it was folded: Fabulous Indian Treasure Found in New Mexico.

"It says here that the artifacts are worth millions," commented a captain. "Where is this finding currently located?"

"It's still in New Mexico." His men looked at Don Daniele with surprise. That state was a long way from their usual place of operations. "Along with the rest of the treasure."

The captains looked at each other with expressions of disbelief, greed, and confusion. Now the operation no longer seemed so simple or immediate.

"It doesn't say anything here about there being more artifacts," the same man insisted, holding up the newspaper.

"Because they don't know of its existence. What was found is only a small part of that fortune, gentlemen."

Some of those present swallowed noisily.

"The rest of the treasure is hidden in the mountains of New Mexico," Monreale explained. "But among the pieces found there is an artifact that is key to finding the others. Once we get the complete treasure, we need to transport it to safety, divide it, and sell it."

Monreale looked at his subordinates. He saw that their faces reflected ambition, disbelief, despair, and even fear. The emotions of all criminals before starting an illicit activity that could well mean glory... or death.

"What should we do, boss?" asked the first of them, who recovered from the shock.

"We have to organize the hit, the transport and the security of the entire operation. The part of the treasure that was found is well guarded," explained the *capo*. "We will need brave and well-armed men. You will have to choose a hidden and well-protected place to store the treasure after the robbery. And our fences must be prepared to sell the artifacts and make profits that appear legitimate."

It would be a titanic task. To encourage them, Monreale added:

"We will be so rich that no one will be able to oppose us. The other gangs will fall without the need to fire a single shot. We'll just buy fucking New York!"

There was several applause around the table, but not as enthusiastic as Monreale had anticipated. However, he was not daunted. After all, these men were nothing more than well-dressed bandits. Undoubtedly, the enormous scope of the operation was beyond the comprehension of their narrow minds. But Don Daniele did not care that they were unable to assimilate his plans, as long as they carried out his instructions.

"No," said a deep voice suddenly coming from across the table. "It is an impossible task."

Monreale sighed. He knew that if there was any opposition to his plans, any qualms, it would come from that man.

Luciano Ferrante was the oldest and most respected of the captains of the Monreale clan. He was over sixty years old, but he retained a robust and agile appearance. He had arrived in the United States at a very young age and during the previous century had led one of the largest and wildest gangs of the Sicilian mafia. His men were specialists in grand robberies and ruthlessly eliminating the competition. After several years of success, the police finally managed to arrest Ferrante and he was sentenced to twenty years in prison for murder and robbery. He only served a little more than ten years, but it was enough for his career to come to an end.

In the first decade of the twentieth century, the Sicilian mafia was already in the hands of younger men who used more modern methods to commit their crimes. The old guard was in retreat, although they were still respected men with good contacts in the Motherland. Ferrante's gang had split. Many of his soldiers had died at the hands of rival gangs, and other men had simply switched sides to survive.

Most of those survivors had joined Monreale, the *capo* who was on his way to dominate the New York underworld. Reluctantly, Ferrante decided to do the same. However, he understood his own position as that of an advisor to Monreale and not as a simple dependent. That difference of vision had been a permanent source of friction between the two men, but Ferrante punctually paid his tributes to the *capo* and renewed his oath of loyalty every time they met. Monreale, for his part, distrusted the former mafioso and kept him out of his main operations.

"Our territory is this city," Ferrante said. "What lies beyond is... *sconosciuto*. If we cross our border, we are in danger of being discovered.

We must operate among our people, so that our business remains *cosa nostra*."

The same thing again, Don Daniele thought. He saw that several captains nodded at the old man's words. He had to put an immediate end to those old-school ideas.

"*Lucio, amico mio*. New York is not the world, nor are Italian countrymen the only ones who have money. We are no longer in Sicily. The United States is our new homeland."

"*Ma il nostro sangue è ancora siciliano!* But our blood is still Sicilian!" replied the old man in a harsh tone. "Wherever we go we must honor our traditions."

"And so it will be," Monreale agreed. "But I don't want to live hidden all my life, hidden among my people. With this plan that I propose to you, we will conquer America!"

The men looked at him in amazement. The audacity of the boss knew no limits. At the same time, Ferrante laughed. His laughter prevailed over the murmurs of the others, until a heavy silence fell heavily over the conference room. Monreale stared at his captain until he stopped laughing.

"Always with your delusions of grandeur, Danny," he said reproachfully. Then he added in a serious tone, "You're going to bring ruin to all of us."

The atmosphere in the room became tense. No one could openly contradict the Don, not even an old comrade. The other men looked down and waited for their boss's reaction.

Monreale nodded slowly. Finally, Ferrante had made his last slip. The time had come to demonstrate to those men the true power of Don Daniele Monreale.

"You disrespected me, Lucio," the *capo* declared.

At the same time, his mind said, 'You'll die for this'.

Luciano Ferrante shuddered. Monreale watched him in silence, but his mind issued an order: 'Get up and go next to that sideboard'. Ferrante hesitated, but at last he stood up and took a few hesitant steps toward the sideboard in the corner of the room. The captains seated around the table held their breath. Ferrante was dishonoring himself by humiliating his boss. However, Monreale said nothing and limited himself to staring at his rival.

'Open that drawer and take what's inside'.

Ferrante was sweating profusely, but he was not speaking either. He opened the drawer and pulled out a gleaming Thompson submachine gun. Franco Gagliano jumped up and ran to protect his boss, but he ordered him with a gesture not to move. The other men leaned back in their chairs or half got up. Several shouted at Ferrante not to do anything crazy.

The old mobster held the gun pointed forward, but he seemed distracted, as if he didn't know what to do with it.

"Are you trying to kill me, traitor?" Monreale asked aloud.

"No," Ferrante stammered, in a voice of confusion.

'Do it now', Monreale's mind commanded.

Immediately, Ferrante rested the barrel of the submachine gun under his chin and pulled the trigger. The burst of rounds destroyed his head. His brains splattered the ceiling as his body spun lifelessly on itself until it fell heavily to the ground. The captains, accustomed to violence and death, were disoriented. Several paled intensely and more than one had to hold back a few gags. Gagliano kicked the Thompson away from the bloody corpse. Monreale looked coldly at his men.

"Whoever does not have the courage to accompany me in my plan, let speak now."

No one moved. The men held their boss's gaze for as long as they could.

"Franco will give you your orders. The meeting is over."

The men left the room muttering. It was evident that Ferrante had managed to hide the submachine gun in the drawer in advance with the intention of killing the boss. It was a treacherous, if audacious, coup. But in the end the old mobster had lacked courage. He had paid for the mistake with his own life.

One of the soldiers standing guard outside

the conference room gestured to Monreale to speak apart.

"D'Amato has just arrived, boss."

Don Daniele stiffened.

"Where is he?"

"In the basement."

Monreale ignored his men and went immediately to the basement of the building, which was used as a storage room. Stefano D'Amato was sitting at a simple table, desperately eating and drinking. He looked unkempt and pale. It was evident that he had been in hiding since the failed hit.

"D'Amato," said Monreale. "What happened?"

"Don Daniele," the soldier knelt in front of his boss and took his hand. "It wasn't my fault, boss!"

"Get up and talk like a man."

D'Amato stood up and spoke hurriedly.

"We struck at the right time and place, chief. Roselli and Rocco carried the tools and I drove. When I arrived at the site, I crossed the car on the pavement, in front of the other vehicle. Roselli and Rocco immediately got out and began to spray fire. But one of the targets fired back and knocked off both our men!

"One minute. Are you saying that those men were armed?"

"At least one of them, Don Daniele. He was very fast and had excellent aim!"

"What nonsense is this, D'Amato?" Monreale

took him by the lapels of his jacket and shook him. "Those men are bookworms!"

"I swear that's how it happened, boss. Maybe that man was a bodyguard."

"I can't believe it," the *capo* murmured. "And the other targets?"

"I saw two falling, the oldest ones. I think the boys caught up with them with their bursts. Then the armed guy tried to kill me. I hardly backed up with the car and managed to flee. The car was left like a sieve, boss!"

Monreale gaped at his soldier. A very simple task had ended in complete disaster.

"Roselli didn't manage to get close to those men?"

"It all happened very quickly, boss."

"*Porca miseria!*"

Incredibly, his captain had failed him. Roselli only had to obtain some relics that Monreale had described to him in detail. Obviously, in addition to the robbery, the men who had the artifacts in their possession would have to die. No witnesses could be left alive. The ideal place to strike was in the street, at night. There was less movement and few onlookers. Of course, no one had counted on an armed bodyguard. Now Monreale realized that he should have foreseen it, considering the high value of the pieces. That man was to be a private detective, or a police officer assigned to the protection of the scholars. Monreale had to plan a new attempt before his plan was damaged or someone gave him away.

He turned abruptly and found his lieutenant, Gagliano, who was watching him expectantly.

"There has been a setback, Franco.

"Give me the order, boss. I'll do it."

Monreale shook his head.

"This time I'll take care of it myself. There can be no more mistakes. The Roselli disaster will be in the newspapers and will attract attention to us."

They both moved away from the soldier, who had sat down at the table with a dejected face.

"What will we do with D'Amato?" Gagliano asked in a low voice. "Someone may recognize him."

"He must disappear," Monreale ordered. "Permanently."

4. MOUNT SINAI HOSPITAL

It was the longest night of his life. He sped through Harlem on a large avenue until he came face to face with Central Park. Without getting out of the car, he asked for the hospital and asked passers-by for directions. He ran into drunks, indifferent, tourists and immigrants. Most of them had never heard of Mount Sinai. Others didn't even know what that Manhattan neighborhood was called. After several stops, someone was able to direct him to the hospital. By this time Sir John had fallen into unconsciousness. Upon arriving, Hunt stopped with a screech of tires in front of the main entrance of the imposing building and dropped over on the horn.

He could not see his boss for hours or know anything about his state of health. A nurse told him in passing that Sir John was being operated on. The police arrived shortly after, along with the press, several directors of the American Geographical Society and staff of the British consulate. Hunt had to repeat the story several times, the press was expelled from inside the premises, and he was left alone only when someone noticed that he was about to fall exhausted.

The attack had evidently been perpetrated by the Mafia, but no one dared to give reasons for the motive for the crime. Gangsters had never attacked academics or scientists. In a second wave of visitors, authorities from the city, the state and the federal government arrived. Information about the identity of the attackers had spread during the morning. Hunt thanked the outpouring of support with red eyes and a knot in his stomach. Finally, in the middle of the afternoon, he was able to break free from the whole gale. He asked for Sir John and was informed by a doctor in the surgery area that the patient was recovering.

"Come with me, son."

The doctor, an older man who introduced himself as Dr. Steinberg, guided him to an unoccupied room on the same floor.

"Get some sleep. Sir John is in good hands. But you seem to be on the verge of fainting."

Hunt awoke abruptly when it was already dark. He had been dreaming that they were trying to kill him. He sat up on the bed and, when he saw where he was, he realized that it was not a dream. Simply, his mind had recreated everything that had happened since the fateful previous night. He got out of bed and found that he hadn't even taken off his shoes before sleeping. He went out into the corridor and tried to find his way back to the surgery department counter.

At that time the place was calm. Most of the lights in the hallways were turned off to give the floor a nighttime atmosphere. Through the half-open doors, Hunt spotted several patients sleeping or simply resting in their beds after surgery. He thanked the air of tranquility that was breathed in the recovery area. The police interrogations and the insistence of journalists had left him exhausted. For now, the important thing was that Sir John should recover from the attack. Then Hunt would go in search of the killers.

He had engraved in his mind the names of the two gangsters the police had mentioned: Roselli and Rocco. According to the head of the investigators, who had reported himself at the hospital, both men belonged to a gang that operated in Italian Harlem. Roselli himself was suspected of being the leader of the group, but he was undoubtedly answering to a more senior *capo*. The key question of that affair still hovered in the captain's head: Why had the mafia attacked some academics? As he did not believe in coincidences, he told himself Sir John would have been right. The attack was related to the gems and the finding of the treasure in New Mexico. Somehow, the attackers knew that the gems were in the possession of the SGA and had decided to steal them.

However, it was too risky a hit, even for the mafia. Hunt understood that the gems had a very high value, perhaps incalculable, but it still seemed far-fetched to steal archaeological pieces that were difficult to sell on the black market. This, without counting on the visibility of the hit. After a moment's reflection, Hunt deduced that the gangsters never imagined that the attack would be countered by any of their targets. Much less did they suppose that any of them would even be arrested. Not to mention being injured or killed. Obviously, their goal was to leave no witnesses to the attack.

The surgery department counter was located under an opening in the wall, at the beginning of a corridor. On the other side was a small office where a middle-aged nurse nodded off in her chair. However, when she heard approaching footsteps, the woman straightened up and pretended to check some medical records.

"Good evening, nurse. I look for Sir John Connelly's room."

"That patient cannot receive visitors."

Hunt smiled at her, despite the nurse's sour

face.

"I'm Captain Peter Hunt. Am..."

"Ah, you're the man who caused such a fuss this morning. They told me that all that was missing was for the president to come and visit us."

Hunt kept his smile undaunted.

"Dr. Steinberg left instructions that you were allowed to enter," the woman explained. "Room 182. Going around that corner."

"Thank you very much."

Hunt quickly walked away in case the nurse bit as well as barked. Outside Room 182 was a chair leaning against the wall, but it was empty. The door was ajar. Hunt entered the room and closed the door behind him. Sir John was lying on a bed with metal railings, covered by the sheets up to his chin. He breathed softly. His arm was connected to a rubber hose that supplied him with serum from a bag hung on a metal stand.

"Sir John, can you hear me?"

He spoke to him in a low voice, so as not to startle him. Since his boss didn't answer, Hunt repeated the question in a louder tone. Nothing. The director of Department X was fast asleep. Or maybe he had been put to sleep with some painkiller. At least, Hunt guessed he wasn't in a coma. Hunt wished he could talk to a doctor about his boss's condition, but by that time it seemed that the surgeons had already left. Perhaps there was a doctor on duty in the emergency room, but it was unlikely that he knew the case of a patient in the surgery department.

Hunt would have to wait until the next day to speak with Steinberg or another doctor. He stared at Sir John for a moment. He was furious about what had happened. He was in charge of his boss's security and hadn't seen the attack coming. It was true that it was something unforeseen and very fast, but he felt guilty anyway. In addition, the driver of the car had managed to flee. If he had stopped him, he would have been able to interrogate him and find out who was behind the attack. To make matters worse, Professor Robert Lester, his host in America, had been killed. Hunt promised himself that he would investigate the reasons for the attack and find the culprits... at any cost.

Suddenly, he remembered the gems. Sir John had put the puzzle box in one of the pockets of his jacket. Hunt turned round. He looked for the jacket his boss was wearing, but there was no item of clothing in the room. Surely his suit was covered in blood and had been discarded or even incinerated. Had anyone noticed the lump in the pocket and looked inside, discovering the small solid gold box? Although the device was an obvious temptation, Hunt was confident in the integrity of the hospital staff. Maybe the police searched his belongings, he thought.

Then he discovered that there was a bedside

table on the other side of the bed, next to the bedroom window. He went around the large bed and opened the top drawer of the bedside table. He almost laughed. There was the puzzle box along with Sir John's pocket watch and his old fountain pen. The trusty briar pipe had been lost forever. Hunt took the box and operated the mechanism that opened the lid. The seven gems glittered in the light that filtered through the window. Hunt dropped them into the palm of his hand and examined them closely.

The door opened with a soft creak. Hunt immediately turned around. He held the puzzle box behind his back and put the gems away blindly. A nurse was standing by the bed. In her hands she held a tray with some medical supplies.

"Good evening, sir. You shouldn't be here."

Hunt noticed a slight accent as she spoke. The girl was very beautiful. She wore an immaculately white uniform, with a bib and skirt, and wore a cap on the nape of her neck that held the bun in which she gathered her wavy black hair fixed. That hairstyle allowed the beautiful features of her oval face to stand out, on which seductive lips stood out. The eyes, deep green, stared at Hunt, questioning him with serious professionalism.

Hunt smiled at her as he put the puzzle box in his jacket pocket.

"I'm Captain Peter Hunt. Sir John is..."

"I know. Matron told me that you would come."

The girl arranged the tray at the foot of the bed. She briefly auscultated the patient, took his pulse, and then changed the IV bag. Hunt watched with interest as she performed her tasks with simple efficiency and speed. When she finished, she looked at him and smiled politely.

"You'll have to go soon, captain. Visitors are not allowed at night."

Suddenly, Hunt remembered the empty chair outside the room.

"Do you know if there were any policemen standing guard in the hallway?"

One of the visits that morning had been from the police commissioner. Hunt was sure that the man, with the district attorney, had promised him that there would be a permanent guard while Sir John was hospitalized.

The nurse shrugged.

"I am sorry. I just started my shift."

Hunt peered into the hallway. It was deserted and dimly lit. Nor were voices or noises heard coming from the counter or the doctors' room. Hunt returned to the room. A rush of adrenaline ran through his body.

"What is your name?" He asked the nurse.

She must have noticed his uneasiness, for she looked at him suspiciously before answering.

"Allison MacGregor. Is something bad going

on?"

He smiled forcefully.

"You need not worry, Allison. Can I call you Allison?"

She nodded. Hunt sensed that the girl was more and more worried.

"Are you Scottish, Allison?"

"Yes. I arrived in America at a very young age, with my family."

New York, a city of immigrants, Hunt thought. He took the girl by the arm and led her to the bedside. The girl's green eyes widened.

"I need to get my boss out of here."

"Impossible!" Now she looked at him with disapproval. "The patient is still in serious condition and under heavy sedation. He cannot get up, even with help."

Hunt bent down and inspected the lower part of the bed. Fortunately, the legs ended in wheels.

"Then we must move the bed. Are there any empty rooms in this floor?"

The nurse took a couple of steps away from the captain and crossed her arms.

"I don't know what's going on, but I assure you that..."

Hunt confronted her in a serious tone.

"They'll come to kill us any moment," Hunt said.

The girl turned pale. She stammered another protest, but he silenced her with a gesture.

"There should have been a police guard outside, but he's not there," he insisted. "There are also no doctors or other personnel nearby. Someone cleared this sector, or perhaps the entire floor."

"But that's impossible!"

"We were attacked in the middle of the street last night," Hunt explained. "With machine guns! I'm afraid the same men will try again tonight."

Allison's mind was buzzing with questions. Hunt noticed it in her eyes. Before the girl continued to deny reality, he grabbed her by both arms and held her firmly in front of him.

"You must help me, Allison. The killers will stop at nothing."

Without further explanation, Hunt approached the serum holder and tried to take it down.

"I'll do it," said the girl. "You grab the bed."

The nurse secured the catheter that Sir John had in his forearm. Then she took down the IV bag and left it on the patient's chest. Hunt released the levers that held the bed wheels on brakes, then grabbed the railing on its side. Allison grabbed the other side and together they pushed the bed toward the door. The wheels made a slight squeaking sound and then started moving.

They passed the bed through the door opening and then turned it so that it could be moved down the corridor.

"I think there's a spare room at the other end of the floor," said the nurse. "Mrs. Klein was discharged this afternoon."

"Very well. Let's go."

The bed was quite heavy. Although it had wheels on each leg, it was difficult to overcome the inertia to move it. In addition, the creak of the metal frame flooded the quiet corridor. Hunt wanted to go faster, but he restrained himself to avoid the loud noise that the bed would make. He assumed that the murderers were already inside the hospital. He deduced that they had contacts in the police to have managed to remove the officer on duty. Regarding the medical staff, he imagined that it would not be difficult to create some distraction with a dying patient in the emergency department that required the presence of several doctors.

Together with the nurse they turned the bed in a corner of the corridor. The girl was pale and kept turning her head in all directions. Hunt had scared her to death, but there was no other way to convince her to help him. And the threat was very real.

"Maybe we should call the police," the girl whispered. "There is a telephone at the department counter."

"They won't come," Hunt replied curtly.

Allison gaped at him. He gestured for her not to stop advancing.

At the end of the corridor was the counter, which protruded slightly from the wall, serving as the sill of the opening that connected with the matron's office. Amid the infuriating squeaks of the bed, Hunt and the girl managed to get there. There was light in the office, but no one could be seen inside.

"The door is on the other side," Allison explained. "I will go and confirm that Mrs. Klein's room is unoccupied."

The nurse went out to the waiting room and went around it to go to the door of the office. Before she got there, Hunt poked his head over the counter. The matron lay on her back on the floor. Her eyes were wide open and there was a thick red mark on her neck. She had been strangled.

"Allison, come here!"

The nurse stopped just before entering the back hallway. She stepped back into the waiting room and from there asked:

"What's wrong?"

"We don't have time," Hunt hurried. He didn't want her to see her boss's corpse. He was sure that the impact would be very great for her. "Come on, let's continue."

Allison made a sign of resignation and went back to the other side of the bed. As they moved the bed, Sir John shuddered in his deep sleep. Allison examined him for a second, but then signaled to Hunt that they could go on.

They went through the waiting room and took the next corridor. The nurse nodded that the unoccupied room was at the other end of the hallway. Hunt's heart was pounding. Now he was sure that the assassins would arrive at any moment.

The girl opened the door to the room while the captain turned the bed to orient it towards the opening. Allison pulled the headboard, and he pushed its feet. The bed was passing through the opening when Hunt heard footsteps coming from the previous hallway. Still pushing the bed, he half-turned and saw three men walking briskly in his direction. They all wore dark suits and their hats tightly capped. And each one had a gun in his hand.

"Lock the door and don't open it until I tell you!" Hunt ordered the girl.

He pushed the bed with all his might and finished bringing it into the room. With a scared rictus, Allison rushed to close the door from the inside. Hunt ran to the entrance to the hallway, where it opened into the waiting room. He drew his Webley Mk VI revolver. He had reloaded the six cartridges before falling asleep in the bed lent to him by Dr. Steinberg. He took a knee on the ground, raised his weapon, and pointed it at the assassins. They abruptly moved away and stuck to the walls of the other corridor. Only the waiting room separated the two opposing sides.

The gangsters fired immediately. The

entrance to the corridor was filled with lead. Hunt dropped to the ground and returned fire. His shots went nowhere. His opponents were firing furiously, simply filling the entire space of the hallway with gunfire. Hunt rolled across the floor and backed away, without firing again. He could not waste his rounds. The noise of the gunshots was deafening. No doubt the shooting could be heard throughout the hospital. Maybe there was already someone calling the police, but it would all be over by the time law enforcement arrived.

It appeared to Hunt that the killers were armed with Colt M1911 pistols. That meant they had seven cartridges in the magazine plus one in the chamber. At that rate of fire, they would soon have to reload. He saw an instant later one of the gangsters step back and replaced his magazine. Lying on his face on the floor, Hunt took careful aim and fired. The man fell backwards and lost his gun. One less. Another of the gangsters exhausted his ammunition and also walked away to reload. This time Hunt stood up, got into a shooting position, knees bent, and shot the man. He only managed to wound him in the arm, but it was enough to disable him.

The third gangster seemed to be the oldest of the three. He was also the bravest. He had reloaded his ammunition quickly and lunged forward while still firing. Pieces of plaster sprouted from the walls of the corridor when they were hit by the powerful .45 ACP bullets. The air was filled with gunpowder smoke. Hunt had to back off almost blindly. He fired a couple of times forward, but the assassin's shots did not stop. Suddenly, a piece of cement from the wall hit the captain's face. He instinctively put his hand to his face to protect himself. Then he felt a pain in his arm and his revolver slipped out of his hand.

"Don't move!" A voice commanded. Amid the smoke from the cordite and the dust from the plaster coating on the walls, Hunt saw only a vague figure pointing its gun at him a few inches from his body. "Where's the box?"

"What box?" asked the captain in turn, although he knew perfectly well what the murderer meant.

The man cocked his pistol loudly.

"The puzzle box! I know you have it. Give it to me or I'll kill everybody, including the nurse."

Hunt knew when he had been defeated. However, he also knew that if he handed over the box, he would still be killed. The mafia did not leave any witnesses alive.

"It's in Room 182," Hunt said, with a mock tone of resignation. "In a drawer on the bedside table..."

The shot rang out loudly next to his ear. Hunt cringed in sudden pain, as a sharp beep pierced his brain.

"The next bullet will blow your brains out.

We already searched the room and there is nothing there. Don't play with me, English, or you'll regret it."

"OK! But don't hurt us."

Hunt crouched down submissively. He took the puzzle box out of his pocket and handed it to the gangster. He snatched it from his hands. Hunt ducked a little deeper and prepared to launch himself like a projectile at the killer. He was staring at the box and seemed almost forgotten about Hunt. Hunt took a strong breath. He was about to charge when the gangster shouted in surprise and then he was startled. A nauseating vapor emanated from his clothes. A noise of glass crashing on the floor was heard in the midst of the smoke in the corridor.

The killer shouted in pain and ran towards the exit. Hunt turned and saw Allison MacGregor standing in the hallway, a few feet behind him.

"There's a cart with cleaning products in the room," the girl explained.

"It must have been hydrochloric acid," Hunt said. "Are you ok?"

She nodded vigorously. The captain ran to the other corridor. There were only a few blood stains on the floor; the three men had fled.

* * *

Daniele Monreale was driving the car in a state halfway between euphoria and irritation.

Although he had achieved his goal of obtaining the precious puzzle box, at the same time the hit had been on the verge of failure. Again. In a reflexive gesture, he held the steering wheel with one hand and with the other he felt the pocket of his jacket where he had kept the small gold receptacle. He had opened the box surreptitiously as he got into the car—he knew the opening mechanism beforehand—and had almost cried as he saw the seven gems shining inside. Now all that remained was to activate the gemstones and get the jackpot.

Slowly, he became more relieved as the car sped away from the hospital. The newspapers were right about that Englishman. That same morning he had read the news about the shooting in Washington Heights. The article described Hunt, the man who shot back the attack, as a former military man and researcher at the British Museum, with extensive experience in exploratory expeditions. Anticipating a new confrontation with the Englishman, Monreale had taken with him Greco and Vizzini, two of the toughest soldiers of his own clan. However, the morons had started shooting left and right when they saw Hunt draw his gun. Monreale didn't mind shooting inside a hospital or killing innocent people who crossed his path, but he hated losing control of an operation.

The Englishman had asserted his training

and discipline on the brute strength of his men. Monreale wanted to deal with that guy again, but for now he had other problems. To begin with, the liquid that that bitch threw at him had caused burns on his skin and stung his eyes. He would also have a bullet reserved for her in case he saw her again. Damn, he thought. He could have become deformed, or blind. At least he had gotten off lightly, not like his two henchmen who moaned in pain in the back seat. Greco's arm was inert and covered in blood. Vizzini would be lucky if he got alive to the next day.

Monreale maneuvered to enter through the rear access to the Bowery building. Several of his men came out to meet him and dragged the wounded down.

"Are you okay, Danny?" Gagliano asked.

"A fucking bitch threw acid at me, or something. Can you believe it, Franco?"

His lieutenant stared at him with wild eyes. The suit was still smoking and Monreale had a cheek and part of the neck red.

"I'll call the *dottore* ," said Gagliano. "You should see those burns."

"That he attends to the guys first. Vizzini is on his last legs."

Monreale took off his jacket and threw it on the ground. He held the puzzle box tight in a fist.

"I'll be in my office. Let no one bother me," he ordered.

"Yes, boss."

"She hasn't arrived?" Gagliano shook his head. "Well, look for her. I want her here now!"

* * *

This time the police had invaded the hospital's surgery department. Agents swarmed all over the floor. Nurses and aides had to cry out for investigators to step aside so they could move patients from nearby rooms. The damage to the waiting room and both corridors was considerable. The press camped outside the building waiting for an official report on the shooting. The establishment's board of trustees angrily complained about the lack of vigilance, while the mayor and district attorney tried to calm the frightened surgeons. The authorities promised to catch the perpetrators of the murder of the matron as soon as possible. British consulate staff moved Sir John to a location that would be kept in reserve.

Meanwhile, Hunt was subjected to further interrogations late into the night. In the end, the homicide investigator instructed him that a police artist would make a portrait of the suspect who had nearly killed him. The cartoonist turned out to be a young, bohemian-looking man who wore a loose shirt and had long hair. He unfolded a sketch book with blank sheets of paper in front of the captain and prepared several freshly sharpened charcoal pencils.

"Very well, sir. Please describe in great detail the man you saw. It is important that you point out the features of the face, the color of the hair and eyes, and any distinctive signs that the suspect may have had."

Hunt closed his eyes for a moment and conjured up the serious, cold face of the killer. Between the smoke of the gunpowder, the dust of the plaster and the barrel of the gun that was pointed between his eyes, there was not much he could remember of that man. However, he concentrated and slowly described the characteristics that came to his memory. Gradually the mental portrait became clearer and was able to refer to the color and length of his hair, the expression of his face, the shape of his eyes and the deadly rictus of his mouth.

The sketch artist would make a version of the features described and then show the drawing to the captain. The latter directed him by closing his eyes again.

"No, thicker eyebrows... Darker hair... Yes, the eyes are fine... Cruel traits... Older, in his fifties..."

"Wait a minute," said the illustrator after half an hour. "You don't need to go on. I know this man!"

Hunt looked at him in surprise.

"You see, I'm of Italian descent." Hunt's pulse quickened. Obviously the killer was some kind of gangster renowned among his compatriots. "But

I have nothing to do with these *mafiosi*."

"No, of course not," the captain assured him.

The sketch artist bent down to speak to him in a low voice.

"You were very lucky, sir. This man is one of the most dangerous bosses in the mafia." He held up the sheet of paper and showed him the finished drawing. The resemblance to the killer was remarkable. "Daniele Monreale. 'Dan The Man'. The king of Little Italy."

A little later, Hunt left the room and found himself alone in the hallway. The interrogations had been carried out in the premises of the hospital management. No one was around there at that hour. Hunt leaned his back against a wall and sighed. It seemed that this day would never end. What promised to be a quiet academic trip to America had quickly turned into a bloodbath. New York was a violent city full of corruption. It was no different from the seedier corners of Cairo and Shanghai where the captain had been before.

Delicate footsteps approaching down the corridor roused him from his reverie. Suddenly he found himself face to face with Allison MacGregor. Now she was wearing her street clothes. A simple long dress and a thick wool coat. She looked very different without her stern nurse's uniform and her hair pulled back under her cap.

"Oh, you're still here!" she exclaimed.

"I've just finished with the police. And you?"

"The police also got me. And then the board of directors. They wanted to make sure that the hospital had nothing to do with this matter."

"I bet. Can I invite you to dinner?"

"No thanks. I just want to go home to sleep."

"You saved my life. It's the least I can do. Besides, you must be hungry," he insisted.

He was sure she wavered in her decision.

"Starving, to tell the truth." She paused. Finally, she nodded. "I guess I deserve a nice dinner for saving your life."

She had a beautiful smile. Hunt smiled too but shook his head at the same time.

"You mean breakfast. Have you seen what time it is?"

He offered her his arm and they went to the exit together.

5. BOWERY

The clinking of plates and cups echoed through the empty tea room of the Biltmore Hotel. It was not yet dawn, but the breakfast staff was already serving the earliest customers. The waiters were accustomed to the coming and going of guests at all hours, especially considering that the hotel was directly connected to the adjacent Grand Central Railway Terminal. Within minutes, Hunt and Allison were separated by a table full of scrambled eggs, fried bacon, hash browns, sausage, toast, pancakes, waffles, and other kinds of cold cuts and pastries. Between the plates, different jugs of hot water, milk, cream, and sugar rose like towers.

"This is what they call an American breakfast," Hunt said. "Not even at lunch could I eat all this."

Allison, who had already tasted the contents of almost every dish, looked at him with her mouth full. He smiled at her.

"It was true that you were starving."

The girl laughed discreetly, trying not to choke. Hunt poured himself another cup of coffee and tried some toast and jam. He would gladly have eaten eggs and bacon, but he had lost his appetite after he learned who his enemy was. His stomach felt full of bile, produced not by fear, but by anger. He was sure that he would have a new meeting with Daniele Monreale. And on that occasion the mafioso would not flee again.

"A penny for your thoughts," said Allison, rousing him from his reverie.

Hunt noticed that he had been absorbed in his thoughts for several minutes.

"I'm sorry, my dear. I can't stop thinking about the man who attacked us. I had heard that these gangsters were violent guys, but I never thought they could go as far as to start a shooting in a hospital!"

"Yes, it's quite unusual. However, they constantly assassinate their rivals or burn down the businesses of those who reject their offer of protection."

"Evidently, this Monreale guy wished at all costs to seize the object that was in Sir John's possession."

He avoided giving details about the puzzle box and its contents. Allison seemed like a good girl—and had saved his life—but he didn't really know her. However, the girl was stunned when she heard his comment. Her cup of coffee was stopped halfway to her mouth and her eyes widened.

"Danny Monreale? The king of Little Italy?"

Hunt stiffened in his chair.

"Do you know him too? But how?"

"I live in the Lower East Side, the district next to Little Italy. Most of the district's residents are immigrants, or descendants of immigrants," Allison explained. "As in all poor neighborhoods, there are several gangs that control gambling, liquor smuggling, and extort money from shopkeepers."

"Wow. It seems that the mafia is more widespread than it seems."

The girl shrugged and continued talking while still eating.

"The mafia is the criminal organization of Italians, particularly those from Sicily. But there are also Irish and Jewish gangs. On the street where I live, operates a gang of Scottish loan sharks. Stores and establishments that do not pay the loans, have their windows broken. If the owner falls behind on payments again, his legs are broken."

"My god! I thought those practices had disappeared before the war. Crime has fallen in London's East End. And in Birmingham, the Peaky Blinders have all but disappeared."

"Perhaps that will happen in England," said the girl. "But many practices brought from the Old World by immigrants are still in force here. One of my cousins is involved in one of these groups and tells me that all of Manhattan is divided among dozens of criminal gangs, all made up of immigrants. In Brooklyn and the Bronx there are also several of those groups."

Hunt was impressed by the girl's knowledge. Organized crime appeared to be common among immigrants in New York's poorest neighborhoods. The people who lived in those places were used to that way of life or, rightly, accepted it as something normal. The local authorities did not care about improving these neighborhoods and eradicating criminals, so they reigned freely among their own compatriots.

"Fortunately, I have a good job," Allison said. "I hope to raise an amount of money soon that will allow me to leave the Lower East Side and take my parents to a better neighborhood. You can't imagine the rental prices in Midtown, or even in the northern area!"

"I really hope you can make it soon, Allison. You're a good girl."

"Call me Allie. My mother's name is also Allison, and you make me feel as old as her."

They both laughed. It was the first time Hunt had seen her cheerful.

"You're going after Monreale, aren't you?"

The girl's sudden question caught him off guard. Almost without realizing it, he nodded his head.

"That object he stole," she asked. "Was it very

valuable?"

"More than its economic value, which is quite high, it has a very important... *cultural* value," Hunt explained.

He had been about to say 'mystic', but he didn't want to have to explain himself to the girl so much. However, she still surprised him by saying:

"I can help you find it."

He shook his head.

"You don't need to get involved in this matter, Allie. I thank you very much for what you did, but those guys are very dangerous."

"Didn't you hear anything I told you?" The girl left her cup forcefully on the saucer. The porcelain clanked loudly in the empty room. "I've lived with gangsters all my life. I'm tired of seeing them strutting around the street, as if they were the owners of the neighborhood. And now, to top it off, they attack the place where I work."

The girl's beautiful face had turned crimson from her contained fury. Hunt tried to pacify her with a gesture, but she shook her head.

"I have more reasons than you to hate Monreale and others like him. Let me help you retrieve that item, Peter. I finally have a chance to do something that hurts them."

In spite of himself, Hunt realized that he was nodding. He didn't know anyone else in town and could use all the help he could muster. Allison looked at him expectantly. After a moment, he smiled at her.

"Finish your breakfast," he said. "We have a lot of things to plan."

The train dropped Hunt off at the Grand Street station of the Third Avenue Railroad. From the raised platform you could see the upper floors of the buildings of Little Italy and the Lower East Side, on whose sides hung large advertising signs. Down below, at the corner of Bowery and Grand, there was a great hustle and bustle of passers-by and a busy motor cars traffic. Hunt mingled with the crowd that had descended from the train at the station and lowered the metal staircase that led to street level among the other passengers.

He immediately found himself surrounded by employment agencies, small restaurants, cheap hotels, second-hand clothing shops and ethnic food stores. A dozen different languages filled the air beneath the noise of trains running on the elevated tracks that obscured both sidewalks of the avenue. For a moment, the captain felt lost, but suddenly a hand grabbed his arm and made him turn around. Allison MacGregor smiled at him, amused.

"It wasn't hard to find you. You stand out from the crowd like a lion in the pond where the gazelles drink."

"I hope it's a compliment," he murmured.

"Dressed like this, you will never be able

to approach Monreale," she said, whispering the name of the mafioso.

Even though there was a lot of noise in the street, the girl was still afraid that she might be heard by some nosy person.

Hunt forced himself to remember that he was now in his enemy's territory. And he realized that he was out of place there. He wore a sleek, new-looking navy suit, a light gray Homburg hat, and shiny black Oxford shoes. On the contrary, passers-by wore worn, dark and anonymous clothes. At most they covered themselves with flat caps. In addition, the captain was one head taller than most of them. He felt a little ridiculous for not having foreseen that he must go unnoticed in that place. The girl was right. There he would easily attract attention.

After finishing breakfast, they agreed that the girl would guide him on a tour of the neighborhoods in which Monreale moved. It was a risky maneuver, but Hunt needed to do a reconnaissance of the terrain. Meanwhile, Allison would try to find out where the mobster was hiding and if anyone had heard on the street about the attack on the hospital.

The captain went to sleep for a few hours in his room and the girl immediately returned home. They would meet in the middle of the afternoon at the Grand Street station of the elevated railway. He could catch a train of the same line near his hotel. After waking up, the captain grabbed a quick lunch and then boarded the train at the 42nd Street station. Together with the girl they walked away from the station.

"What shall we do?" He asked Allison.

From that moment on, she would be the one who would take the initiative.

"A while ago I was talking to my uncle, the father of the cousin I mentioned. He is furious that his son mixed with the gangsters, so it was not difficult to make him talk."

Hunt was in awe of the girl. She was proving to be a vitally important ally.

"He told me that Bowery forms a border between the territories of the Sicilian gangs and those of other immigrants," she explained. "Here, business is done between like-minded groups and disputes between rivals are settled."

"A neutral zone. Will you be able to find out anything about the Monreale clan?"

As they talked, they walked south, in the shadow of the huge, elevated train tracks. The girl pointed her chin at an establishment of dubious quality located further on at the same street. Hunt carried the revolver under his jacket, but he would only use it as a last resort. However, he unbuttoned his jacket when they entered the premises. Above the dirty window it had painted a sign with green letters: Óglach.

"This restaurant is owned by an Irish friend of my uncle. I suggest you don't speak in front of him." Hunt raised an eyebrow. "At the very least, try to hide your Eton accent."

"I didn't go to Eton," he murmured.

She silenced him with a gesture.

Hunt knew right away that he was going to have trouble inside the restaurant. *Óglach* meant 'young man' in Irish, but, by extension, it translated as 'young soldier'. That was the name given to the members of the Irish Republican Army, the paramilitary organization that had fought in the war of independence that ended with the creation of the Irish Free State in 1922. The owner of the premises must have been a supporter of the IRA and it was very likely that the restaurant would serve as a meeting place for supporters of the organization.

The interior of the premises was poorly lit, but it looked clean. A couple of middle-aged patrons sipped beer from large glass mugs at a table in the corner. The men gave the newcomers a suspicious look and then turned their backs on them. Hunt ignored the cold welcome and motioned for the girl to sit at a table near the entrance. That way they could flee quickly if necessary.

A short red-haired man, but thick as a barrel, came over to serve them. His arms looked like two legs of ham.

"What do I serve you?" He asked sharply.

He had a strong Irish accent. You could tell he didn't like strangers.

"Two beers," the girl asked.

The publican gave Hunt a cold look. It was obvious that he had sussed him as an intruder. The captain maintained a neutral expression but did not take his face away from that gaze. He did not wish to be seen uneasy or even less intimidated. The owner of the place returned in a brief moment with two pints of beer. Allison cleared her throat before asking:

"Are you Liam O'Connor?"

The publican squeezed his eyes and looked at the girl with obvious suspicion. This is a bad idea, Hunt thought.

"Who asks?"

"My name's Allison MacGregor. My uncle Brendan told me you could help me."

O'Connor looked at both strangers for a few moments before asking the girl:

"Brendan MacGregor from Orchard Street?" Allison nodded. "Brian MacGregor's father?"

"Brian is my cousin."

"Yes, I know them. Tell your cousin to come and pay me what he owes me for... er, he knows."

"Yes, I'll tell him."

O'Connor turned to Hunt. He folded his arms and asked him in a hoarse voice:

"And who are you?"

"A family friend," Allison replied quickly.

The Irishman did not take his eyes off the captain.

"Is he mute?"

"Hunt," he introduced himself.

He spoke in a low, neutral accent, but O'Connor didn't change his sullen expression.

Hunt was beginning to get restless. Perhaps it would be best for them to leave immediately. Before he could gesture to Allison, she said:

"Er... we need to ask you for some information, Mr O'Connor. My uncle Brendan said you were *trustworthy*."

"Of course I am. Come, let's talk back."

Allison nodded smilingly and got up right away. Hunt made a very discreet gesture of denial, but the girl did not notice. It was an obvious trap. As they followed O'Connor to the back room of the restaurant, Hunt reached under his jacket to grab the revolver. The publican opened the door and waited for them on the other side while they went into the back room, that it was even darker than the main room. In the dim light, Hunt spotted several wooden boxes with liquor bottles. The place was also one of those so-called *speakeasies* where they served illegal alcohol.

O'Connor closed the door behind them. At his back, Hunt felt the bartender move and reacted immediately. He drew the revolver as he turned toward the man. He raised the gun and pointed it directly between the eyes of O'Connor. The knife O'Connor was holding gleamed in the dim light, inches from the captain's neck. Both opponents remained motionless, ready to attack at the slightest carelessness of the opponent.

Allison stifled a scream of terror.

"I know what you're thinking," Hunt said, calmly. "But I'm not a policeman and I don't work for the government."

"However, you have a good piece, eh?" O'Connor lowered his eyes to study the revolver. "Webley Mk VI, the standard-issue weapon of the officers of the army of oppression."

"A memento of the war. And no, I was never stationed in your country. Listen, I have no problem with your cause or your republic."

"But I do have a problem with you, my friend. The English are not welcome here."

"We'll go the way we came," said the captain. "It is clear that it was a mistake to come to you."

Allison stepped forward and stood next to both of them.

"Please, Mr. O'Connor. We just want to locate Daniele Monreale."

The publican did not move the knife a millimeter and his eyes remained fixed on Hunt. However, he turned to the girl.

"What do you want with that *wop*?" O'Connor used the pejorative term to refer to Italians.

"I must recover something that Monreale stole," Hunt confessed.

The Irishman stared at him for a few moments. Then he took a step back and lowered the knife to waist height. Still, he kept it pointed forward.

"Those mafiosi are nothing more than thieves. Are you a private detective, English?"

"Believe it or not, I work for a museum."

O'Connor laughed. Finally, he put the knife in the sleeve of his shirt, where he kept it hidden. Hunt holstered the Webley under his suit jacket.

"I've never had a problem with that *wop*," the publican said. "But I don't trust him. Come, I'll show you his lair."

He led them to the entrance of the restaurant. From the doorway he pointed a thick finger toward the opposite side of the Bowery.

"Do you see that brick building, on the next block? It is the warehouse where Monreale hides his liquor. I heard that he also has his headquarters there, on the upper floor."

"Thank you very much, Mr. O'Connor," said Allison. "We are sorry to have bothered you."

"Don't worry. You'll pay me back the favor," said the Irishman, indicating that he really intended to collect the debt from the MacGregors. Then he turned to Hunt. "A warning for you, English. Don't come back this way. The boys are not as nice as I am with intruders."

Hunt nodded at him, took the girl by the arm, and they both hurried away. They waited until they were back at the railway station to speak again. Allison breathed hard.

"That was intense," she said.

"Your uncle must have warned you that the damned O'Connor was from IRA! We almost didn't make it.

"But we got the information," the girl reasoned. "Now we can keep a close eye on Monreale."

"I don't think so, Allie. Monreale must have informants all over the neighborhood. Maybe I should go to the authorities and let them investigate the matter."

Allison stared at him with bulging eyes.

"Peter! That man has half of the city's police and prosecutors in his pocket. That is why he was able to take Sir John's guard off and then attack the hospital. I knew nothing would happen to him!"

"We are at a disadvantage, my dear. We must carefully plan our next steps."

The girl shrugged and finally nodded, disheartened.

"I suppose you're right. What do you suggest?"

"For the moment I will go and see how Sir John is doing. You should go home to rest. I'll pick you up tomorrow at the hospital. I'm sure I'll come up with something by then."

"Good afternoon, Peter. Be careful."

"You too, Allie."

She kissed him lightly on the cheek as he prepared to climb the ladder to the railroad platform. He smiled at her. He couldn't know that there wouldn't be any meeting the next day.

* * *

Allison stared for several minutes at the stairs Peter had climbed. She knew that what she would do would not have his approval, but it was necessary. Until the night before, she led a quiet but solitary existence between her home in the immigrant neighborhood and her work at the hospital. The attack had changed everything. The courage and determination of that Englishman had inspired her to rebel against the injustice and abuse of those mafiosi. As she had told Peter, she knew very well how criminal gangs operate, whether they were Italian, Irish, or Jewish.

Several people had died because of Monreale, including her own matron. Allison wanted to show Peter that she could also contribute to his fight against these men. Thinking of this, she turned and walked back to the brick building that Mr. O'Connor had shown them. Now that she was alone, she walked calmly down the street knowing that she belonged to the neighborhood and, therefore, did not attract attention.

She passed in front of the entrance to the Monreale building, a darkened and anonymous portal from which no sign hung indicating its function or tenants. The door was locked, but no one could be seen watching it. There were only a couple of sinister-looking young men circling near the entrance, seemingly with nothing to do. Allison deduced that they were Sicilians who stood guard on the sly. She continued on her way without paying attention to them, but one of them whistled at her and made a couple of comments in Italian. It must have been some kind of dirty compliment, as the other young man laughed his ass off.

Between the brick building and the next construction ran a wide alley. Allison took a breath and entered the passage. Her heart was beating faster and faster. In her mind she invented various excuses in case someone asked her the reasons for being there. The alley went halfway down the block. There was a high gate closed with boards. Allison deduced that on the other side was the courtyard of the building. She looked around to make sure no one was there, and then bent down to peek between the boards.

In the courtyard some trucks could be seen parked. The doors of the cargo beds were open. Some men carried boxes inside the vehicles. Allison imagined that it was some kind of contraband. The gate was only attached to the wall with a metal chain wound over the lock. It would be easy to open the gate, but the chain would make noise. The men inside would see the girl immediately. She told herself that perhaps she should try another access, or wait until it was dark to try to open the gate.

"Can I help you, miss?"

The voice behind her startled her. The same young man who had whistled at her as she passed by was a few meters away from her in the alley. He looked at her with a sarcastic expression, but at the same time he kept a hand in his trouser pocket. God, he's got a gun, Allison thought.

"What are you doing here?" The boy insisted, this time in a more serious tone.

One of the excuses she had made immediately came to her mind.

"They told me that they were hiring here."

"Hiring? In an alley?" The young man glared at her.

"Of course not. Don't be absurd." She laughed, but her laugh sounded dry and fake. "They told me it was on this block, but I lost the note with the address."

"Are you looking for a job then?"

She nodded and tried to pass by the boy's side. He intercepted her and also smiled falsely.

"Come with me. My boss can give you a job."

She couldn't think of any excuse to refuse if she had just said she was looking for a job. The other option was to run away, but that boy would catch up with her right away. All she could to do was nod and accompany the boy. They left the alley and headed for the entrance of the building. The other guard saw her pass by and winked at her. Allison blushed. She followed her guide through a vestibule to a door behind the stairs leading to the upper floors. The door led to a large cellar full of boxes of alcohol bottles. On the opposite wall there was a wide gate leading to the courtyard. Several employees carried the boxes from the warehouse to the trucks parked outside and then returned for another load, without stopping.

Daniele Monreale supervised the loading standing under the opening of the gate. Allison recognized him immediately. She felt a shudder of terror that made her stumble. The mobster noticed her and went to meet her.

"What's the matter?" He asked his guard.

"I found this woman sniffing around in the alley." Allison stiffened and prepared to speak. The boy added, "She says she's looking for a job."

"Oh, but she already has a job." Monreale approached her until they were confronted less than a meter away. The mobster smiled ominously. "Isn't that true, nurse?"

Allison felt like fainting. Monreale made a gesture and between two of his henchmen they took her and dragged her away. They flew her down the stairs, to the lower level of the building. There they left her in a small room dimly lit by a light bulb hanging from the ceiling. Allison sat down on the only stool she could find and hid her face in her hands. How had she been so foolish? She only wanted to confirm that Monreale was in the building, to tell Peter the next day when they met in the hospital. But she had been captured and the mobster had recognized her immediately.

What would they do to her? Those mafiosi were savages. But if Monreale had wanted her dead, he would not have hesitated to eliminate her immediately. There inside his building no one would say anything and then they would get rid of her body. Didn't gangsters put the corpses of their victims inside barrels that they left abandoned on a dark corner or in an alley? Allison was sure she had read those stories in the papers. Her stomach churned at the thought that this might be her fate. Perhaps Monreale planned to interrogate her first, to find out more about Peter. Then he would kill her. Tears fell down her cheeks. No one knew that she was a prisoner in that mafioso's lair. They wouldn't miss her until the next morning, and by then it would be too late.

No one came until it was already dark. Suddenly the door opened and Monreale appeared.

"Come on," he ordered in a dry tone.

The rest of the basement was empty and quiet. Allison wondered where were all the men who had swarmed around a few hours before. That loneliness made her even more uneasy. The gangster led her down a long, dark corridor. She estimated that they were moving away from the Bowery building.

"Where are we going?" Her voice sounded nervous and weak.

"Since you are here, Miss MacGregor, you will be able to witness a very special ritual."

"How do you know my name? What ritual?"

She stopped, but Monreale grabbed her arm and forced her to continue.

"I made some quick inquiries after you arrived. As for the ritual... You'd better wait and see."

The corridor led to a large circular room with a low ceiling, which seemed to Allison to be a kind of temple. On the walls hung pieces of painted leather, beaded necklaces, and wooden hoops with a woven net inside, decorated with feathers. A wooden bench ran along the entire circular edge of the wall. In the center of the room a fire burned over a brazier, the smoke of which escaped through an opening in the ceiling, just above the fire. The air in the place was hot and charged with the smell of burnt herbs.

Monreale motioned for the girl to sit on the bench on the wall. He took off his jacket and left it on the bench as well. Then he knelt by the fire and placed a small object on a platform in front of him. The object emitted a golden glow under the dancing flames of the fire. It seemed to Allison that it was a jewel box or similar container. Monreale turned the lid and from the inside of the box he extracted seven gems of a bluish green color that he also left on the platform.

"Your friend Hunt had no idea what he had with him," the mobster commented.

His face, lit from the side by the fire, showed an ecstatic expression. Allison herself felt a little drunk. She assumed it was the product of the smoke emanating from the burnt herbs.

"What is all this?" She managed to ask.

"This is my *kiva*," the man replied. "The place where I practice ceremonies to increase my power."

In the midst of her drowsiness, Allison opened her eyes and tried to wake up.

"What power?"

Monreale took the seven gems in one hand, stood up, and placed himself in an empty space in the room. He looked at the girl, without saying anything, but she felt his eyes penetrate her brain.

'Now, keep silent'.

She became involuntarily agitated. Had he said something to her? The order had echoed within her. She wanted to say something, but she was unable to open her mouth.

'Watch and marvel'.

Allison focused her attention on the man's fist, clenched over the gems. Now she was sure he was saying something, but she didn't understand his words. It did not appear to be English, but neither did it appear to be Italian. It was a litany in an ancient, guttural language.

Suddenly, the man moved his arm and threw the gems into the air. The small spheres separated, spun over the mafioso's head, and then remained suspended there, forming a kind of spiral. An instant later, each gem cast a light that joined the rays thrown by the others, forming a translucent cascade between them all that engulfed Monreale. To the girl, the shape of the light seemed like a constellation seen in a night sky.

"At last the map unfolds in front of me." Monreale spoke again. Allison felt her mind clear. "Now I just have to follow the route and I will get the beacon that will allow me to deploy my power."

"Beacon? What beacon?" The girl asked.

The smoke dried out her throat. She felt more and more sleepy, and the man's voice sounded distant and diffuse.

"The medallion! It's been hidden for hundreds of years, but now it's shown me the way."

Monreale raised both hands and walked them through the light formed by the gems that still floated in the air. The cascade of fine golden dust shuddered between the mafioso's fingers. Allison tried to decipher the design of that strange cloud, but to her eyes it looked only like a sandstorm frozen in time. The man, for his part, smiled in wonder at that illusion. The girl coughed and closed her eyes. She was going to fall asleep at any moment.

'Allison, listen to my voice'.

She was sure he wasn't talking to her, but the voice still echoed in her mind.

'I hear it'.

'Peter Hunt will come for you'.

Her body shuddered at the sound of that name. Peter...

'When he comes, you'll be waiting for him'.

'Yes, I'll wait for him'.

'We will have a surprise for him'.

Allison smiled involuntarily; her eyes closed.

'It will be our secret'.

Shortly after, she fell asleep.

6.
MANHATTAN

It was almost midnight. Hunt had been guarding the entrance to the Monreale building since the early hours of the afternoon. He had not seen the mafioso circulating there, but he had seen dozens of his henchmen. The place was quite crowded. The gangsters went alone or in groups, stayed a few minutes in the building, and then left. No doubt they went there to report to the chief or to receive some assignment. Hunt realized that it would be impossible to enter the building from the front without being seen. Even at that time of night there were some young people who looked like guards. If he wanted to rescue Allison, he would have to find another place to infiltrate the mobster's headquarters.

Early that morning, Hunt had gone to Mount Sinai Hospital to meet the girl. Another nurse informed him that she had not gone to work. No one was surprised among the medical staff, considering what she had been through. Hunt tried to play it down on his part, but as he left the hospital all his internal alarms had gone off. It was obvious that something bad had happened. Hunt didn't have Allison's home address, but it didn't take long for him to get it from the same co-worker he'd talked to. He immediately went to the Lower East Side and went to the MacGregor family's apartment. Mrs. Allison, a plump middle-aged Scotswoman, told the captain that her daughter had not arrived all night.

Hunt tried to calm her down, but even he didn't find his excuse very convincing. After assuring the woman that he would contact her as soon as he heard from the girl, the captain went straight to the R. H. Macy & Co. store in Herald Square. There he bought some American-style clothes, in plain and dark colors, and a pair of flat caps. On the previous visit to Bowery he had realized that he must mingle with the inhabitants of the area if he wanted to go unnoticed. Finally, he went to visit Sir John, who was recovering from his surgery. Thanks to his high-level contacts, the director of Department X was housed at the British Consulate General, opposite Battery Park.

"I'm afraid Monreale has Allison," Hunt said.

"First the gems... And now that girl."

Sir John's voice was faint. He was lying in bed in a room on the top floor of the consulate building. A large window offered views of the park and the harbor. His recovery would be slow and difficult.

"I intend to retrieve the gems tonight. And the girl, of course," said the captain.

"I think Monreale intends to use the gems for some other purpose," said Sir John with difficulty. "He wouldn't have gone to so much trouble... just for the puzzle box."

"Maybe he wants to steal the rest of the treasure. The American Geographical Society has not disclosed where it keeps the find."

"The mafia has informants... among the authorities or in the Society itself," Sir John assumed. "It wouldn't cost him anything... find out the treasure cache. I think it's about... something else."

A maid from the consulate brought them lunch. Roast beef for Hunt and a porridge for the director. The woman herself served it to him by the spoonful. While she remained in the room, both men ate in silence. As soon as the maid withdrew, Sir John made a feeble gesture to the captain to come nearer. Hunt set his tray aside and stood by the bed.

"You must recover those gems... Peter. Obviously, Monreale knows its importance and usefulness. In his hands... shouldn't be good at all."

"Don't worry, Sir John. I will try to find out everything Monreale knows."

"Be careful, Peter. These mobsters are

savages."

Hunt leaned out the window. In the distance he could see the Statue of Liberty. He wondered how it was possible for Americans to value freedom so much, especially in New York, and at the same time allow the city to be full of criminal gangs that terrorized its inhabitants.

"It will all be over tonight, Sir John," said Hunt, speaking over his shoulder. "I have to settle an account with that man."

"I do not doubt your abilities, Peter. But I suggest you go prepared. Something tells me... that they will be waiting for you."

Hunt grabbed his cap and prepared to leave.

"I'll be back with the puzzle box, Sir John," he said confidently.

And with Allison, he thought. The girl was an innocent victim in that affair and by now she was probably dead. As he left the consulate, Hunt cursed himself for allowing the girl to help him in his investigation. If something happened to her, he would be the only one to blame.

Shortly after midnight, with the territory well studied, Hunt decided to act. For a few moments, he took refuge behind one of the pillars that supported the elevated train tracks. Under the tracks it was pitch black. For the same reason, only a couple of drunks and some prostitutes who had already given up hope of finding a client wandered around. From his hiding place, the captain waited until the place was calm to approach the building located on the corner of the same street. At the top of the façade ran metal zigzagging fire stairs.

Hunt gathered momentum running, jumped, and managed to hang from the last flight of stairs, which was raised at the height of the second floor. Under the weight of the captain, the last flight spring was triggered, and the ladder descended with a metallic screech until it was resting on the pavement. Without hesitation, Hunt began to run upward. Each flight of the stairs climbed up one of the five floors of the building, until it reached a balcony from which the next flight emerged. On each of the balconies there were three windows arranged in a line through which the stairs could be accessed in case of emergency. However, Hunt did not attempt to test any of the windows to see if they were open. He simply reached the top of the stairs and from there propelled himself to the roof of the building.

He lay down on the roof and waited for a few moments, revolver in hand. He heard no voices or footsteps approaching the building. Only then did he half rise, until he crouched, and advanced along the flat roof of the building towards the adjacent construction. He passed over the division between the two buildings and continued on the next roof. Thus he advanced back to the building occupied by Monreale's gang. As Hunt had envisioned, security was concentrated at the entrance, at street level, but not there at the height.

The mobster's headquarters did not have an emergency ladder at the front. Perhaps it had been removed for security reasons. However, in the center of the roof stood a hut with a metal door. Hunt deduced that the inner stairs ended there. The door was locked, but Hunt was prepared for such a contingency. From the inside pocket of his jacket he pulled out a set of lock picks. He tried a couple of the thin tools until the lock gave way and the door clicked open. He was inside. Now came the most dangerous part of his mission.

He descended the stairs with his revolver in front of him, taking light steps like a tiger about to pounce on its prey in the jungle. Hunt felt like a hunter. And of the worst kind of wild animals: the ruthless criminals who attacked other men. The city that had seemed so fascinating to him now felt like a concrete jungle. The captain was fed up with being the prey hiding in the thicket. Now he would be the one to make his enemies flee.

The top floor of the building appeared to be deserted. Hunt walked down a hallway with several doors open. He saw some offices that seemed to belong to different companies. There was also a spacious meeting room and a couple of law firms. The door at the end of the hall was locked. Before trying the lock picks on the lock, he glued his ear to the door. There was no sound from the other side. He desisted from opening the door and descended to the lower floor.

After a while he understood that all the companies located in the building must be fronts for the mafioso. Painted on the windows of the doors were only Italian names and various combinations with the name of Monreale. Hunt continued to descend and only heard voices as he approached the ground floor. From the last flight of stairs, plunged into darkness, he spied the lower hall. A couple of men—he remembered that they were called *soldiers*—spoke in the Sicilian dialect. After exchanging a few jokes – they both laughed – one of them said goodnight to the other and left. Hunt waited for him to disappear through the front door and seized his chance. He strode down the last steps and planted himself behind the man before he could react.

"I'm looking for the girl," he whispered in her ear. "If you want to live, don't tell me you haven't seen her."

The soldier shuddered as he felt the barrel of the revolver against his neck, but then nodded.

"I saw a girl this afternoon, but I don't know..."

Hunt plunged the barrel hard into the base of his neck.

"The boss had her with him! I swear!"

"Where, damn it You must have a hiding

place for the people you bring by force."

"They generally use the basement..."

Hunt knocked him out with an accurate blow from the Webley's butt to the back of his head. The man slid to the ground like a rag doll. Hunt hid the body under the stairs and then continued down the next flight of steps that descended to the lower floor. The stairs ended in an open space that served as a storeroom. For the most part, the space was occupied by stacked boxes of alcohol bottles. Prohibition was making all the criminals in the country rich.

On one of the side walls there was a door. It was locked. Hunt could no longer waste time. He kicked the door hard and blew the lock off. On the other side was a small room with a single stool in one corner. Hunt turned around immediately but stopped abruptly and re-entered the room. A soft smell of perfume hung in the air. Hunt had smelled it before. Allison had been locked up there! He returned to the storeroom and looked around. He didn't see or felt other traces of the girl. Then he noticed an open corridor in a corner. It looked like a recent work, crudely dug under the street.

Hunt stepped into the darkness. The corridor was quite long. The captain realized that the route went away from the building and probably ran several blocks below the city. Perhaps there was a mechanism to activate some light, but Hunt preferred to move forward in the dark. He did not know what he would find at the end of the road and preferred to keep the element of surprise. He groped his way forward, but still holding his revolver aloft. Something inside him told him that Monreale's dirty secrets were at the end of that tunnel. The rarefied air of the excavation dried out his throat. As he progressed, he began to feel hot and soon his face was covered in sweat. Soon after, he saw a dim light at the end of the tunnel.

The long, dark passageway ended in a large circular room. Under the dim light of a bonfire in the center of the enclosure, Hunt made out some ornaments and rustic paraphernalia, similar to those of native peoples. The air was charged with a sweet, pungent aroma. His eyes, which had already become accustomed to the gloom, distinguished a figure stretched out on a bench that surrounded the entire length of the wall. The captain's heart pumped blood hard as he recognized Allison. The girl was motionless. He bent over her and checked her pulse and breathing. Relieved, he gently shook her to wake her up.

"Allie, it's me, Peter."

"Peter?"

Her voice sounded lethargic. Hunt helped her up.

"Are you ok?"

"Yes..."

"Can you get up? We have to get out of here

right away."

She nodded, but only managed to stand up slowly, as if her body was dull. Hunt put an arm under her armpits and helped her walk. Then he noticed a shiny object resting on a platform near the fire. Without letting go of the girl, he reached out to pick up the puzzle box. With difficulty, he opened the lid and discovered with relief that the seven gems were inside. He put the gold box in his pocket and went on.

Both went into the corridor. As they progressed, Allison felt better and was able to walk on her own. The escape became faster. When they reached the storeroom, Hunt stopped abruptly and the girl bumped into his back.

"What happened?"

The captain ordered her to be silent with a firm gesture. Then she heard it too: footsteps running down the stairs. Hunt gestured for Allison to hide behind a stack of boxes. He took cover behind another pile and raised his weapon.

"We found Giuseppe unconscious under the stairs," one of the men explained to another who ran beside him. "Intruders must be in the basement..."

An accurate shot hit him in the chest and made him roll down the remaining steps of the stairs. The other mobster fired blindly into the storeroom, but Hunt also shot him. The captain came out from behind his hiding place and took Allison by the hand.

"Stay behind me!" He ordered. "We'll have to shoot our way through!"

He ran up the stairs, with the girl crouching behind his back. In the lobby on the ground floor he spotted three soldiers from the Monreale clan. As soon as he emerged from the stairwell, he shot them in quick succession. One of the men sprang in pain, but the other two returned fire. Hunt went under the top flight of stairs – someone had taken this Giuseppe away – and from there he continued shooting. The mafiosi had nowhere to hide. One of them tried to climb the stairs, but Hunt cut him off with a shot that knocked him down with a crash.

The last man simply crouched in a corner and from there emptied the magazine of his pistol into Hunt's hideout. The gangster accompanied his burst with a shout of fury. The captain squeezed into the cramped space, protecting the girl, as a hail of wood and brick splinters leaped everywhere. Hunt reloaded his revolver with a steady hand and waited for his opponent to replace his magazine as well. When he heard the metallic click of the gun, Hunt threw himself to the floor and slid face down the polished tiles of the lobby. Upon reaching the other side, he got up with one knee on the floor and shot the soldier.

Then he ran back to the girl.

"We won't be able to get out in front," he whispered, panting. "Outside there are more guards."

"There's a backyard," Allison said. "I think it connects to the next street."

Both ran to the loading and unloading area. They made their way through the piles of liquor boxes and reached the courtyard, which was lit by a pair of outdoor lamps. The silhouette of a truck could be seen at the opposite end of the yard. They ran to the vehicle just as they heard footsteps pouring into the cargo zone. Shouts in Sicilian dialect filled the night air. Hunt clearly heard the sound of several guns being cocked.

He opened the door of the truck, grabbed Allison by the waist, and pushed her into the cabin. Then he jumped after her. Bullets whistled all over the yard. The noise was deafening, and the flash of the shots lit up the night. Half-crouched, Hunt turned on the ignition of the truck and started the engine. Without getting up from his seat, he spied the courtyard through the edge of the windshield. He discovered the exit gate to the back street. Out of the corner of his eye he saw that several gangsters were running towards the truck, without stopping shooting. The glass in the cabin shattered. Allison gave a shout of terror.

The captain stepped on the gas and threw the truck into his attackers. Several of them threw themselves away from the onslaught, but a couple of men failed to dodge the vehicle launched at full speed. Their bodies were thrown by the impact. Hunt managed to lift his head so he could see the way. He took a sharp turn in the small space of the courtyard. The truck swung dangerously on two wheels but managed to head towards the gate. More shots hit the rear cargo bed and hit the bodywork. Hunt threw the truck like a battering ram toward the gate. The two halves of wood burst open, splintered, and warped by the shock. Hunt turned again into the street and drove away in a northerly direction. The last shots and shouts were left behind. They had managed to escape.

The truck stumbled through the deserted streets of the city, blowing smoke from the engine. Finally, they had to abandon it in Midtown and from there they continued on foot to the Biltmore Hotel. This time, Hunt took Allison straight to his room.

"You must rest," he said. "I'll have a doctor see you."

"No need. I am fine."

He made her lie on his bed. The girl's eyes began to close immediately. As Hunt wrapped her in a blanket, Allison murmured:

"I'll tell you all about it later..."

The girl slept almost all day. When she woke up, the sun was setting and its oblique rays bathed the room in orange hues. She blinked several times and looked around the room until she found Hunt. The captain was setting the dinner that had been brought to him in a cart. He laid his plates down on a coffee table and brought the food to Allison on a tray. She sat up to eat and found that she was now lying under the covers. Completely naked.

"You did it?" She asked Hunt.

She felt her cheeks flush.

"I had to do it," he explained in a serious voice. "It started to get cold, and you didn't wake up. I had to cover you and... Well, you couldn't sleep with your clothes on, could you?"

She pouted in disbelief, but willingly accepted the tray. She made short work of her dinner immediately. After eating for a while, she was finally able to explain Hunt her frustrated visit to Monreale's headquarters and the way she had been captured.

"My God, Allie! What you did was very dangerous."

"Fury clouded my thoughts, Peter. That man is a monster! First he attacked you in the street and then in the hospital. I'm tired of criminals controlling people's lives."

Hunt shook his head in a reproachful gesture. He poured himself a glass of water. He cursed for not being able to drink some Glenlivet. He looked at the girl as she continued to eat.

"What was that place at the end of the tunnel? Why were you there?"

She looked down and was slow to respond.

"I don't know. I must have fainted as soon as I was taken to the basement. I have only a vague memory of a hot and sweltering place."

Hunt remembered the fire burning in the center of the circular room. A heavy aroma floated in the gloom. Maybe they had thrown some drugs into the flames. In a reflexive gesture, he took the puzzle box out of his jacket pocket and opened the lid.

"Don't you remember if Monreale was there with you? Did you see if he tampered with this box or the gems?"

He dropped the seven spheres into the palm of his hand and showed them to Allison. She stared at them, as if hypnotized.

"Allie?" he asked, after a while. "Is something bad going on?"

"Those stones. It's as if... they called me."

Hunt clenched his fist and the spell was broken. The girl's expression relaxed and she smiled at him as if nothing had happened. Hunt felt uneasy.

"Maybe Monreale did something to make you forget what happened in that room. Something with the gems."

"I don't know. I don't really remember, Peter!"

A couple of tears fell down her cheeks. Hunt sat down next to her on the bed and took her hand.

"Excuse me, my dear. I didn't mean to disturb you."

"It is ok. It's just that I have a big stain on my

mind." Allison looked up at the captain. Her eyes shone with despair. "I feel like I've never been in that room."

"Don't worry. I'll let you rest tonight, and I'll talk to Sir John tomorrow so we can get you to safety."

Hunt removed the girl's tray and pushed the cart away from the bed. Then he grabbed a pillow and threw a blanket on the floor.

"What are you doing?" She asked, surprised.

"I'll sleep on the floor. Don't worry, I'm used to it."

As he passed her by, Allison stopped him by holding his hand.

"Don't you want to... sleep here?" She glanced at the bed. Hunt raised an eyebrow. "After all, you already saw me naked."

"Are you sure? I don't want to impose anything on you, Allie."

For all response, she sat up on the bed and let the sheets slide over her breasts. Hunt undressed without taking his eyes off her. Then he crawled under the covers next to her. Allison pressed against him, and they kissed. Hunt felt the girl's warm body lying beneath his.

"Make me forget all this, Peter," the girl whispered in his ear.

Hunt woke up in the middle of the night. He was covered in sweat. To his surprise, Allison had behaved... franticly. He still felt her body burning next to his, in constant movement, with no desire to stop. Perhaps the proximity to death had made her feel alive like never before, giving free rein to her passion. After more than an hour, the girl had fallen over, breathing heavily. Hunt had gone to get her a glass of water, but when he returned, she was already asleep.

Remembering it, the captain smiled in the darkness. He reached out to stroke Allison's soft body but couldn't find her on the other side of the mattress. He raised his head, his senses alert, and turned to light the lamp on his bedside table. He stopped with his hand stretched out when he heard noises in the room. His body tensed. He waited for his eyes to get used to the gloom and then he looked around the room. A silhouette was crouched next to the chair where he had left his weapon.

"Allie?"

The girl turned to him, his revolver in front of her. She was still naked.

"What are you doing?"

She didn't answer. She took a step towards the bed and raised the revolver. Hunt slowly pulled the sheets away from his body.

"Allie, you're confused. Put down the gun and let's talk."

What troubled the captain most was the girl's silence. He could barely see her face in the dark, but he would have said that her eyes were dull, as if she saw nothing. Her breasts rose and fell to the rhythm of her breathing. She didn't seem to be agitated. It was evident that during her captivity the girl had been hypnotized or somehow induced to kill Hunt. He himself had once suffered an attempt at mind control and knew how difficult it was to overcome the voices that invaded the mind, the feeling of emptiness and the loss of personality.

The captain understood that he was not facing only a criminal who led a gang. Behind the theft of the gems was something much bigger and more sinister. Dark forces were operating in the shadows and now they had taken over the poor girl. Hunt ruled out throwing himself on her. He would not be able to sit up on the bed and jump on the girl before she fired. The only alternative was to try to free her from her mental prison.

"Listen to my voice, Allie. I'm Peter."

Hunt had been using his revolver for many years. He knew how it worked, and each piece that made it up, by heart. Thanks to the absolute silence of the room, he heard a slight metallic click. He knew right away that Allison was pulling the trigger. Without hesitation, he slammed back and threw himself on the floor next to the bed. The shot rang out loudly and the flash lit up the room. Hunt poked his head over the mattress to see the girl, but a second shot forced him to take cover again.

"Allie, you must fight it! Hunt shouted. "Resist anything..."

The third shot shattered the lamp on the bedside table and the fourth splintered the wall. A little cloud of gunpowder hung in the air, and the smell of cordite had filled the room. Hunt crawled across the soft carpet toward the foot of the bed. A fifth shot sank into the floor, just inches from his head. He cursed in his mind for having left the revolver close at hand, fully loaded. It was an old habit that could now cost him dearly. The girl had only one round left. He decided to wait for her to fire before trying to move.

Several seconds passed without the last shot coming. Maybe Allison was waiting for him to peek over the side of the bed so she wouldn't waste her last bullet. Hunt cursed again. He didn't intend to stand still like a sitting duck, waiting to die. He raised his head once more and felt a horror that squeezed his heart. Allison had the Webley pressed against her temple. She kept her finger on the trigger, but she seemed to hesitate.

"No!"

Hunt sprang up, climbed over the bed, and threw himself with all his might at the girl. He felt his body move in slow motion, as if he were drifting through the air. With bulging eyes, he saw Allison pull the trigger.

7. NEW MEXICO

Hunt couldn't concentrate on reading. The gentle swaying of the train, which at other times had given him a sense of tranquility, or even lethargy, now only managed to distract him. He put aside the magazine and entertained himself by looking at the landscape that paraded in front of the window. However, he wasn't able to pay much attention to it. He had been traveling for more than two days, but his mind was still on New York, unable to overcome the incredible events that had occurred after he had rescued Allison MacGregor from Daniele Monreale's lair.

The girl had shot herself in the temple before he could reach her. But the very hesitation of her hand, produced by her natural attempt at mental resistance, saved her life. The moment she pulled the trigger, in an impulse of survival, she turned the barrel of the revolver a few millimeters. The bullet only grazed her temple, and the burning powder burned her skin, but they were minor wounds. Allison fell to the floor in a daze. Hunt was right by her side. Immediately the captain tore one of his shirts and wrapped the cloth around the girl's head.

She blinked several times until she managed to focus her gaze on Hunt. It seemed as if she was seeing him for the first time.

"Peter? Where am I?" Then her eyes widened. "I'm naked!"

"Don't you remember... anything?"

She shook her head, and her eyes filled with tears. Hunt dressed her with considerable difficulty, trying not to graze her head wound. Then he put on his clothes too. The girl gaped at him when she saw him naked. With another glance at the bed she understood what had happened. Her face visibly reddened. Hunt called the British Consulate General and then the consul himself spoke to the police to avoid a new scandal over the bullets that had awakened the entire floor of the Biltmore Hotel. The hotel manager was alerted to what had happened and reassured the other guests, without disturbing the occupants of the room from which the noise had emanated. A consulate car arrived shortly after and took them both to Mount Sinai Hospital.

It was several hours before Hunt could see Allison again. Her parents also arrived at the hospital, but they kept a safe distance from that Englishman whom they obviously blamed for the misfortunes their daughter had suffered. Finally, a doctor named Berkowicz came over to talk to the captain.

"She will recover," the doctor told him. "However, her mental state is very altered."

"Were you able to determine what had happened, doctor?"

"It seems to me that she was subjected to a very powerful suggestion. A kind of long-lasting hypnosis. On the surface, she was acting normally, but in reality she was following very specific instructions that someone put in her mind."

Hunt tried to hide his uneasiness in front of the doctor. He knew that it was not just hypnosis, but something much more powerful, of supernatural origin. He could not imagine a gangster involved in these mystical affairs, but it was evident that Monreale had some kind of power to subjugate others. Add to that his desperate search for the natives' gems, and the conclusion was that they were facing an extremely dangerous enemy.

"As far as I could tell," Berkowicz continued, "Allison was forced to—ahem, seduce you... and then she had to kill you."

"Does she remember anything else? It is very important that she knows what happened while she was captive," said the captain.

The doctor shook his head.

"Her memories were suppressed and replaced with the instructions that were implanted in her. It would be very difficult to make her remember what really happened."

"But is it possible?" Hunt insisted. "It's a matter of life and death, doctor."

"I think so, but it could cause a deterioration in her mental state..."

"Listen to me, doctor. The man who did this to Allison is a criminal and murderer. I must stop him, or he will do the same to other people."

Berkowicz studied Hunt professionally. He must think I'm crazy, thought the captain. However, he held the doctor's gaze. After a moment, Berkowicz nodded slowly.

"There is a colleague in Paris, Dr. Pierre Janet, who has developed a very interesting treatment of the repressed subconscious. What he calls *psychotherapy*. In Vienna, Sigmund Freud has worked on similar techniques of hypnosis and psychoanalysis."

"Can you perform these treatments with Allison?"

Berkowicz scratched his chin for a moment. Then he whispered to Hunt:

"Come back this afternoon at seven."

At that time, the hospital's psychiatry department was calm. Berkowicz greeted Hunt outside his office.

"Very well, captain. Let's try," said the doctor. "You must remain still and in absolute silence until I tell you otherwise. Do you agree?"

Hunt nodded. Inside the office, Allison was lying on a couch, her head slightly raised. The curtains were closed and only a table lamp dimly illuminated the room. The doctor pointed to a chair behind the couch in the shadows. Hunt sat and stood motionless, watching in fascination as the doctor induced the hypnosis. Berkowicz held in his left hand a gold pocket watch that glowed brightly in the dim light. He placed it about thirty centimeters in front of the girl's eyes and ordered her to stare at it.

"You have only to think of this watch, Allison," Berkowicz said in a deep, authoritative voice. "Nothing matters more than this watch."

After several minutes without speaking or moving the clock, the doctor raised the index and middle fingers of his right hand and placed them in front of the watch. Slowly, he brought his outstretched fingers closer to the girl's face. Both eyes followed the path of the fingers, moving closer to the nose and narrowing until the eyelids closed involuntarily.

"Your eyes are relaxed, and you can't open them," Berkowicz suggested. "If you try to open them, they'll only close harder. Now, try to open them."

The eyes quivered under the eyelids, but they did not open. Berkowicz took one of the girl's arms, lifted it to the height of her head, and let go. The arm slammed down to the couch.

Hunt watched the trance-like state Allison had reached. The doctor signaled to the captain to come to the couch.

"Allison, listen to my voice. Do you trust Peter Hunt?"

The girl shuddered in her sleep.

"Peter—danger, Peter!"

"Don't worry, you're safe now. Peter is here."

With gestures, Berkowicz indicated to Hunt that he could now speak to the girl.

"Allie, it's Peter. I rescued you from that basement. Do you remember it? Monreale can no longer harm you."

Hearing the mafioso's name, the girl shook on the couch. His fingers stiffened and his whole body tightened. Berkowicz muttered to Hunt to be careful what he said.

"We are a long way off, my dear," continued the captain. "I just need you to tell me what happened there. It's just a bad memory."

Slowly, between tremors in her body, Allison relived her capture and the ritual she had witnessed. The doctor looked at Hunt in amazement as she described the underground room, the mobster's litany in the strange language, and the glowing cloud that had emanated from the gems suspended in the air. Hunt supposed that the doctor had a hard time believing what he heard, but he, on the other hand, knew that the whole story was true.

"He was inside me," Allison said. "In my

mind I only heard his voice. He told me that I should wait for you to come, Peter, and that I should go with you. And then I had to... I should..."

"Don't worry about that, my dear. Do you remember what he said about that strange cloud? Do you know what he used the gems for?"

Allison was sweating. Berkowicz wanted to stop the hypnosis, but Hunt grabbed his arm and shook his head.

"It wasn't a cloud... it was the road... towards the treasure."

Hunt flinched. The treasure? He waited for her to continue talking.

"The hidden treasure... hundreds of years... waiting for its true owner..."

"Did he say what that treasure was?"

"A fabulous... treasure. But he just wants... the medallion. The gems show the way to the medallion." Allison began to speak quickly, almost without pausing between words: "The medallion controls everything, the mind and the body. The medallion will increase his power. The medallion is the key. The medallion, the medallion, the medallion... He must retrieve it, he must go for it, he must follow the path traced by the gems."

The girl's voice was getting raspy. The agitation dried out her throat. Hunt took her hand and stroked her.

"Take it easy, Allie. Did he say where the

medallion was? Where should I go to look for it?"

The girl opened her eyes and stared at Hunt.

"The old village on the cliff. New Mexico."

She closed her eyes and fell unconscious.

It took Peter Hunt two days to make all the preparations for his trip. Before leaving New York, he met with Sir John Connelly. The professor was already more recovered and was sitting in a chair in front of the window of his room in the consulate, looking out over New York Harbor.

"So the gems displayed a kind of map, didn't they?"

"Rather a specific route to find the medallion," Hunt said. "Apparently, the relics that were found in the Spanish saddlebags are only a part of a vast indigenous treasure."

"Cibola," murmured Sir John. "And the most important piece would be that medallion."

Hunt nodded.

"Monreale plans to use it to increase the power to control minds. He called it 'the beacon'."

"That's why he abandoned the gems in the room where the girl was," said the director of Department X. "They were no longer of any use to him."

"It was all a trap, Sir John. Allison had to seduce me into letting my guard down. Then she would kill me, and finally she would have to take her own life."

"How is the girl?"

Hunt shrugged.

"She's young and strong. It will take her a while to recover from the experience, but she will finally make it. Dr. Berkowicz informed me that her parents will take her from New York. Apparently, they have relatives in Montana, or somewhere close to it. They are confident that a calm environment will be beneficial for her."

"I am sure that it will be so. Was you able to say goodbye to her?"

The captain looked dejected.

"They didn't allow me to see her. They said that my presence could relive the whole traumatic episode." Hunt shrugged. "I left her a letter with Berkowicz. I hope she receives it."

"I'll make sure she gets it, Peter," his boss assured him. "You should leave this matter behind you, too. Many dangers await you on your way."

The next day, the captain set out on his long journey to New Mexico. After leaving most of his luggage in storage, he took the private elevator that connected the lobby of the Biltmore Hotel to the adjoining Grand Terminal Station. From the hotel's special arrivals hall, he went to the exclusive platform that the New York Central Railroad had for its express service to Chicago. Considering the length of his trip, he stopped for a few moments at a kiosk to buy something to read. He acquired a fantasy magazine called *Weird Tales* and Agatha Christie's most recent novel, *The Man in the Brown Suit*.

The platform was covered by a red carpet that had the name of the train, 20th Century Limited, engraved on it. According to the brochure that Hunt was handed while boarding, it was the most famous and spectacular train in the world. The captain guessed that the company of the Orient Express would have something to say about it. However, at the end of his journey he had to admit that the trip had been quiet and the service on board excellent. The train departed from the New York station at exactly 2:46 in the afternoon and began its twenty-hour journey to Chicago.

Hunt tried to forget the events of the last few days by reading the adventures of Miss Anne Beddingfeld in her search for the suspicious man in the titular suit. Later he dined in the dining car. When he returned to his section, the seat had been turned into a bunk bed isolated from the aisle by a curtain. Hunt put on his pajamas in the bathroom and eventually the accumulated fatigue helped him sleep during the journey through Buffalo, Cleveland, the rest of the states of Ohio and Indiana.

The train arrived at LaSalle Street Station at 9:45 a.m. local time. A previously warned porter hurriedly unloaded Hunt's luggage and took it to a taxi that was waiting outside the station. From there the captain went to the nearby Dearborn station, located less than a mile away, where he boarded the California Limited train, of the Atchinson, Topeka & Santa Fe company, which departed at ten o'clock. Hunt slumped exhausted in his seat.

That country was really vast, Hunt told himself several times during the trip. Along the way, he had seen all kinds of landscapes, climates and passed through three time zones. The service on the train had been formidable once again. Meals came from the famous restaurants of Fred Harvey Company and each car had comfortable rooms to talk or having a drink. There was also an observation car located at the end of the convoy, provided with large windows to admire the scenery. On the afternoon of the second day of travel from Chicago, the train entered the state of New Mexico.

Hunt was immersed in reading a story about the occult, included in the magazine, called *The Statement of Randolph Carter*. The story was fascinating, but the captain had a hard time moving through its pages. Perhaps the proximity to his destination had made him more restless. As he thought of Monreale and Allison, his pulse quickened. As he had done many times during the long train ride, he reached into his jacket pocket and checked that the gold puzzle box was safe there. He had decided to carry it as an amulet so that it would constantly remind him of the purpose of his mission.

In the narrow circle of occult science

experts, Hunt was known as the 'mystery hunter'. It was not a nickname he liked very much, but it had spread among the museum's academics and benefactors. But for this time, he decided to embrace its meaning. Only now he would hunt for more than mysteries. He would be just a hunter. And every moment he was closer to his prey.

The first stop in the state of New Mexico was in the town of Las Vegas. The train stopped for a few minutes and then went through a pass between the Sangre de Cristo mountains, heading west. Interestingly, despite the name of the railway company, the train did not pass through the city of Santa Fe. To get to the state capital, you had to take a branch line from the town of Lamy. On the other side of the mountains it was already dark night. The train arrived in Albuquerque, the state's main city, after midnight. There the stop was longer, but most of the passengers continued to sleep.

A porter woke Hunt up around five in the morning to get dressed and gather his belongings. About six o'clock, the train made a brief stop at the town of Gallup so that the captain could get off. It was already dawn, but the cold air of the mountains was still felt over the village. Hunt took the only taxi that served the small station, which took him to an Indian-style inn in the center of the town. As agreed, the captain was to remain there until local authorities made contact with him.

He had breakfast at a nearby café, where he was watched undisguisedly by the locals, who were mostly natives. Hunt smiled at them and touched the brim of his hat in greeting. He ate without haste, ignoring the gazes of the patrons. When he finished, he immediately returned to the inn. Since he had nothing to do, he simply lay down on the bed and fell asleep on the spot. Less than an hour later, he was awakened by a firm knock on the door of his room.

When he opened the door, he found a large man, with a good-natured face, wearing a riding uniform and a campaign hat.

"Captain Peter Hunt? I'm Major Samuel Nash of the New Mexico Mounted Police."

"Good morning, Major."

"They asked me to come and get you, sir. Come on, we have a command post in the town hall."

They walked a couple of streets to a Spanish colonial-style building. The heat was intense outside, but inside it was cool. Major Nash led Hunt to a boardroom that had been converted into a police station. A dozen uniformed officers were bent over the central table, studying maps and documents. Someone was giving instructions at the center of the group. When the new arrivals entered, the agents stepped aside to let pass the man who had been talking to them.

The man was the same age as Hunt, but his

features were unmistakably American. The hair the color of wheat, the blue eyes, the affable smile. He was wearing a black suit, white shirt, and a black tie, fastened with a gold clip. His fedora hat was similarly black. He pulled out a leather wallet which he opened to show Hunt a badge with a five-pointed gold star. Then he put it away and held out his hand to the captain.

"Special Agent Hyam Noone, United States Secret Service."

"Secret Service, huh?" Hunt shook his hand. "It sounds mysterious."

Agent Noone widened his smile.

"We are one of the oldest federal law enforcement agencies in the country," he explained. "Our missions consist of safeguarding the financial system, preventing counterfeiting of currency and ensuring the security of the president."

"And find lost treasures," Hunt added.

"Especially if the treasure is worth billions of dollars," Noone laughed. On a more serious note, he added: "Actually, the American Geographical Society is in charge of the search and the security of the operation is provided by the mounted police."

"I thought you gave the orders here, Agent Noone."

"I'm not here, captain," the agent said, winking. "Major Nash is in charge."

The mounted policeman blushed. His

position was probably symbolic. Hunt deduced that the federal government was actually in charge of the operation. Noone greeted the major with a nod of his head and then put a hand on Hunt's back to guide him out of the boardroom.

"Let's go to a quieter place so we can talk."

They settled in the terrace of a nearby restaurant and ordered coffee. Noone lit a Lucky Strike cigarette and offered another to Hunt, who declined.

"Would you mind telling me everything that has happened in New York since you arrived, captain?"

"No problem, agent."

Hunt gave an orderly and detailed account of the events. He left out only some aspects that seemed to him to be at odds with the law. After all, he was talking to an agent of the federal government. Noone nodded his head a few times, but he didn't interrupt the story at any moment. But it seemed to Hunt that the agent was memorizing everything he was telling him in detail.

"So you rescued the girl by yourself, eh? Impressive, my friend."

"The impressive thing is that Monreale is still free. He should have been arrested and put on trial."

"Don't count on it." Noone shook his head with a look of regret. "These mafiosi have the police, prosecutors and judges in their pockets.

They could not act otherwise. The same is true in Chicago, Atlantic City, and elsewhere across the country."

"It seems incredible that no one is going after these criminals," muttered Hunt.

He did not want to offend Noone, but it seemed to him that it was an unusual situation. However, the agent did not seem to feel alluded to.

"The Treasury and the Bureau of Internal Revenue have the mafia in their sights for the liquor smuggling," he explained. "But they have few staff and little support from the public."

"So, do you mean that Monreale will not face justice?"

Noone lifted the brim of his hat and looked at Hunt with an enigmatic expression.

"There are several kinds of justice, Peter. I can call you Peter, right? If we are going to work together, we should address each other by our names."

"That's fine, Hyam."

They shook hands again. Hunt felt that he finally had a powerful ally in his fight against Monreale.

"It's almost lunchtime," said the agent. "Here they sell the best chili con carne west of Albuquerque."

Noone ordered the food for both of them. They were served pork marinated with chili sauce, accompanied by corn tortillas and sautéed vegetables. The dish was quite spicy. Hunt felt an immediate burning in his stomach, but Noone seemed accustomed to the strong dressing. The American ate voraciously and asked for another portion.

"Green chili is the star product of this state," he explained. "I've been here for several weeks now, and I've gotten used to its taste."

With a gesture he indicated a huge string of chili peppers that hung from the ceiling of the terrace. When dried in the sun, the peppers were turning a deep red color.

"A little intense for me," Hunt said.

"Wait until you try Mexican food. They put lots of chili on all the dishes."

Have you been to Mexico?

"Not officially."

Noone laughed. He fired up a Lucky and ordered more coffee.

"Is this whole Houdini thing really true?" He asked the captain.

Hunt raised an eyebrow.

"You know. Mind control, gems flying through the air..."

"Well, I didn't witness any of those situations," Hunt said cautiously. "I knew from experience that it was very difficult to make people believe in paranormal phenomena. Besides, truth be told, there were always several explanations for mystical events. The important thing is that Monreale believes in those powers and that is what makes him dangerous."

"Or maybe he's totally nuts, don't you think?"

Noone stared at him, waiting for an answer. Hunt realized that the man knew much more than he appeared. He was apparently an ideal agent for the Secret Service. Finally, Hunt chose to just shrug.

"I just want to stop him, Hyam. He is a criminal and murderer."

"Don't worry, buddy. We are in the same boat."

"Will the federal government go after the mafia?"

Noone raised both hands to stop him there.

"Those are big words, Peter. Let's say that, for now, we want to prevent the treasure of the Anasazi from falling into the wrong hands."

Hunt tried to avoid his disappointment. Wasn't there any federal agency willing to put an end to organized crime? Could it be that the mafiosi also had federal agents in their pockets?

"By the way," said Noone, interrupting his thoughts. "Do you have that gold box with you?"

Hunt put it down on the table and taught Noone how to open the lid. The agent's face showed no emotion as he looked at the turquoise gems. He inspected them for a few moments, then closed the box and put it in his pocket.

"I'll put the box in a safe place. After all, it belongs to Uncle Sam."

"I understood that the treasure found in the

saddlebags was being analyzed by the American Geographical Society."

"I am afraid that after the latest events," replied Noone, "it will be necessary for the Service to take care of it."

"Very well. What's next?" Hunt asked.

He was impatient to begin his work in this remote place.

"Now, my friend, we will go in search of the treasure. Like Captain Flint!"

Noone got up, and Hunt followed.

"Captain Flint hid the treasure, my friend," Hunt said. "Jim Hawkins is the one who goes in search of it."

The officer laughed and patted the Englishman on the back.

"Those British novels are not my thing, Peter. I prefer Mark Twain!"

Noone escorted Hunt to his inn.

"Rest, Peter. We will leave early tomorrow."

At dawn the next day, Hunt went back to the town hall. The mounted police had a car and a truck to transport the entire contingent. Major Nash got behind the wheel of the car, with Noone at his side. Hunt settled into the back seat. A police sergeant occupied the front cabin of the truck, and the rest of the men were seated on the benches of the rear cargo bed of the vehicle. They set off immediately.

Soon the sun hit hard over the mountains. The vehicles drove away from the town at a slow pace, advancing along dirt roads and trails that could barely be seen a few meters away. The sparse vegetation consisted mainly of parched shrubs that covered the prairies and valleys between the mountains. In the highest areas there were some groves of stone pines and junipers. However, most of the landscape was arid and rocky.

The journey continued in silence, only interrupted by the shouts of the men in the truck when one of the policemen saw a prairie dog or a dusky grouse fluttering along the road. Shortly after, a detonation startled the occupants of the car. The three of them flipped just as a second shot came from the back of the truck.

"What the hell?" Noone asked when a third shot was heard.

Major Nash leaned out of the window and shouted what was going on.

"Guzmán thought he saw a bighorn sheep among the trees, sir!" The truck driver replied.

"Tell those idiots to stop shooting," Noone ordered the policeman.

"We're not on a hunt, sergeant!" Nash shouted. "Put that damn rifle away!"

The journey ended without further incident. After half a day of travel, the vehicles arrived at a camp located in the shade of some trees. About fifteen tents were spread out in a circular shape. In the center burned a large fire that served to heat the camp and cook. Another dozen policemen were waiting at that outpost. The newcomers joined them and sat on the ground by the fire to eat their rations. Soon it would be sunset. At night, the temperature dropped sharply in the mountains.

The detachment commanders and Hunt met in the command tent. On an easel table were several maps of the area. Leaning over the maps there was a middle-aged man dressed in a denim shirt and khaki pants. He wore a red cloth bandana tied around his neck and a cowboy hat over his head. Noone made the introductions.

"Neil Grant, Peter Hunt. Professor Grant is an archaeologist with the SGA. Captain Hunt is our advisor from British Museum."

"Oh, you were with Professor Lester when—"

"I'm sorry for what happened," Hunt added, seeing the archaeologist look embarrassed. "I tried to save the professor, but I couldn't."

"You are a hero, captain! You have nothing to excuse. It is an honor to finally meet you."

They all gathered around the maps. Grant took one of them and unfolded it in the center of the table.

"The saddlebags were found here." He pointed on the map. "From the background that the Society has gathered, and the testimony of the girl who was held captive by Monreale, we believe that the rest of the treasure may be in this area."

With one finger, he drew a circle over the

THE CURSED TREASURE

region north of the camp. Noone nodded and said:

"Tomorrow we will form four patrols that will divide the terrain into grids to explore it. If someone finds traces of the treasure, they must throw a flare. If there is no success, the next day we will adjust the quadrants."

Each patrol, of five men, set out early at dawn. In that area there were no longer roads or trails. The ground was stony and uneven. Cars were replaced by horses. Hunt, Grant, and Noone formed a group with two men from the mounted police. Hunt was given a large, strong mount, accustomed to riding in the mountains. Once he had adjusted the reins and harness, Hunt followed the other members of his patrol. The mounted police officers were originally from that region and knew the mountains well. They led the march.

The land they had been assigned was an area of several square kilometers. In order to encompass everything, the patrol headed for the higher mountains, from where the men could observe the paths and valleys below. Hunt simply rode behind them, gazing in fascination at the stunning scenery around them. After several hours, they reached the top of a large mesa that commanded a good view of the entire surrounding landscape. There they would rest for a few moments. They drank water from their canteens and then the two police officers surveyed the surroundings with powerful field binoculars.

"What's that buzzing sound?" Professor Grant asked.

Hunt heard it too. It was a low noise, but intense. Suddenly Hunt stiffened.

"Hyam, the puzzle box!"

The Secret Service agent reached into his jacket pocket. He pulled out the box and the buzzing increased in intensity. He opened the lid by aligning up the notches. Inside, the turquoise gems vibrated by hitting each other. The three men stared at them in amazement for a few moments, until Hunt said:

"Throw them in the air, Hyam."

Noone picked up the gems in his fist and then tossed them up. The gems rose several meters, but instead of falling to the ground they were suspended in the air, forming a kind of spiral. Rays of light shot out of the gems and coalesced around the figure, forming a nebula of delicate lights that floated above the astonished men. The policemen also came to observe, open-mouthed.

"I just saw that," said one of them. The others turned sharply to the man. "Er... that drawing. Over there," he added, pointing over his shoulder.

Hunt and Noone grabbed their binoculars and peered over the edge of the plateau, trying to follow what the policeman was telling them.

"There, at the foot of the plateau," said the officer.

Hunt pointed his binoculars in that direction and soon saw what the policeman was showing them. The figure that formed the interconnected light of the spheres corresponded to the beginning of a narrow canyon that disappeared winding between two rock formations. The geographical feature was hidden from view by the huge mesa, and it was only possible to see it from above and looking at a specific angle.

"To your horses!" Noone ordered.

He picked up one of the gems and the others immediately fell to the ground. He put them back in the box and jumped on his mount. They descended the mesa down the less steep slope, advancing in single file along a narrow path barely marked on the hard surface of the rock. No one spoke. Everyone was tense by the discovery and expectant of what they would find at the end of the canyon. Even the horses seemed anxious. They neighed and refused to advance. The horsemen had to constantly spur them on to force them down.

At last they reached the canyon. It was a high and narrow passage, through which almost no light reached. The wind blew strongly inside, causing thunderous whistles. The horses were rearing up and resisting the orders of their masters. The progress became slow and difficult. The constant curves of the road prevented the end of the route from being seen, further disturbing the spirits of the explorers. The canyon did not extend more than a kilometer, but it took the horsemen like forever to travel its entire length. When they finally came out on the other side, the horses stopped abruptly and refused to continue. The men dismounted and gathered holding the reins tightly, to prevent the frightened animals from fleeing.

On the other side stretched a small horseshoe-shaped valley. At its other end rose a cliff whose wall curved inwards, forming a high and open cave. Inside the cavity was built a village of stone houses several stories high. The houses blended in with the cliff wall due to its sandstone color and were hidden by the wide edge of the top of the ravine. It was an impressive place, but from which an air of desolation emanated.

"It's an Anasazi village," Professor Grant murmured.

As the others watched in fascination, Hyam Noone raised his hand and fired a flare into the air.

8. UNDER THE CLIFF

Excavation work began two days later, when Professor Neil Grant concluded his preliminary analyses. Together with his two assistants, he spent those days taking photographs of the site, measuring the distances and surfaces of the village with a theodolite, and drawing sketches and plans of the structures. They also collected samples of the rocks and adobe with which the structures were built. State mounted police officers patrolled around the cliff day and night, watching the desolate valleys and surrounding mountains on horseback.

Hunt and Noone, on the other hand, didn't have much to do. Both wandered through the ruins of the village, trying not to interrupt the work of the archaeologists while they looked for vestiges of the treasure that could be found with the naked eye. To pass the time, they talked about their specialties. Hunt had greater knowledge of occultism and paranormal phenomena, while the American seemed to be an expert in organized crime, radical groups, and bank robbers. They exchanged their knowledge while continuing to walk along the cliff, from the top to the cavern that housed the village.

"You can't imagine the kind of criminals we face. There's a guy they call Baron Lamm," Noone explained. "He is a German who was apparently a soldier in the damned Prussian army."

"And now he's a robber?"

"One of the best. He has a gang of pros who meticulously plan each heist. His methodology is known as 'The Lamm Technique'".

Hunt stared at him in bewilderment. The Secret Service agent nodded to reinforce his words.

"I tell you this, Peter. Crime is evolving." Noone shook his head angrily. "In Atlantic City, the county treasurer himself, Enoch Johnson, is also the head of the county's criminal organization. He lives in the Ritz Hotel on the boardwalk, always travels by limousine and wears raccoon coats worth more than a thousand dollars."

"A few years ago, at the end of the war, the anarchist group of the *Galleanists* sent almost forty bombs by mail to politicians, businessmen and judges. By mail, good God! And now, the head of a New York mafia clan can control people's minds. Where will we end up?"

Noone led Hunt to one of the tents in the camp. The place was deserted. All the police officers and men of the American Geographical Society were at work in the village under the cliff.

"Is it true, Peter?" asked the American when they were alone in the tent. "Is it *really* true what that man can do?"

"The psychiatrist who treated Allison MacGregor diagnosed that she acted under a strong hypnotic induction or metal suggestion," the captain confirmed. "How Monreale managed to do it... I don't know."

"But you have a theory, don't you?"

Hunt remained unmoved by the agent's insistence. Noone waited for the answer for a few moments. In the end, he smiled. He took a flask from inside his black jacket and poured the contents into two glasses he found on a table.

"The best Kentucky bourbon," Noone said.

He handed the other glass to the captain. Hunt raised an eyebrow.

"Damn, I don't work in the Prohibition Office," the American explained, shrugging.

They both drank the liquor in one sip. Noone rinsed the glasses with water from a basin and left them where he had found them.

"Professor Grant told me all about Department X of the British Museum," the agent remarked. "He feels great admiration for your work."

"The department's task is to investigate

occult and paranormal phenomena," Hunt conceded. "But many times the analysis ends up ruling out a fantastic or supernatural intervention."

"Come on!" Noone exclaimed. "In the years that I have been investigating crime I have seen incredible things, my friend. I don't think anything can surprise me anymore."

Hunt sighed, then said:

"Ok. I think Monreale has learned some kind of indigenous ritual that allows him to mentally control people. Among the pieces of the treasure is a medallion of great mystical power. Monreale needs it to increase his power and become a crime lord in New York, or perhaps the entire country."

Hyam Noone was surprised anyway. He stared at Hunt in amazement for a moment, until he managed to internalize what the Englishman was telling him.

"A gangster with mental powers! I had never seen that before!"

Then he laughed. His laughter increased, until he had to sit in a folding chair so as not to fall. Hunt watched him silently, but with growing concern for his sanity.

"I'm fine," the agent panted as he caught his breath. "It's just that the situation seems to me... madness!"

"Monreale would not have taken so much trouble if he did not believe in the success of his plan," Hunt reflected. "Don't you think so?"

Noone got up and panted, still tired from his outburst.

"I suppose you're right. I'll talk to Professor Grant and Major Nash. Tomorrow at dawn we will start digging. I want to find that medallion as soon as possible!"

However, this was easier said than done. Most of the town's homes were in ruins. The ceilings, built of wooden beams, had long since given way. Many rock walls and stairways had also fallen, knocking down a significant part of the structures. As Grant explained, the mortar used to join the stones was made of mud, water, and ash. Those were materials that degraded easily over the centuries, as a result of the intense heat and strong winds that blew over the cliff.

"It is possible that this site was abandoned more than six hundred years ago," explained the archaeologist. "And I would say that it has been in ruins for at least a couple of centuries."

"That means the treasure is hidden under the rocks," Noone concluded.

Grant nodded.

The professor and his assistants lifted the rocks carefully, recording every movement. Then they cleaned various areas of the ground with brushes. It was a slow and frustrating task. The excavation progressed for several hours. Hunt and Noone assisted in the removal and grouping of the debris so that archaeologists could catalog it. The Secret Service agent complained that these were only stones, but the professor began a long dissertation on the importance of preserving the original work. Noone muttered something unintelligible and continued to work in silence.

The first discovery was made by one of the professor's assistants, a young man recently graduated who was doing his specialization with a scholarship from the SGA. He was pushing some rocks away from an ancient outer wall when he started shouting and jumping up and down in excitement. The others ran to meet him. In his hand he held a ring with a turquoise set in it. It was somewhat dented and dirty, but it was evident that it was an old piece of jewelry. The young man wiped it with a cloth and revealed the unmistakable shine of solid gold.

Everyone admired the object for a few moments, until Grant picked it up to take pictures and make some drawings. That finding, although small, renewed the team's hopes and made them all work harder. Soon the pieces of the treasure began to resurface from the ruins. Other jewelry items, vessels, ornaments, and some weapons. All the objects were made of gold. After several more hours, the pile of golden finds was already almost a meter high.

In the evening, Noone, Grant, and Hunt sat down to rest. Near the horizon, the sun bathed the mountains in orange hues. The wind was blowing, and the temperature was dropping rapidly. The men were exhausted but satisfied with their work. The Secret Service agent stared at the pile of artifacts and shook his head several times, as if doing some mental calculations.

"This is only a small part of the treasure, isn't it?"

Grant nodded.

"How many of these piles should there be among the rocks?"

The professor shrugged.

"There are no exact records of what Salamanca found in Cibola, nor how much he took with him. But by my estimation, this pile of objects is not even a tenth of the treasure."

"That's what I was afraid of," Noone murmured.

"What do you think, Hyam?" Hunt asked.

It was evident that something had the American uneasy.

"It took us a whole day to find this pile of artifacts," he said. "So, it will take us almost two weeks to recover all the treasure if we continue at this rate."

"I would have brought a full team of diggers," Grant said. "But the authorities only allowed two of my assistants, for security reasons."

"We're not the only ones after the treasure, Professor," Noone explained. "The fewer people who know, the better."

"So what are we going to do?" Hunt asked.

"I would like to find at least that medallion that Monreale spoke of. That way we could move it to a safe place while the SGA finishes digging up the other pieces."

"And we'd get the mob away from the dig site," Hunt agreed. Suddenly he jumped up, "I've got it! The gems, Hyam!"

The agent looked at him without understanding.

"The spheres have an unusual magnetism," Hunt explained. "I want to try something."

Noone went to get the puzzle box from his tent and returned with the gems to the village. Hunt held them in the palm of his hand. Just as he had guessed, the little spheres began to vibrate and make small leaps. With his palm outstretched in front of him, Hunt began to walk around the perimeter of the site. In the cave, there was less and less light. The sun was about to set behind the mountains.

"Quick, some flashlights!" The captain asked.

Several rays of light illuminated his path. He soon discovered that the vibration increased if he walked in a certain direction and decreased if he moved away from there. The gems were working like a compass. After a few attempts, he understood how to use them to orient himself. His steps then became more secure, and he understood that he was heading directly towards the highest structure of the village.

"The tower!" Grant exclaimed. "The medallion is in the tower!"

An ominous, unsettling sensation emanated from the partially demolished structure. As Hunt got closer, the turquoise gems began to bounce harder and harder on the palm of his hand. In the end, he had to form a bowl with both hands to prevent the spheres from shooting out. Although it was already dark, the tower cast a shadow even darker than the rest of the ruins. The hairs on the back of Hunt's neck stood up. He clenched the gems in his fist and stared at the damaged structure. Death nestled inside it.

Hunt gave the gems to Noone, who kept them back in the puzzle box.

"It is dangerous to go into the ruins at night," Professor Grant warned.

Noone ignored him. With a battery-powered flashlight in hand, he climbed over the fallen rocks until he found an opening that allowed him to enter the ancient structure. Hunt shrugged and followed immediately. Grant and his assistants waited for them at the base of the tower. A cold wind had risen and blew strongly over the cliff. Black clouds completely hid the moon and stars. The darkness was absolute.

The first level of the tower was completely covered with rocks that had previously formed the side wall. Hunt watched the American crawl forward, pushing aside debris and pointing the beam of light at the ground. He managed to catch up with him on his ascent. They both nodded. A crumbling ladder, leaning against the opposite wall, ascended in the darkness to the upper levels. Noone tested the steps by carrying his weight with one foot first. The ladder creaked, but it resisted. The agent went up to the next level, followed by Hunt. Half of the wall on that level was down. The top of the tower was only intuited, for it was submerged in the most absolute blackness.

Both men ran the beams of their flashlights on the ground, but they soon realized that there was nothing there either. Only the upper level of the structure remained. This time there was no ladder, but the height of the ceiling was less than two meters. The Secret Service agent stood under the opening, raised his hands, and grabbed onto the rafters that formed the floor of the next level. With the momentum of his arms, he propelled himself upwards and disappeared through the hole.

Hunt followed suit, but as he hung from the edge of the opening, the beams gave way and a good deal of the floor collapsed. Hunt stepped aside just in time to keep the large wooden beams from falling on him.

"Are you ok?" Noone asked from the upper level.

"Yes. But I'd better wait for you here. The combined weight of the two of us could knock down the entire floor."

"Speak for yourself, my friend. I exercise every day."

Hunt heard him laugh. From below he saw the beam of light passing through the upper chamber of the tower. The agent's footsteps creaked the worn beams that formed the floor.

"Wait a minute!" Noone exclaimed after a moment.

"What did you see, Hyam?"

Noone did not respond. Hunt heard another couple of footsteps, but suddenly there was silence.

"Hyam?" The captain insisted. "Hyam?"

"Wait a moment, Peter." The agent's voice came muffled. "I think... Found..."

Hunt waited for his partner to finish his sentence, but he did not hear his voice again. What the hell was going on up there? Hunt hung himself again from the beams that formed the upper floor. The wood creaked under his weight. The stillness in the upper room was abnormal. Hunt pulled himself up with the strength of his arms, but only poked his head over the edge of the opening. On the other side of the chamber he saw a figure standing, completely motionless.

"Hyam?"

The beams were going to crumble at any moment. The floor creaked audibly, and some timbers were cracking. Hunt cursed and lunged up as best he could. Several beams detached from the floor and fell to the lower level. Hunt rolled across the floor until he felt safe. He got up in the midst of the dust and the noise. However, the figure remained motionless the entire time.

Hunt approached the agent. Noone was standing turned to the wall, with a departed expression on his face. The captain immediately understood what was happening.

"Hold on, Hyam! Don't listen to the voice..."

The blow caught him off guard. He felt a strong pain in his jaw that made him stumble backwards. Noone had punched him well. Hunt shook and confronted his partner. But Noone attacked him again. This time the captain was ready. He dodged the blow and shouted at the agent, but Noone was completely possessed. He threw fierce punches and kicks in his direction, with genuine intent to harm him.

"It's not you, Hyam!"

The agent's eyes were empty of expression, but he did not relent in his attempt to hit Hunt. Hunt had no choice but to push him away, but then Noone threw himself on top of Hunt and they were caught in a lethal embrace. Hunt felt the air slipping away from his lungs. He tried to free himself, but the other man had a firm grip on him. He foamed at the mouth and grunted wildly. Hunt struggled with him, but instead of breaking free, they both fell to the ground. Noone still did not loosen his grip.

They rolled on the ground, which creaked and warped under their weight. Hunt yelled at his partner again, but to no avail. Noone was squeezing harder and harder with both arms, preventing Hunt from breathing. The captain gasped for air, but the lack of oxygen began to weaken him. Both fighters were on the edge of the opening. Hunt could see the rocks on which they were about to fall. It could be a death blow.

"Hyam, listen to me, damn it!"

The beams were giving way. The ground level dropped several centimeters. In desperation, Hunt sharply raised his head and slammed his forehead at the deranged agent. Noone was distracted for a single moment, but it was enough. Hunt rolled with him to the other end of the room and managed to stay on top of Noone. He carried all the weight of his body on the elbow that he put on the agent's chest. Noone groaned in pain. The grip was finally released. The captain knew he had no choice. He picked up a loose stone from the ground and smashed it against Noone's temple. The agent exhaled and lay motionless. He was unconscious. Hunt wheezed up. He rested his hands on his thighs and stayed like that for a while, catching his breath. He heard he was called from below.

A large part of the outer wall was demolished. Hunt peered through a crack and saw Grant pointing his flashlight at the tower.

"We heard screams!" exclaimed the professor. "What happened?"

"We're fine!"

Noone breathed quietly. Hunt stepped over him and approached a pile of rocks stacked against a corner that formed a pile a meter and half high. Some rocks had been pushed aside by Noone. Below them was a faint golden glow. Hunt removed the remaining rocks, throwing them on either side. When he managed to open a major hole, he stared at what was underneath.

"Captain Hunt!" Grant shouted from the foot of the tower. "Have you found anything?"

Indeed, thought Hunt, as he contemplated the remains of the conquistador Don Rodrigo de Salamanca. The skeleton was still dressed in his threadbare doublet and a rusty helmet. The bones of his right hand were held tight to his sword. In the other hand, clenched in a fist made up of decrepit and contracted bones, one could make out the gleaming medallion and the chain of which hung inert over the remains of the body.

Hunt shouted for the others. Several rays of light peeked through the ruins. He assumed that archaeologists were going to make several checks before moving the valuable skeleton. Besides, he didn't want to touch the medallion for anything in the world. He turned away from the ominous artifact and tried to clear his mind. The influence of the object was harmful, like a nauseating smell that sticks to the clothes and remains for several days in the nostrils. He leaned against the edge of a crumbling wall and took a deep breath for fresh air.

Hyam Noone woke up the next morning. He had a large bruise on his temple and his head hurt terribly. When he opened his eyes, he saw Peter Hunt leaning over him, smiling.

"I'm sorry, my friend. I hope I didn't hit you too hard."

The agent put a hand to his head.

"This... was it you?"

"Don't you remember?" Hunt put a hand on his shoulder. "You found the medallion, Hyam. But at the same time you fell under its power of mind control."

Noone's eyes widened. Then he laboriously rose from the field cot where he lay. Hunt helped him to his feet and out of the tent. The agent was walking with difficulty.

"There was a voice in my head," Noone murmured. "It gave me orders! It told me that I should protect the medallion... to expel intruders..."

He stopped suddenly and took the captain by the shoulders.

"God, Peter, I won't—"

Hunt tried to play down the matter with a gesture.

"It was quite a close match, my friend. And you got the worst of it. Let's say we're even now."

Over the course of the morning, Noone recalled fragments of what happened. The gaps in his memory were filled in by Hunt. When the agent felt more recovered, they went to Grant's tent to examine the medallion.

"It gives me chills to see it," Noone said.

He didn't even want to touch the artifact. He lit a Lucky and kept a safe distance from the table on which Hunt and Grant were leaning.

"It's a fascinating object," the professor commented. "From the tenth century, approximately. I had never seen anything like it."

"Do you know who made it?" Hunt asked.

Grant shook his head.

"It should belong to the Anasazi culture, but it is nothing like the other relics that have been found." The other two men looked at him puzzled. "I suppose it must have been made by some lost civilization. The inhabitants of Cibola."

"So the legend is real."

"It seems so, captain. There are no gold deposits in this region, but all the pieces we have found are made of this metal."

"Perhaps the people came from another region and migrated in ancient times to Cibola."

Grant nodded.

"It's possible. But there is something that I still cannot explain." He glanced at Noone sideways. "What happened in the tower..."

For a few moments, no one said anything. The Secret Service agent looked uneasy. He lit another cigarette with trembling fingers.

"How is it possible that this thing could... control me?" He asked.

"I'm afraid it wasn't the medallion, Agent Noone," the archaeologist replied. Noone looked at him in bewilderment. "It is impossible for an inanimate object to have that kind of power."

"What do you mean, professor?" Noone hurried him.

"I think you were attacked by Salamanca."

"What the hell are you saying? That man has been dead for more than two hundred years!"

Grant held up his hands to appease him.

"Indeed, the spell must be housed in the medallion. But it is only activated when someone carries the artifact next to the body. It must be a mixture of mystical and vital energies," the professor explained. "This kind of magic is very powerful. And Salamanca still had the medallion clutched in his hand."

"Even after death, the conquistador was still the bringer of magic," Hunt concluded. He looked up and exclaimed, "That's it, the beacon!

Quickly, he told them what Allison MacGregor had heard Daniele Monreale say during the performance of the ritual.

"Somehow, Monreale got the mind-control spell, or learned the magic, or whatever," Hunt concluded. "But he needs the medallion to amplify its power."

"So, Salamanca was a kind of sorcerer?" Noone interjected.

"I don't think so," replied Grant. "It is likely that Salamanca, in obtaining the treasure of

Cibola, simply took the medallion. That activated the artifact's powers, and then the medallion consumed him."

"That's why the magic works so far," Hunt added.

The archaeologist nodded.

"Among the ruins of the village are several bodies," Grant informed them. He and his assistants had found the skeletons. "They are all Spaniards, from the time of the Conquest."

"The men of Salamanca," Hunt concluded.

"They all perished in the village. Violently."

"Did they attacked them to steal their treasure?" Noone ventured.

"The treasure is under the ruins, agent. The attack was not to steal or to recover the objects.

"Vengeance?" Hunt asked.

The professor nodded, still looking at the medallion.

"A cursed treasure," murmured the captain.

"That's right. The Spaniards stole it from the holy place and that brought the curse upon them. It is possible that there was some kind of guard meant to protect the treasure."

"Like the *medjay* of Ancient Egypt," Hunt said.

Grant nodded, admired. Noone finally approached them. He was more serene.

"We must get the medallion out of this place before Monreale knows we've found it," the agent said. "If it falls into his hands, there will be no way to stop him."

"Do you think the mafia will try to seize the artifact?" Grant asked.

He looked around with a frightened expression, as if he feared an imminent attack by the gangsters.

"Monreale deciphered the map formed by the gems, professor. Therefore, he knows that the medallion is in this place. And I believe that he has the means to organize a search operation like ours."

Now Grant looked genuinely scared.

"Don't worry, professor. There are about twenty police officers guarding the camp. Not even Monreale is crazy enough to face such a large force."

Noone and Hunt immediately went to meet with Major Nash to arrange for the removal of the medallion. They agreed that the next day a contingent made up of half of the police officers, in addition to the two of them, would leave. They would take the medallion back to Gallup and take the first train to Chicago. From there they would go to Washington, where the artifact could be kept in a federal building. Everyone agreed that it was very dangerous to take it to the headquarters of the SGA in New York, where it would be within reach of Monreale.

Over dinner that night, Grant was informed of the plan.

"I regret that I cannot continue my study

of the artifact," said the archaeologist. "But I recognize that I will feel relief when I know that it is far away."

"Will you continue to excavate the ruins of the village, professor?" Hunt wanted to know.

The archaeologist nodded.

"It's a fascinating place, captain. Even without considering the treasure, the ruins represent an excellent opportunity to learn more about the Anasazi culture."

"Ahem, Professor?"

Everyone turned to the voice coming from the next table. One of the archaeologist's assistants, the younger and quieter of the two, had one hand raised, as if he wanted to ask a question in the classroom. It took Hunt a moment to remember his name... Conway?

"What's wrong, Nick?", asked Grant.

That was it. Nicholas Conway. Hunt saw that the boy had blushed.

"I haven't felt very well these last few days. I think the food has made me feel sick."

"What a pity, Nick."

"I was wondering if I can go back to Gallup tomorrow with the others."

Grant looked at Noone. The agent shrugged.

"I'm sorry to lose you, but it's better for you to go. We will be here for several more days and you must recover."

"I'll try to come back as soon as I feel better, professor."

"Don't hurry, boy. The important thing is that you recover."

They left at dawn. Noone was driving the car, with Hunt at his side. They had kept the medallion in a duffel bag that Hunt deposited on the floor of the car, next to his feet. Nick Conway was in the back seat, his eyes downcast and silent as always. In the truck were a dozen of the best marksmen from Major Nash's detachment, armed with rifles and shotguns.

Hunt feared they would be attacked in the middle of the road. It would be the ideal place, in the middle of the remote mountains. However, it would take a large force heavily armed to defeat the police. As they moved in the scorching heat, Hunt kept looking at the nearby hilltops and the groves beside the roadside. He saw that in the back of the truck the men were tense, clutching their weapons tightly. The eyes of the policemen also relentlessly scanned the surroundings.

The trip seemed eternal. When they spotted the small village, several of the men breathed a sigh of relief. The two vehicles stopped next to the town hall. Hunt slung the bag over his shoulder and got out of the car. Noone met him immediately. Conway waved goodbye nervously to both of them.

"That was intense," the boy murmured.

"Nothing to worry about," Noone boasted. "Take care, kid."

"You'd better get a doctor right away, Nick,"

Hunt said. "You look pretty pale."

"That's what I'll do, captain."

He shook hands with them and hurried away.

"Curious kid," commented Noone.

They entered the city hall and forgot about him. However, Conway did not forget about them. As soon as he was out of sight, he took a side street and ran toward the post office. Once inside, he took a message form and wrote some notes in a hurry. Then he handed the sheet of paper to the clerk.

"I must send this by telegram. Urgently!"

9. CALIFORNIA LIMITED

They boarded the train from Flagstaff just in time for dinner. Major Nash offered to have a couple of his agents accompany them at least to the state line, but Noone declined. Men in uniform would draw too much attention, just what they wanted to avoid. In addition, between Noone and Hunt they would be perfectly capable of guarding the medallion. They had purchased tickets in a sleeping car compartment and would be safe there during the trip.

"We should go to dinner," the Secret Service agent suggested. "After all, no one knows we're traveling on this train "

The California Limited consisted of the locomotive, the tender and six passenger cars. The dining car was located in the second place of these, behind a mixed car that was divided between the luggage compartment and a smoking lounge. On one side of the corridor there were tables with four chairs and, on the other, tables with two chairs. Hunt and Noone occupied one of the latter. Almost all the dining room stalls were occupied. Hunt glanced covertly over the diners. He thought he saw businessmen, a couple of families on vacation, and a posh man who might be a movie actor.

"I'm not much of a fan of movies," Noone said, peering over the captain's shoulder, "but I'd say it's Milton Sills.

Hunt shrugged. He watched even fewer films than the American.

"Last year he starred in *The Sea Hawk*," the agent explained. "Very entertaining."

"If we get out of this, I'll try to watch it," Hunt said.

"Do you think Monreale will try anything during the trip?"

"I'll bet."

Noone cursed under his breath.

They ate in silence the splendid dinner served by the famed service of Fred Harvey Company. Hunt enjoyed the hearty portions served on fine porcelain plates and the efficient waitresses' service. However, it was not a quiet dinner. Hunt was unable to relax at any point during the evening. At every moment he kept an eye on the other diners and all the passengers who passed through the car. He was looking for signs of someone who was interested in them or who seemed willing to attack them. After finishing dinner, Hunt told himself that the trip would likely last forever.

"I'm exhausted," Noone said. "But I'm not able to go to bed. Will you join me to smoke?"

They went to the next car, which functioned as a bar and lounge. It was located immediately behind the locomotive. It consisted of a large smoking room, a barbershop, and the luggage compartment. Hunt and Noone occupied large adjoining rattan armchairs. The agent immediately turned on a Lucky Strike.

"The next stop is in Albuquerque," he announced. "We must be attentive to passengers who board there."

"Maybe we should get off before we get to Chicago," Hunt proposed. "To mislead anyone who is watching us."

"Good idea. I think Kansas City would be a good option. We'll be there in a day and a half."

"Well, I see that we will have a long journey ahead of us."

Noone slowly smoked his cigarette. By the time he was done, the other smokers had already retired to sleep. Hunt would have liked to drink a good whisky, but the damned Prohibition prevented him from doing so. It was unusual that in a country like that the government should completely eliminate alcohol to control the habits of its population. Hunt had read that Prohibition was largely ignored, especially in the big cities, but it would be impossible to find any liquor on board the train. Not even his travel companion had a reserve. During his stay at the camp, Noone had completely emptied his flask.

"We'd better try to get some sleep," Hunt suggested. "It's too late."

"Come, let's talk to the conductor first."

They found the man responsible for operational and safety duties of the train in his position in the last car, next to the observation room. Noone showed him his badge and told him what he needed. The conductor nodded vehemently and promised to keep them informed. Only then were Hunt and the agent able to go to sleep in their compartment. Shortly thereafter, the train made a brief stop at the Albuquerque station and then continued on its way through the arid terrain of New Mexico.

During the night, the speedy machine crossed the central plain of the state and then entered the Sangre de Cristo mountains through the Glorieta Pass, where a decisive battle had been fought during the Civil War. Dawn bathed the eastern slope of the mountain range in an intense reddish tint, from which derived the name that the Spanish conquistadors had given to those mountains. Following their own instructions, the train conductor woke up the Secret Service agent and his partner early in the following day.

"Here's the information about the passengers who boarded in Albuquerque," Noone told the captain. "Two men and a woman. They all travel separately."

"Well?"

"One is a reporter returning to Chicago after an assignment in Albuquerque. The other is a Catholic priest who was visiting the city's archdiocese."

"And the woman?"

"Her occupation is registered as an artist. It does not indicate reasons for the trip."

"Artist?"

"Yes. Moon Goldeneagle, Albuquerque resident."

"Strange name," Hunt remarked.

"You know how artists are," said Noone. "I think I'll keep an eye on that reporter. I think he's suspicious."

Hunt nodded absently. For some reason, he thought that woman more suspicious. An artist traveling alone, boarding the train in the middle of the night, in a remote place like Albuquerque... He decided that he would keep an eye on her.

When he finally met her, Hunt understood at once that Moon Goldeneagle was not a stage name, but a name of native origin. And she wasn't a mature woman wrapped in a robe and with a mysterious look, as he had imagined her. On the contrary, she was a young and very beautiful woman. Her indigenous features – high cheekbones, slanted eyes, jet-black hair – gave her a captivating air and an exotic beauty.

Hunt saw her soon after, having breakfast in the dining car, and knew at once that she was the new passenger. She wore an elegant and discreet dress, under a coat, and covered her head with a delicate cloche hat.

Noone was in another car, following in the footsteps of the reporter who seemed suspicious to him. That left Hunt the opportunity to approach the woman. He walked over to her table and picked up the other chair.

"Good morning, miss. Is this seat free?"

She nodded with an almost imperceptible gesture. Hunt immediately sat down and smiled at her. A waitress arrived promptly to take his order. The captain made his request mechanically and the woman left. Moon had only a cup of coffee on the table, still intact. On her knees she held a sketchbook. She seemed amused sketching out something that Hunt couldn't see from across the table.

"Are you an illustrator?" He asked.

The woman looked up and gazed at him as if she had just noticed his presence.

"I like to draw," she replied in a neutral tone.

Hunt forced himself to maintain a friendly expression.

"Captain Peter Hunt," he introduced himself, holding out his hand.

The woman sighed lightly, and then held out hers.

"Moon Goldeneagle. Are you in the army,

Captain Hunt?"

"Retired from the British Army."

"Then you don't have any rank at all, right?"

"Retired officers, from the rank of captain on, can continue to use their rank and be called by it," Hunt explained, as if quoting Debrett's etiquette handbook.

"I see. In England, titles and names are very important, aren't they?"

"I guess." He laughed and shrugged. "By the way, your name is very peculiar. Where does it come from?"

"From my parents, obviously."

Touché, Hunt thought. It was evident that his charms had no effect on this woman. She seemed somewhat amused by his attempts to strike up conversation, but her eyes showed that she really wanted to get rid of his company. He understood that he had only one way out.

"Maybe I'm bothering you. I'll call the waitress to get me another table."

He made a gesture to call the young woman, but Moon stopped him with a gesture.

"Don't bother, captain. I was already leaving."

She got up from the table and left at once. Hunt barely managed to get up in a polite gesture, but he couldn't say anything to her. The woman had already disappeared through the door leading to the car paltform. Hunt sat down again, and for a moment stared at the cup on the other side of the table, still full of steaming coffee. He, for his part, continued to eat his breakfast. He did not know what to make of the outcome of their encounter, but he told himself that this woman was too beautiful and cunning to fit in among the dull passengers on the train.

Noone met him a few minutes later.

"I managed to talk to the reporter," he announced. "It seems legit."

Hunt refrained from telling him 'I told you so'. He just nodded politely.

"Now I'll focus on the priest," the agent said. "I've never trusted them, you know?"

"I was talking to the artist. Moon Goldeneagle."

"Trying to hook her up, huh?"

Hunt tried not to get exasperated.

"I think she may be a mob agent, Hyam."

The Secret Service agent looked at him with a gesture of disbelief.

"A woman? It's not the style of those mafiosi, dear friend. Did she look Italian?"

"Of course not. I would say that she was rather of native origin."

"A redskin?"

"I understood that this term was offensive."

"You know what I mean, Peter," Noone said, shrugging.

"I can only say that the girl was very reserved. And beautiful."

"Bad combination." Noone laughed. "I

suggest you stay away from her, boy. And listen to me: let's concentrate on the priest."

Hunt couldn't help but smile at his partner's insistence. He put the cup in his mouth but did not get to drink the coffee. The train slowed down abruptly, giving a strong jerk. The crockery clinked on the tables. The patrons in the dining car looked up and several of them uttered exclamations of fear and surprise. Then the convoy gave another tug, this time more intense. From under the cars the screech of the brakes could be heard, which swept through the length of the train like lightning. Finally, the train stopped completely. Hunt and Noone looked at each other with senses on alert.

They both ran to the platform at the end of the car. On both sides were doors with windows that allowed passengers to get off the train at the stations. Hunt looked outside through one of the windows, while Noone stood at the opposite door.

"We are just at the foot of the mountains," the agent commented. Through his window he could see the reddish mountains spanning the entire horizon. "I don't like this at all."

Hunt discovered at that moment the cause of the sudden stop.

"Hyam, here!"

The agent stuck to the same window, and both gaped at what was coming. About twenty horsemen were galloping along the side of the train, from the locomotive to the dining car. It looked like a scene out of a western novel. But those men were not cowboys. Hunt knew at once that these were people sent by Monreale. Somehow they had managed to stop the train – with some barricade, surely – and now they were looking for him and Agent Noone.

The American cursed under his breath.

"We have to get out of here, Peter. Inside the train we are trapped."

"Let's go back to the front to find a way out," Hunt said.

He reached under his jacket and drew his revolver. Noone also drew his weapon, a .45-caliber Colt 1911 pistol. Through the hall they passed to the preceding car, which consisted exclusively of compartments. Halfway up the car, the compartments were on one side and the corridor on the other, and after a central vestibule the arrangement changed in the opposite direction. Hunt took cover in the central space and peeped down the next corridor.

"Clear," he whispered.

They ran to the end of the car and went through both platforms to move on to the next car. It had a compartment at each end and ten open sections in the middle, each with two seats facing each other. The passengers in the car had gotten up and were peering out of the windows, wondering the reason for the unexpected arrest. Seeing the two men with guns passing by, some women screamed, and some children hid in the seats.

"Secret Service!" Noone shouted. "Federal agent! Stay in your seats!"

They crossed the central aisle, pushing the curious away, without answering the questions that the passengers hurriedly asked them. The compartment at the end was the one they occupied. Hunt wondered if there was anything of value that needed to be taken out of there before he fled, but a negative gesture from his companion dissuaded him from even trying.

"They're surrounding the train," the American agent explained.

Hunt peeped through the windows while still moving forward. He saw riders on horseback on both sides. The noise of the galloping hooves of the animals was deafening.

"We must hurry," Noone insisted. "They must have already boarded the train somewhere."

The penultimate car in the convoy had the same configuration as the one in front of it. Before reaching it, the fugitives heard screams coming from inside. Hunt peered through the opening of the next platform and saw several armed men coming in the opposite direction. They hastily pushed passengers who stood in their way and brandished their weapons to frighten them.

"We won't be able to get through," the

captain warned. "Let's back up and try to descend through a platform that is not guarded."

"We won't get very far," Noone reasoned. "Outside it is open field."

The agent's eyes shone with fury. As they backed away, Hunt put a hand on his shoulder.

"We can't start a shooting inside the train."

"I know, damn it!"

"There they are!" A voice shouted behind them.

Hunt half turned and saw three men running in his direction.

"They have seen us!" he exclaimed through gritted teeth.

Through the windows they could see that the men on horseback were converging on the car in which the targets of the assault had been spotted. Noone cursed and barricaded himself in the platform where they were, between the two cars.

"We'll have to take them down, Peter."

Then, he fired a couple of times into the next car. The shots rang out loudly within the enclosed space, but the shrieks of terror were even more intense. The passengers tried to get out of the line of fire, pushing each other and darting in all directions. The assailants fired back, not caring that they could hit an innocent person. Chaos and screams took over the car.

The passengers behind the fugitives heard the heartbreaking shrieks coming from the next car and began to back away in disarray. The horsemen leaned out of the windows of the cars and hit the glasses with the butts of their weapons. Hunt told himself that there would soon be too many men over them to stand up to them. He no longer had an alternative. He shouted at people to get on the floor and also started shooting.

The first shots went too high. Hunt was afraid of accidentally hitting one of the passengers. He waited for one of the attackers to be in a line of clear fire and only then fired again. The man gave a groan of pain and fell on his back. Hunt opened fire again, preventing the other two men from advancing.

"We can't stay here!" He shouted to Noone.

The agent was further back, sheltered behind a seat. Fortunately, the passengers in that car had managed to evacuate it in its entirety. Noone fired to cover Hunt as the captain backed away. The bullets from the .45-caliber pistol cracked like thunder inside the train. Hunt hid in the seat on the other side of the aisle and from there covered Noone in turn so that he could back up. The attackers continued to advance between their own shots.

"Let's try the next platform," the American proposed. "I'll soon run out of ammo."

"I agree!"

The assailants were already at the entrance of the car. From there they had free rein to shoot into the car. The air was already thin with gunpowder smoke. Bits of bulkhead lining and plush on the seats were flying everywhere. The car was in ruins. It would take a long time for that train to get back on track, Hunt thought. That is, if the company got passengers willing to travel on it.

One of the attackers stepped forward, firing incessantly, and giving a war cry, like an outlaw from the old west. Hunt threw himself to the floor to dodge the burst. The attacker's reckless action had left him exposed. Hunt shot him from below, hitting him in the belly. The assailant bent forward and stopped screaming. He took a couple of hesitant steps and then fell sideways between some seats. Only two attackers remained, who took cover to avoid following the fate of their partner.

Hunt and Noone managed to take turns backing up to the opposite end of the car. They only had to move from one platform to the next and there test the side doors to see if they had free pass to the outside. If they wanted to have the slightest chance of success, they had to manage to flee quickly enough that the horsemen patrolling the outside of the train would not discover them. It seemed like an impossible task, but it was the only option they had left. Hunt hoped they would get far enough away from the convoy to hide among the rocks. From there they would have to quickly enter the surrounding vegetation.

They both crouched and backed away through the small space of the platform. The attackers advanced crouching down the central corridor, their weapons raised. At the first sign of a head raised above the seats, or of a hand stretched forward, the opposing side would fill the car with bullets again. Hunt gestured for Noone to approach one of the platform doors and peek through the window. For his part, he stayed behind a bulkhead, in a firing position.

"Now, Hyam!" He whispered.

Hunt jumped into the middle of the hall and raised his revolver. The enemies were hidden between the seats of the car in front. At the slightest hint of a furtive movement, he could reach them cleanly with one shot.

"Quickly!" He ordered, without taking his eyes off the previous corridor. "I have them within reach and..."

He heard a soft metallic click that he identified as the unmistakable cocking of a gun. He turned his head slightly and saw that Hyam Noone was standing by the side door of the platform. However, he wasn't looking out the window. His eyes were fixed on Hunt. His head was slightly tilted forward, in a strange and unnatural position. For a moment, Hunt thought his partner had been wounded, but then discovered that he had a small object pressed against the base of his neck.

Hunt took a step back into the platform and could see the strange object better. It was a small pistol, no bigger than the palm of a hand, fitted with four barrels. Despite their small size, Hunt knew that derringers were deadly at close range. John Wilkes Booth had used one of these devices to kill President Lincoln at point-blank range. Moon Goldenegale held hers pushed tightly into the agent's skin. The woman came out from behind the bulkhead that hid her and looked hard at the captain.

"I can fire all four shots in quick succession, Captain Hunt." He nodded, indicating that he believed her. "But the first shot would be enough to kill agent Noone."

Hunt grimaced but nodded again. He knew she was right.

"Shoot him, Peter!" The American muttered. "Don't let her get her way."

"Are you willing to exchange my life for that of your partner, captain?" She pressed the small pistol tighter to the back of her captive's neck. "I assure you that I will not hesitate to pull the trigger."

Hunt kept his revolver pointed toward the platform. He noticed that the two attackers who were still standing had advanced down the hallway. They carried their guns raised in front of them. Hunt cocked his revolver and stopped them with a gesture.

"Tell your men to stop, Miss Moon." Hunt's

voice sounded cold and calm. "Maybe you can shoot Hyam once, or maybe twice, before I shoot down those killers. And then I'll still be able to shoot you without you hitting me with that pepperbox in your hand."

For the first time, the woman smiled. Hunt was right. Derringers were called "pepper shakers" because of their appearance and size, which allowed them to be easily hidden. But that same characteristic diminished their precision and power beyond a few meters.

"I have no doubt that you are a good marksman, captain," said Moon, with a smile on her lips. "But I'm sure one of my men will shoot you, and even if you don't hit him, it will distract you enough to try to shoot you after I kill agent Noone."

"So we're on a Mexican standoff, aren't we?" Hunt concluded. "Do you know the expression, Miss Moon?"

"In a duel between three opponents, no one manages to have the advantage to get the victory," she said.

At the same time, she nodded. Now it was Hunt's turn to smile.

"As soon as I saw you, I knew you worked for Monreale," Hunt remarked.

He had pretended to sound angry, but it was evident that his voice had a tone of admiration.

"Don't I look like an artist?"

"You don't look like a mafioso, either. It's

your eyes, Miss Moon. Too calculating."

She laughed, showing perfectly white teeth. Then her face hardened.

"Enough compliments, captain. What will we do, then?"

"We'll give you the medallion and you'll leave at once."

"No, Peter, damn it!" Noone shouted, furious.

He tried to get away from the woman, but the four barrels pressed against his neck dissuaded him. He still held his pistol in his hand, but he had it pointed at the floor. Hunt knew that his partner felt humiliated and frustrated, but he had to make him understand that the only chance they had of getting out of this situation alive was to deliver the device to the assailants.

"Hyam, give the medallion to Miss Moon."

Noone looked at him with eyes bulging with fury. His face was flushed, and the knuckles of his hand had turned white from squeezing the butt of the pistol. After a moment, he gave a guttural scream and dropped his weapon. He brought his free hand to the inside of his jacket and slowly pulled out the medallion. The piece of gold glistened in the sunlight that came in through the side door window. Noone lifted the medallion over his shoulder, and Moon Goldeneagle grabbed it from behind.

Hunt brandished his revolver at the assailants. The men slowly backed up the hallway, still looking at their opponent. They had their guns pointed at the floor. Hunt hurried them with a gesture. Shortly afterwards they disappeared at the other end of the car. Then Moon opened the door to the platform and jumped on a horse waiting for her outside. She spurred the animal on and galloped away, followed by all her henchmen. Noone immediately ducked, retrieved his pistol, and began firing toward the group of assailants.

"Damn, Peter!" He shouted in the middle of the shootout. "Now they have the fucking medallion!"

Hunt put a hand on the agent's shoulder and yelled in his ear.

"Stop shooting! You're not going to reach them!"

Noone turned sharply to the captain.

"What shall we do, then? We're stranded in the middle of nowhere!"

"We'll go after them."

The Secret Service agent looked at him with a gesture that betrayed what he was thinking. That the Englishman had gone mad.

"And how the hell..."

Before he could continue complaining, Hunt grabbed him by the shoulders and turned him outward. They both peeked through the open door and the captain pointed towards the back of the convoy. Two horses, both without their riders, were looking for some grass with their heads down on the side of the train. Noone gawked at the animals.

"I hit two attackers during the shooting," Hunt explained. "In a hurry to flee, the other members of the group abandoned their mounts."

Noone laughed wildly. He patted Hunt on the back and got off the train.

"Come, my friend! I've always wanted to be like Wild Bill Hicock!"

They ran towards the horses, which meekly allowed themselves to be caught. They jumped on them and shot off into the mountains.

10. SANGRE DE CRISTO

The outlaws were quite ahead of them. But they were a large group, which delayed their march. They also left a large number of tracks in their wake. For half an hour Hunt and Noone easily followed the deep tracks left by the horses as they galloped across the ground. Then the ground became stonier, and the footprints began to fade. The pursuers were forced to slow down their ride so they could look for hoof marks on rocks or broken branches in the bushes. In front of them, the mountains rose imposingly.

"They must have a shelter somewhere," Noone said. "The nearest town is several hours away and is in that other direction."

He pointed to the side of the place where the increasingly faint tracks of the fugitives were leading them.

"If they exchange horses for motorized vehicles," said Hunt, "we shall never catch up with them."

Noone nodded, uneased.

The horses they rode were large and robust animals, accustomed to the arid terrain of the mountains. They allowed themselves to be guided docilely and were not afraid of heights or ravines. On their flanks they carried leather saddlebags that the riders quickly examined as they climbed the mountains. The outlaws were well prepared for their raid. In their saddlebags they carried camping implements and several full canteens. Hunt rummaged through the bags for maps or signs of the bandits camp. He was unsuccessful.

"They can't have gone very far," Noone muttered after a while.

The trail had completely disappeared. Both men looked around. They only saw forests, ravines and mountains that grew in height ahead, until they reached peaks of almost four thousand meters towards the center of the sierra. Hunt dismounted from the horse and bent down to examine the ground.

"I think we strayed from the trail further back," said the captain. "I'll back up this path to look for some mark."

Noone stayed with the animals while Hunt explored the surrounding terrain. The sun was high in the sky and the heat was becoming oppressive. Hunt drank from his canteen and suddenly felt hungry too. It was assumed that there was abundant native fauna in those places, but they did not carry long weapons to hunt a deer or an elk. And they couldn't spend the bullets of their handguns to get lunch.

Hell, Hunt thought. I'm reasoning as if I'm going to spend several days in this place. He hadn't talked about it with Noone yet, but he was convinced that they couldn't chase the bandits for more than a few hours. If they couldn't find them by then, they would have to go back to the railway line and wait for the next train or try to get to the nearest town. In any case, their stay in those mountains surely was going to be arduous.

The terrain was wild and steep, even for horses. Landforms made proper surveillance difficult. There were too many places where even a large group of horsemen could hide unseen. Dense clumps of trees, deep ravines, canyons that meandered in the shade of the mountain slopes. In addition, the captain wondered, what would they achieve by finding the fugitives? The outlaws vastly outnumbered them and had more firepower. Hunt was confident that he could eliminate some if necessary, but in the long run, they would win. They needed the state police promptly to deal with the bandits. With a full detachment of mounted agents, they could dig the ground well and engage the bandits with gunfire.

Monreale had set up a good operation. It had to be admitted. No doubt he had been laying out his plans for several months, perhaps even before the four Spanish saddlebags were found west of New Mexico. A little more than three months had passed since that discovery, insufficient time to organize all that. Perhaps in New York he had an army of gangsters at his service, but he had also managed to organize a band of outlaws more than three thousand miles away.

The subterranean temple that Hunt had seen in rescuing Allison MacGregor showed that it was a long-winded operation with careful preparation. Monreale's interest in the mystical practices of the natives must have begun much earlier, perhaps years. Hunt had described the room to Professor Neil Grant during his stay at the camp. Grant had been very interested in the matter.

"Well, it must be the recreation of a *kiva* of the Anasazi," the professor explained. "It is a circular-shaped room that was used for religious ceremonies, rituals and political meetings."

"I thought I saw similar structures in the village we found under the cliff," Hunt recalled.

"That's right. There are in most of the villages built by the Anasazi."

"Why would a mafioso of Italian origin have a... *kiva*, under the headquarters of his business in Manhattan?"

"I can think of only one reason," said Grant. Hunt raised an eyebrow. "To practice the same rituals as the Anasazi, obviously."

The mobster's relationship with native religion continued to intrigue Hunt. How on earth had Monreale come to know those rituals or the very existence of the medallion? After all, the treasure of Cibola had been lost for more than two hundred and fifty years and there were no records of it even being found by the Spanish conquistadors. Hunt thought again of the elusive Moon Goldeneagle. Clearly the woman was originally from that area, although she did not resemble Hunt's image of the American Indians. Moon was resolute, bold, and very modern. Perhaps she had lived elsewhere for some time or had been raised far from her village, the captain deduced. But it was still hard to relate her to the New York mob.

Hunt abruptly interrupted his reminiscences. He crossed a grove of poplar trees and found himself on the edge of a cliff. At the foot of the mountain ran a stream that meandered through the valley, down the mountains. In the distance, at the water's edge, Hunt saw horses and men drinking from the stream. He wished he had binoculars, but he was sure it was the group of bandits anyway. Or, at least, a part of them. He ran through the grove until he came to the path that ran along the opposite boundary. Noone and his mounts were a little higher up the mountainside.

"I found them!" He shouted. "They are up the

valley, on the other side of these mountains."

They jumped on the mounts and went through the poplars. When they reached the cliff they could see that some riders were entering a ravine.

"They're quite far away," Noone said. "We should continue along this side of the valley until we reach them. If we try to cross here and then follow the same path, we will lose a lot of time."

They did it that way. They led the horses to the top of the mountain. Then they continued to the top of the next elevation. Noone found a few pieces of dried beef in one of his saddlebags. He shared them with Hunt as they climbed the mountain range. The thin strips of meat were crispy and salty, but at least it calmed their hunger. Although not their thirst. They drank the entire contents of the canteens, confident that they would soon find a source of water to refill them. After an hour, both horsemen had dry throats and were sweating profusely. Noone took off his black jacket and hung it from the saddle.

"Why do you always wear black?" Hunt asked.

Now that he thought about it, he hadn't seen the agent wear clothes of any other color.

"My father was a very strict Methodist pastor," Noone explained. "Not only did he promote plain dress, but he also demanded the omission of any color or flashy adornment. As a result, my whole family wore rigorous black." He shrugged over the saddle. "I guess I got used to it. Besides, this way I avoid having to choose different clothes in the morning when I wake up."

Hunt laughed.

For a while they advanced in silence, skirting a high mountain covered with tall pines. Hunt began to wonder how much farther they could go into the mountains. Soon night would fall, it would be cold, and the conditions for staying there would become harsh and dangerous. He was about to voice his opinion aloud when Noone, who was in the lead, stopped abruptly. Hunt stopped his horse next to the other animal and discovered the reason for the sudden stop. There was nowhere to go on. The top of the mountain ended in a steep precipice.

"Damn!" The Secret Service agent exclaimed.

"We should go back to that pass we saw a little while ago," Hunt proposed.

"We would lose almost an hour in finding a route that would keep us close to the bandits," Noone estimated. "I think the only option left is to go down to the stream and cross on the other side."

"It's faster," Hunt said, "but we'll be more exposed."

They stared at each other for a moment, mentally gauging their options. In the end, they both nodded. They immediately led the horses up the eastern slope of the mountain, facing the valley where the stream flowed. The descent was quite steep, but the animals held on tightly to the ground and managed to reach the plain safely. From there to the edge of the creek it only took a few minutes. They stopped for a moment, and both horses lowered their heads to drink water. The riders dismounted and refreshed their faces and necks. After almost a day riding, they were covered in dust and sweat. They also stuffed the canteens.

"It's going to get dark soon," Hunt said. "If we don't find the bandits soon, we will be trapped overnight in the mountains."

"You're right," Noone conceded. "There is no more food in the saddlebags, and we only have a couple of thin blankets."

"Maybe we should go back and notify the state police."

"By the time they reach the mountains, Moon and his men will be gone."

"Then we must make a plan," Hunt insisted.

"Our only advantage is surprise. Besides, we can go faster than them."

"If we get ahead of the group of bandits, we can ambush them from somewhere high," the captain proposed. "The horses know the terrain and will be able to guide us in the dark."

"We're two against twenty, Peter. " Noone smiled sadly. "Our chances of success are minimal."

Hunt shrugged.

"It's either that or abandon the search right now."

Noone put one foot on the stirrup and stood up on his saddle.

"Let's go, my friend!"

They forded the stream a short distance upstream. When they reached the opposite bank, they immediately threw themselves after the bandits. It did not take long for them to find traces of the passage of the large group through the adjoining forest. The ground was covered with the tracks of the animals and several of the trees had the lowest branches cracked by the passage of the riders. Hunt and Noone hurried their march, eager to close the distance with the fugitives. The slope of the mountain on this side of the valley was less steep and could be easily climbed. The horses advanced with a sure step, firmly fastening their hooves on the regular ground.

The peaks of the higher mountains cast long shadows on the lower hills. Hunt calculated that night would soon fall. For a long time they rode in silence, following the tracks left by the fugitives. The captain was already beginning to notice the exhaustion of the expedition. His backside ached from being in the saddle for so long. The pants of his suit, made of a mixture of mohair and wool, were completely unsuitable for a long ride. In addition to offering little protection against the constant rubbing of the saddle's leather, they were hopelessly wrinkled.

"I hear something," Noone said as they emerged from a forest near the top of the mountain.

They both stopped and pricked up their ears. Near them ran a canyon that snaked through the middle of the spur in which they stood, which derived from the main chain of mountains that rose towards the center of the sierra. From deep in the gorge came the unmistakable sound of the hooves of several horses pounding against the rocky ground. The group advanced at a brisk pace, no doubt trying to make distance before nightfall. Noone pointed to Hunt to a promontory ahead, which stood like a watchtower above the canyon. There they could hide and confront the bandits from high ground.

They made the horses advance on the grass and fallen leaves, to prevent the noise from giving them away. When they reached the promontory, they hid the animals next to some pine trees and they crouched behind some large rocks. The sunset was behind them, so from below any observer would be dazzled when they looked up. Both raised their weapons and waited for the group of horsemen to twist a bend in the gorge so that they were on open ground and in sight from their hiding place.

The group of bandits appeared shortly

after. Moon Goldeneagle was leading the way on an imposing palomino horse, followed by the twenty horsemen who had surrounded and assaulted the train after crossing the Glorieta Pass. All the men looked rough. They rode skillfully and had sun-tanned skin. Several of them seemed to be Indians, who rode fierce-looking pinto horses. At least ten of the men carried rifles slung over their shoulders.

Hunt glanced at his partner and they both nodded. The time for confrontation had come. The captain raised his Webley revolver, pointed it at one of the bandits, and fired. The rider was startled and fell on his side, sliding from the saddle until he was lying on the ground. The shot rang like thunder in the gorge. The horses reared up and the riders tried to control them before they fled in terror. Noone fired in turn and knocked down another of the bandits.

By this time, Moon was already shouting orders to his men to disperse. Hunt and Noone opened fire repeatedly, easily hitting the horsemen trapped in the narrow bottom of the canyon. Both tried to eliminate the men carrying rifles. However, after the shooting, there were still several mounted and well-armed men who had already taken cover behind some ledges on the slopes of the mountains. Hunt and Noone lowered their heads as the rifles returned fire from the ravine.

Fortunately, the bandits had the sun in their

eyes and were shooting almost blindly. Hunt signaled to Noone to look for a new shooting position. As bursts of shots swept across the rocks of the promontory, the two men crouched back in search of another hiding place. After a few moments they reached another rocky area on the top of the mountain. Sheltered between the large rocks, they fired again at the canyon. This time it was not so easy to hit the targets. The horsemen were scattered and sheltered in the cavities of the irregular slope.

Hunt reloaded the revolver. He tried to take care of his bullets but wasted most of the shots anyway. Noone suffered the same fate. They had lost the element of surprise.

"Let's get out of here, Peter!" Noone shouted over the roar of the bandits' gunfire.

There were at least three rifles still in the hands of the bandits. Five other men were still firing with their revolvers. It was too much firepower to stand up to. Hunt cursed in his mind. He lay on his face on the stony ground and peered through the cracks in the rocks. Below, at the bottom of the barrel, floated a dense cloud of gunpowder smoke. Through the fog, the heads of the shooters could barely be seen. The noise was deafening. The thin gorge bounced the sound of gunfire and the neighing of horses. Amid all this cacophony, the voices of some men could be heard shouting orders or complaining of some wound.

Moon was nowhere to be seen. His striking palomino horse had disappeared. Surely she had returned through the same ravine. The woman was not carrying any weapon useful to be engaged in a shootout. She had simply backed off to leave his men in charge of the engagement. Hunt bet she was carrying the medallion.

"Can you entertain them for a while?" Hunt asked his partner.

Noone stuck his pistol out of the rocks from time to time and fired without looking into the canyon. Immediately a burst of shots responded to him.

"I have only this magazine left," said the agent. "When I stop shooting, they'll come for me."

"Not if I can catch the woman first," Hunt said.

On the other side of the promontory there was a ravine that in turn faced the other side of the mountain, beyond the canyon. Hunt smiled at his partner and dropped down on the wall of the ravine. The hillside had a steep slope, but at least it was of solid, smooth rock. The captain slid down like it was a sledge. When he reached halfway, a rock made him roll down and from there he fell uncontrollably, tumbling like a sack of potatoes. He hit his back, stomach, and limbs, but at least he managed to hold his head up. He crashed at the foot of the slope still conscious, although in great pain. He lay on his back for a moment, catching his breath. He took a mental inventory of his body and told himself that he did not have any broken bones. However, he was covered in bruises and scrapes. He got up with difficulty and immediately ran through the trees.

As he had supposed, Moon Goldeneagle was on the back of her horse in a clearing in the grove. The sound of the shooting could be heard muffled on the other side of the mountainside, deep in the canyon. Hunt raised his revolver and advanced surreptitiously toward the woman, approaching from the side. He prayed that she would not discover that the cylinder of the revolver was empty. He was careful not to step on the fallen branches, advancing slowly, although without taking his eyes off that enigmatic woman. He was about five meters away when she turned her head and looked at him smiling.

"Did you really think I wouldn't hear you, Captain Hunt?"

Hunt managed to keep his composure. He pointed his revolver at her and spoke in an energetic tone.

"Get off the horse. Don't make any sudden movement!"

Moon gracefully descended from the palomino horse, which was grazing quietly. She stood by the mount and watched him with obvious curiosity.

"You are a man of many talents, captain."

"Flattery will be of no use to you, Miss Moon."

"Please call me just Moon. Can I call you Peter?"

"You can call me whatever you want. I just expect you come with me and call your men to..."

Moon approached him with swift steps. Hunt cocked his revolver loudly. The woman took the gun by the barrel and pushed it away. Hunt cursed in his mind and prepared to hit her with the butt of the Webley. He didn't want to attack a woman, but it was already clear that she wasn't like other women. And it was evident she was not willing to give up easily. Hunt raised his revolver to deliver his blow, but suddenly the four-barreled derringer that Moon was wielding was in front of his eyes.

"My Sharps pocket pistol is not as powerful as your Webley revolver," said the woman. "But at least it's loaded."

Hunt knew that each of the four .22 caliber bullets would destroy his face at that distance. In addition, Moon claimed that she could fire all four rounds in quick succession. Hunt did not wish to test her. He put his revolver in the holster under his arm and raised both hands. The woman smiled.

The sound of a struggle was heard between the trees. An instant later, Hyam Noone appeared in the clearing, dragged by four men. Two others closed the group, pointing their guns at the prisoner. The face of the Secret Service agent was covered in blood, and he was breathing heavily.

Seeing the Englishman, he tried to smile. But he only managed to make a grimace of pain.

"At least I put up a good fight," he said in a trembling voice.

"I didn't even have a chance," Hunt replied. He gave Moon a hard look, and added, "But I'll have it."

She caressed his cheek with the 'pepper shaker' and came over to say in his ear:

"We'll see, captain."

The bandits' camp was hidden in a narrow valley between two high mountains, about an hour's walk from the place where Hunt and Noone had been captured. Both prisoners were tied on their horses, blindfolded, and guided by other riders through ropes tied to the saddles. During the journey to the hiding place, no one spoke.

Hunt was sure that this Moon woman had some kind of special power. She seemed to be always one step ahead of the others, she moved precisely and silently, and her eyes were dark as two bottomless pits. There was something about her that was both unsettling and engaging. It was easy to understand that a powerful and dangerous man like Daniele Monreale would have associated himself with that woman. If the mobster was explosive and violent as fire, Moon was cold and hard as ice. Hunt cursed himself for underestimating his opponent, thinking that there in New Mexico he could get ahead of the mob's plans. Although he had found the medallion before his enemies, they had not only snatched it from him, but had now taken him prisoner.

When they finally removed the blindfolds, it was already dead of the night. The camp consisted of a few tents arranged around a campfire. The bandits sat down in front of the fire and gave sullen glances at the prisoners. Then they seemed to forget about them. Noone was dragged to one of the tents, while muttering curses. Hunt, on the other hand, was left in charge of Moon Goldeneagle. The woman kept his wrists tied behind his back, but she just grabbed his arm and led him to her own tent, which was separated from the others by about ten meters. Hunt had a bad feeling about what was going to happen.

The tent was rectangular in shape, with a gabled roof. It was taller and wider than the others used by the bandits. It was made of a thick khaki canvas. It was almost five meters long, four meters wide, and three meters high in its central part. It appeared to Hunt that the tents and equipment were surplus from the American Expeditionary Force that had fought in the Great War. The fabric was impregnated with a substance that protected against fires and insulated both excessive heat and intense cold.

The interior of the tent was illuminated by a kerosene lamp that projected its twinkling light on the decoration in the manner of the natives. The floor was covered with blankets, on the walls were fabrics embroidered with beads, and from the top crossbar hung an intricately woven dreamcatcher, adorned with long colored feathers. Hunt examined these art samples for a few moments before sitting cross-legged on cushions. Moon sat down in the same way in front of him.

"I made them," she explained. "Authentic native art."

"Why are you working for Monreale, Moon? For some reason, I can't see you subordinate to a mobster."

"I don't work *for* him, Peter. Ours is rather a mutually beneficial society."

Now he understood. That woman had her own goals in that operation. Hunt had to try to get information, but it wouldn't be an easy task. He was still her prisoner and still had his hands tied. He tried the knots on his back, but he could barely move his wrists.

"I'll take off your ligatures if you promise to behave well."

Hunt felt uneasy. Moon seemed able to read his mind. He tried to sound relaxed.

"I have no intention of leaving. My interrogation is going well so far."

She smiled her enigmatic smile again. At the same time, and with a swift movement, he drew a sharp dagger from among the blankets.

Without rising, he leaned over next to Hunt and cleanly cut his bonds. The dagger quickly disappeared. The captain watched it anxiously for a moment but couldn't detect where Moon had hidden it.

"Now it is my turn to get something from you, my dear captain."

"I don't have much to tell," he replied in a bored tone.

"Oh, I didn't mean information!" She laughed. For some reason, Hunt got goosebumps. "When the time comes, you will tell me everything I need to know."

Hunt raised an eyebrow.

Without answering, Moon arranged between them a bowl of darkened clay engraved with intricate drawings. From a jug of the same material, he poured a viscous liquid until she filled the bowl. Moon dipped his hands into the oily substance and then took them away. She stretched both hands toward Hunt's face and motioned for him to lean toward her.

"What is this?" He asked with a note of suspicion in his voice.

The substance appeared to be some kind of resin that smelled like sage and other herbs.

"It's just a cleansing ceremony," the woman explained. "Now, keep quiet."

Still hesitant, he bent down so that she could reach his face with her hands. With delicate gestures, Moon stroked his skin and traced drawings with her fingers on his cheeks and forehead. The strong aroma flooded the captain's nostrils. Moon muttered a chant in an unfamiliar language and kept rubbing her fingertips against Hunt's face. At first, the strange caresses tickled him, but then his skin was impregnated with that oil and the touch of her fingers became lighter and lighter.

Hunt began to relax. Not only was his mind calmer, but so were his tired muscles. The chant had increased in intensity. It seemed like a lullaby to Hunt. If the woman continued with her caresses, he would soon fall asleep. His dull mind warned him that he was falling into a kind of trance, but his body felt too comfortable to try to stop the woman. Almost in the last moment of lucidity, he wondered what it was that she was cleansing and why she should do it. Did she wish to purify his soul? His body? With a mental chuckle, he told himself that he knew other, more pleasurable ways to tend to his body.

He found that his eyes were closed. With a great effort of self-control, he managed to open them. At first he got used to the gloom, but then he opened them wide when he saw what was happening in front of him. Moon Goldeneagle was taking off her clothes with subtle movements, without getting up from his cushions. Her body rippled as if she were following music that only she could hear. Her brown skin shone in the dim light, as if it were covered with the same substance with which she had smeared the captain's face. From her naked body emanated a floral perfume, intense and inviting. Hunt discovered that he was also undressing. But unlike the woman, he would pull off his clothes, desperately. The perfume intoxicated him, and the woman's bare breasts seemed focused on his eyes, hypnotizing him.

Then both bodies became intertwined, and he lost track of time and space. They frolicked on the blankets and felt Moon's hands running down his back, digging her nails into his skin amid the frenzy that gripped them. She moaned under the weight of his body, but then she was on top of him and writhed like a rider taming a wild horse. The woman muttered strange words and squeezed his temples with both hands, as if she wanted to extract all his vital energy. He grabbed her by the hips and increased his thrusts, until they both screamed and fell exhausted on the cushions.

As he caught his breath, Hunt felt the dullness of his mind begin to dissipate. He became fully aware of what he had just done, but he felt no regrets. Moon hugged him, resting her breasts on his chest.

"Don't think you'll make me talk with this," he said, gasping.

She stood up to look him in the eye.

"You've already told me everything I wanted to know. I told you that it would be so."

Hunt pushed her away and sat up on the blankets.

"What are you talking about?"

"While we were enjoying ourselves, you told me everything, my dear."

Hunt was dumbfounded. He didn't remember saying anything, except for a few involuntary gasps in the moments of greatest pleasure. But then he realized that what he had revealed had not been said in words. That was what she did with her hands pressed against his temples. It wasn't his energy that the woman had taken away from him—well, there had been some of it—but his thoughts. Moon had mastered him not only physically, but also mentally. That act had not been the product of passion. It had been an interrogation.

Moon stretched out her arms towards him seductively.

"Come here, Peter. You need to rest."

Hunt approached her as if he were going to hold her in his arms. At the last moment, before bodies became intertwined, he clenched his right hand into a fist and smashed it with all his might against the woman's head. Moon flinched and her eyes widened in surprise. But then they get blank and she fell backwards on the blankets. Hunt stared at her for a moment, naked and covered in sweat. It would have been a most sensual image in any other circumstance. He rummaged under the blankets until he found

the dagger.
  He dressed in a hurry.

11. GREAT HOUSE

The camp was silent. A sentinel had been left standing guard near the central fire, but he had fallen asleep. Hunt tiptoed around the tents, trying to figure out in which of them Noone was being held captive. From inside some tents came unintelligible snoring, but no voice could be heard. Hunt did not dare to peek through the fabric openings for fear of encountering some awakened bandit. Nor could he call the agent, even in whispers. Perhaps his only option was to flee alone and then send aid to rescue his partner.

He dismissed the idea immediately. He could not abandon Noone to his fate. It was very likely that, if he managed to flee, the agent would be killed so that he would never be found. For a moment Hunt stood in the darkness, looking for a way to find his partner without alerting all the bandits. And he had to do it soon. He hadn't had the cold blood to hit Moon too hard. The woman would soon awaken from her unconsciousness. It was her whom the captain feared most. After he had attacked her, he assumed that Moon would retaliate relentlessly.

"Peter!"

The intense whisper startled him. He had already reached for the dagger when he realized that it had been Noone himself who had called him. He turned in search of the origin of the voice. A 'pssss' alerted him to the place where his partner was. Noone was sitting on the ground, his back against a tree trunk, just outside the camp. A thick rope held his chest and arms tied to the trunk. The outlaws' horses were tied to nearby branches. Hunt crept forward so as not to alert the animals. He stood on the other side of the trunk where Noone was and cut the rope.

"Are you ok?" He whispered to his partner. "You must be freezing out here."

"Don't worry. Only my hands are numb."

The agent also kept his voice low. The sentry by the fire lay motionless, but he could wake up at any moment. Hunt helped Noone up.

"Did they at least give you some food?" Hunt asked.

His partner shook his head. The captain's blood boiled. The bandits had left the agent out in the open all night, without any food or water.

"They were all aware of what was going on in the woman's tent," Noone explained. "She was there with you, wasn't she?"

"Yes. She was… questioning me."

"Did she hurt you? Did she torture you?"

Hunt blushed. He was grateful that in the midst of darkness his reaction was not visible.

"I am fine. I managed to resist until the end."

If Noone was curious about his partner's escape, at least he refrained from commenting on it. He approached one of the horses and began to untie its tethers. Hunt stopped him with a gesture.

"We must flee on foot," whispered the captain. "The horses will make a lot of noise."

They had to delay the inevitable pursuit as long as possible. As soon as Moon came out of her unconsciousness, she would sound the escape alarm. In addition, going on foot would leave fewer tracks than on a mount. Noone pointed to a sloping terrain covered with trees. Hunt nodded, and they both went into the thicket. They couldn't run in the middle of the forest and the darkness, but they managed to put distance from the bandits' camp.

"Are you armed?" Noone asked, still making his way through the bushes and the low branches of the trees.

"I took a dagger from Moon."

Noone looked at Hunt in surprise.

"I managed to knock her out after the… ahem, interrogation."

"You should have killed her with the dagger," Noone said, without any emotion.

After that they continued their escape in silence. The terrain became increasingly uneven and steep. Both men tripped several times and scratched their hands and faces with branches blocking the way in the dark. It was cold. Hunt's hands felt numb and his face ached. He tried to be guided by the stars, but the blanket of trees completely obscured the sky. For the moment, he had to content himself with descending the mountain. The most important thing was to get away from the camp before the bandits began the chase. A wolf howled in the distance. Hunt cursed mentally and stepped up his pace.

After an hour they came to a narrow valley crossed by a rushing river. They drank some of the frigid water and then continued to follow the course of the river down the mountain. Hunt reckoned that it was another hour before dawn. He hugged himself with his own hands and rubbed them against his arms to warm up. Noone was a little further back, shivering with cold. At least Hunt had spent part of the night inside a tent... in lukewarm conditions.

"I promise I'll arrest all those bastards," Noone muttered. His teeth chattered loudly. "That is, if I don't kill them first."

"Do you think there is a town nearby?" The captain asked him.

He feared that his partner would faint in the middle of the flight. He didn't feel much better either. Both were hungry and exhausted.

"Perhaps in the day I could find my way," said Noone, snorting. "But now I'm going blind."

Shortly afterwards they heard the hooves of the horses. The bandits came after them. Hunt and Noone glanced at each other, then ran along the edge of the river. There the terrain was even, but at the same time it was also more open, which made them easily visible from a distance. The mighty river sounded loudly next to them, but equally the noise of the horses on the ground was heard more and more intensely over the sound of the water.

"They're already close!" Noone shouted.

The agent motioned for Hunt to go into the trees. The captain followed his partner into the woods, but the sound of thunder paralyzed him halfway through the run. Only it had not been thunder, but the firing of a rifle. Hunt continued his run with his body crouched, just as several shots flooded the valley. The bullets ricocheted off the stones on the ground, dangerously close to his feet.

Hunt threw himself headlong into the trees. He rolled on the ground and took cover behind a thick trunk. Half a dozen horses appeared in the valley, silhouetted against the faint moonlight. Hunt was not surprised to see Moon Goldeneagle leading the way. Even from a distance he could perceive her face tense with fury. Hunt deduced that, if captured, their fate would be death. According to what the woman had said, she had already obtained everything she needed from him. Including his body. The fugitives were no longer of value to the bandits, but they could not let them escape. Hunt corrected himself mentally. He and Noone were no longer fugitives. They had become the hunters' prey.

He pulled the dagger out of his clothes. The sharp blade flashed in the darkness. His disadvantage against firearms was overwhelming, but he would not be caught without a fight. He would only need to sneak up on his enemies. He peeked out of the side of the trunk and could see the bandits better. Besides Moon there were four men on horseback, one of them armed with a rifle. The horsemen reached the edge of the forest and there they dismounted, always keeping their weapons in front. Only the woman remained on her mount further back. The bandits hesitated for a moment before going into the woods, but they were no doubt more afraid of their chief than of darkness.

Hunt pressed his back to the trunk and remained as still as possible. One of the bandits passed by less than a meter away, testing the ground and swinging his revolver in front of his eyes. The captain remained motionless and let the man walk away. The other bandits were still nearby, and he should not attract the attention of others. He would have to take care of two men and Noone the other two. There was still Moon outside the forest, but between them they would have to face her.

He changed positions slowly, taking care not to make a sound. He couldn't see his partner, but he trusted that Noone was sheltered nearby. The darkness was dissolving, and the treetops had taken on a pink hue, a sign that dawn was approaching. They had to act soon, or the light of day would give them away. Hunt approached one of the bandits from behind. The man advanced stepping on the fallen branches, without worrying about the noise he made. He didn't hear someone approaching him until it was too late.

Hunt stabbed him in the back, with all his might. The man squirmed and wailed, but no one could hear him. The captain covered his mouth with his other hand while holding the blade against his body. A moment later, the outlaw's legs faltered, and he stopped standing upright. Hunt held the limp body under his armpits to keep it from falling heavily. He laid it gently on the ground and kept moving forward. He thought he saw Noone moving stealthily along his side, also following a bandit. Every moment there was more daylight, and the silhouettes of the men began to be clearly seen among the trees.

He spotted Noone beyond, approaching an outlaw from behind. Hunt could see him clearly as he tiptoed to throw himself at the man. He was less than two meters from his target when he stepped on a branch that creaked like thunder in the middle of the silent forest. The bandit turned quickly and raised his revolver to fire.

"Here!" Hunt cried instinctively.

The bandit turned to the voice and was distracted just the moment for the Secret Service agent to pounce on him. Noone struggled with the bandit, trying to take the gun from him. Both men fought desperately in the middle of the forest. Hunt ran toward them. At that moment, Noone put his arm against his opponent's neck and dropped with all his weight. Hunt could clearly hear the man's neck snap with a single crack! The agent rolled away from the outlaw's corpse. Then he jumped up and took his gun from him.

"There are two left," he said to Hunt when he reached beside him.

The captain merely nodded. His partner had released all his thirst for revenge.

"Over there! They're over there!"

From among the trees came the cries of the two bandits who were still standing. Hunt's uproar and shout had alerted them to the position of their prey. Hunt looked at Noone and motioned for them to flee. They both ran, separated by about ten meters. Hunt's eyes had grown accustomed to the gloom. Now he could make out the rocks embedded in the ground, the fallen logs, and the bushes that stood in his way. On one side of the forest the ground rose steeply up the mountain, and on the other it ended at the edge of the river.

Both fugitives ran in that direction. If they climbed the mountain again, they would be trapped. Hunt traced a diagonal route that, while taking him out of the woods, at the same time took him away from the spot where he had seen Moon waiting on her mount. The two bandits had already detected them and were running after them shooting through the trees. Hunt crouched and ran zigzagging, trying to forget about the bullets whizzing overhead. Later he saw that the forest ended by the edge of the river. Out of the corner of his eye he saw that Noone was taking a route parallel to his own.

They went out into the open field. The river's coastal strip was about fifteen meters wide. Under the first rays of sunlight, Hunt saw Moon on her horse about fifty meters away upstream. She was looking out over the forest, no doubt waiting for her men. For a moment, the captain fantasized that the woman wouldn't notice them, but just then Noone shouted:

"Don't stop, Peter! They are behind us!"

Moon turned to them and immediately spurred on her horse. The animal responded at once and galloped towards the fugitives.

"It's Moon!" Hunt warned his partner. "Run, damn it!"

The noise of the horse's hooves increased in intensity. Out of the corner of his eye, Hunt saw that the bandits were also chasing them along the edge of the forest, firing while still running. Hunt risked looking over his shoulder and saw that the woman was already almost on top of them. A shot rang out thunderously, very close to him. Behind him he heard a groan followed by a loud bang. He peered back and saw Noone lying flat on the ground. He immediately feared the worst, but then the agent raised his head and muttered in pain.

"Save yourself, Peter, damn it!"

Moon was galloping further back, a revolver pointed at him. Hunt understood that the woman had shot Noone in the back. For a split second, anger consumed Hunt. He calculated whether he would have even the slightest chance of knocking her off the horse when she passed him, but he realized that she would never give him that chance. Before he could get closer, Moon would shoot him head-on and hit him cleanly. The captain saw that the horse took over his entire field of vision and understood that he was lost. The muzzle of the revolver was almost in front of his eyes.

Without thinking, he threw himself with all his strength towards the river. The current swallowed him up right away. The water was icy and running hard down the mountain. His whole body went numb, and he immediately lost his sense of direction. He tried to surface in a desperate gesture that would allow him to breathe, but the torrent dragged him inexorably. His body stirred and spun uncontrollably underwater. The cold was so intense that he almost lost consciousness. He swallowed water and felt dizzy, but he still had a glimmer of consciousness. He told himself that he was speeding away from this woman and her savage henchmen. He smiled in the midst of the whirlwind, but the happiness was short-lived. An instant later he hit his head with a submerged rock, and everything turned dark.

He woke up suddenly. He was lying on a kind of mattress or stretcher. It took him a moment to remember his escape by the river. Then the events of the night invaded his mind like a surge of cold, thunderous water from the stream. He tried to get up, startled, but his body did not respond. He barely managed to raise his head a little. He felt sore and his limbs were numb. He was dry, dressed only in a loincloth. He was inside a room. The air was quite warm. Someone had rescued him from the waters and taken him to that place.

It wouldn't have been Moon and his men, would it? He had been on the verge of breaking his head and drowning during his flight to finally fall back into the hands of the bandits. And what would have become of Noone? He was wounded by a bullet, but at least he lived. Unless the woman had finished him off or left him lying in the valley to bleed. He shook his head to drive away those pessimistic thoughts, but immediately a severe headache invaded him.

"Try to stay still," said a voice. "You are still weak."

He sounded like an old man, with a slight accent that Hunt couldn't identify. He searched for him, turning his head, but the man insisted that he remain still. Then the man stood by the mattress and bent over it so that Hunt could see him. His face was wrinkled and sunburned, but his eyes shone with the intensity of a much younger man. The old man's features, though hard and enigmatic, gave off a vital energy and a calm that immediately reassured Hunt.

"Where am I?"

"In the great house of our village. You'll be safe here, Captain. But you should leave as soon as you are recovered."

This time, Hunt forced himself to sit up on the bed, at least until his body was resting on his elbow.

"Do you know who I am?"

"If I didn't know, I wouldn't have brought you to our house."

Questions ran over the captain's mind.

"Are we still in the mountains? How long have I been here? Who are you?"

The old man interrupted him with a simple wave of his hand.

"Your friend is dying. You must go for him."

"Hyam? Haym Noone? How do you know…"

"We know everything that happens in the mountains, captain. That is why we have survived many years safe from invaders."

Hunt tried to control his despair.

"My friend received a gunshot wound before I fell into the river. He needs to go to a hospital and..."

"We'll cure him, captain. But you must be the one to bring him to us."

"I do not know..."

"I sent my scouts to the camp of those bandits. They must be about to return. Now rest and regain your energy. You're going to need it."

The old man disappeared into the shadows. Hunt tried to stand up to get his clothes and get dressed. He guessed that it had been a few hours since he had managed to flee from the bandits. At that point, Noone must have been dying. He thanked the old man and his people for rescuing him, but he couldn't waste any more time. He could barely sit up on the mattress, but then his vision blurred, and his body relaxed abruptly. Then he noticed the smoke from the fire in the corner of the room, forming a cloud that floated in the hot air of the room. His last thought, before falling asleep, was that the smoke smelled of herbs.

Daylight filtered through the narrow window opening and woke him up. Hunt got up much more recovered. As he dressed in the clothes that had been left at the foot of the mattress, he felt hungry. From somewhere came the aroma of freshly prepared food. Guided by his sense of smell, he passed through the narrow portals opened in the thick walls of the great house and managed to reach the outside. The structure where it was located was made up of several levels of interconnected rooms built of stone. The roofs were made of beams covered with mud. Behind the great house rose the high wall of a canyon, which cast its long shadow over the whole complex.

Hunt realized that the great house was one of those dwellings built by the Anasazi. Only it was not in ruins but was still inhabited. In the central square of the village a small group of people had gathered to eat together. Hunt recognized the old man from the night before and approached him. Community members greeted him with shy smiles but handed him several bowls of food. There were some corn tortillas, stewed meat, and black beans.

"Eat as much as you can, captain," said the old man. "An arduous task awaits you."

Hunt raised an eyebrow.

"My scouts returned while you were sleeping. The bandits will soon set up camp. You must reach them before they leave."

"I could use some help."

Hunt saw in the group some sturdy-looking young men armed with bows and arrows, spears, and battle-axes.

"Our warriors cannot fight other people's wars, my friend."

"But they're well armed."

The old man shrugged.

"If we are attacked, we must defend ourselves."

Hunt ate voraciously. The group of natives disbanded shortly after. Men and women went to fulfill their daily tasks. The old man took the captain to the upper level of the village. They ascended rock stairs dug into the sides of the walls and then followed up wooden ladders that led them to the roof of the great house. From there it commanded a magnificent view of the entire bottom of the canyon.

"This village was built nine hundred years ago," explained the old man. "Now it is the last stronghold of our people."

"Anasazi" said Hunt.

The old man smiled.

"The Navajos called us that. *Enemies*. Then the Spaniards, when they saw our homes, called us *pueblos*. We are, simply, the ancient ones. This is our land, even though white men and foreigners now live in it."

The old man stared at the captain.

"Since the conquistadors arrived, they have stolen our treasures and our land. Our culture is disappearing." He shrugged. "It is the destiny of all ancient peoples. Someday we must die and give way to younger civilizations."

The old man spoke calmly, without resentment or desire for revenge. Hunt was impressed by his fortitude.

"We have fought many battles over the centuries, captain. Now you must fight yours."

"I am only one man against many."

"But you're not just any man," the old man insisted. "You are the mystery hunter."

Hunt shuddered at the nickname. They had already called him that before. But the old man had no way of knowing. His face must have shown surprise, as the old man smiled.

"As I told you, we know a great deal, Captain Hunt. Another thing I know is that you will emerge victorious from your confrontation with those bandits."

"You seem very confident. Did you consult some kind of oracle?"

This time, the old man laughed.

"It is not necessary, my friend. I'm going to give you a lot of weapons."

The two scouts went forward, riding with such dexterity that neither they nor the horses made any noise as they advanced through the trees. Hunt tried to make his mount just as stealthy, but the stout horse was reluctant to obey this stranger. Although the mount followed the other two animals closely, it did so on instinct and not because Hunt ordered it to. After an hour's walk, Hunt loosened the reins and let the horse act according to its own judgment.

Hunt smiled at the long leather sheaths that hung on either side of the mount. In each he carried a Winchester repeating rifle loaded with .44-40 caliber cartridges. In a couple of holsters, tied to his thighs in the style of cowboys, he carried two Colt Single Action Army revolvers, popularly known as *peacemakers*. The old man had led Hunt to a large *kiva* on the side of the village. In one corner there was a chest that he kept hidden under some blankets. The old man opened it with a single blow. Inside were more than a dozen firearms, long and short, all shiny and in perfect condition.

"These were the weapons of the invaders. We captured them in different battles," he explained. "We do not use them, out of principle. But we knew that one day they would be useful."

Hunt could not carry more than four of them. He fastened the rifle holsters to the horse he was given and fastened the pistols under his belt with thick straps.

"Don't you have a hat too?"

He was joking, but the old man gave some orders to a boy, and he returned with a high, crowned, wide-brimmed hat. Hunt laughed. He put on his hat and settled into the saddle. Two young scouts were waiting for him on their mounts.

"May the gods be with you, captain."

Hunt touched the brim of his hat and set off.

The three horsemen advanced for several

hours, always hidden among the trees, going up and down the slopes of several mountains. They barely stopped along the way. Hunt was in awe of these young warriors. It seemed that they did not need to rest, eat, or relieve themselves. They rode on the horses with their bodies erect, attentive to every sound. His keen senses picked up from afar the sound of water hitting rocks on a riverbed, the squawking of eagles in the sky, or the whistling of the wind swaying the treetops. They hardly spoke to each other and only communicated with precise and simple gestures.

As the sun began to set beyond the mountains, one of the scouts slowed down and stood beside the captain's horse.

"It's not long now," was all he said.

The horses used the long shadows cast by the trees to stay under cover. The young natives tensed their faces and then nodded. Even Hunt caught what had alerted the scouts. The wind brought the murmur of voices and the smell of burning wood. The bandits' camp was nearby. A rush of adrenaline ran through Hunt's body. His mount also felt the tension. The captain noticed that the animal was also standing up and tightening its hard muscles. The silence in the forest was absolute.

The guide stood beside him again. Hunt realized that he didn't even know his name.

"When the moon goes down," whispered the explorer, "it will be your time."

Hunt looked up. Above the treetops he saw that the sky was completely clear. The stars shone like diamonds thrown at random on a black velvet cloth. The moon shone like a small sun. Hunt looked for some clouds, but none could be seen.

"But..."

The young man silenced him with a hard look. Hunt knew that the moon would be covered, just as the young native claimed. Then, a strong wind rose and shook the treetops. Night had already fallen, but somehow the darkness grew more intense. Hunt looked up at the sky again and found that a black cloak was covering the stars and speeding toward the full moon. Wolves howled pitifully in the distance. Hunt felt his blood run cold.

"It is the hunter's hour," murmured the scout.

Hunt spurred the horse on and galloped through the trees, toward the edge of the woods. He felt in a state of grace. His mind was clear, and his body relaxed. His eyes caught every detail of the forest, despite the darkness, and every sound, however faint, reached his ears. He heard the noise of the bandits talking, unconcerned. He smelled the smoke of the bonfire and the meat that was roasted on the coals. He could also hear his heartbeat, beating faster and faster, at the same pace as the horse that was gathering speed in its furious race.

As he approached the camp at full speed, the captain's mind came to the verses of Shakespeare's *Julius Caesar*:

> *And Caesar's spirit, ranging for revenge,*
> *With Ate by his side come hot from hell,*
> *Shall in these confines with a monarch's voice*
> *Cry "Havoc!" and let slip the dogs of war.*

12. THE CAMP

The noise of the horse's hooves flooded the night air. The bandits who were resting by the campfire got up in surprise and scanned the surroundings, but they could not determine where the thunderous sound that was over them came from. That deafening tapping seemed to be everywhere. Maybe it wasn't a single horse, but a dozen of them. Many of the men had their weapons at hand but seemed unable to pick them up. They had all been paralyzed by the sudden roar that shook the earth. The bandits looked at each other with their faces pressed with terror. The sudden attack must have come from hell itself.

The pinto horse jumped swiftly like lightning and burst into the middle of the camp. Hunt had already drawn one of his rifles. He pulled the lever, inserted a cartridge into the chamber of the barrel, and immediately shot the first man who crossed his sights. The bandit was thrown backwards in the midst of a stream of blood emanating from his head. Hunt flipped the lever of the rifle and turned on the saddle to look for another target. At the same time, he spurred on the mount. The horse responded at once, and galloped round the campfire, charging at the terrified bandits who still stood near the fire, watching the apparition in perplexity.

Hunt shot a second man. Paying no further attention to him once he had knocked him down, he inserted another cartridge into the chamber and searched for his next target. At that moment, the bandits' survival instinct made them run for cover. The bravest prepared to look for their own weapons to defend themselves. Hunt caught the reflection of some shiny revolvers rising in the middle of the night. He crouched in his saddle, still galloping at full speed, and fired in quick succession at the armed men. He saw some fall, but others managed to evade the fire.

The captain realized that he was already losing the advantage that his surprise appearance had given him. Soon all the occupants of the camp would end up reacting and the situation would turn against him. He was in the center of the camp, surrounded by heavily armed enemies. With his left hand he took the reins and held the rifle only with his right. With sudden tugs of the straps, he ordered the horse to go between the tents to avoid being exposed in the open field. Several bandits opened fire. The night air was filled with the noise of multiple gunshots.

Hunt exhausted the ammunition of the first rifle. He simply threw it on the ground and took the second one. He had no chance of reloading the weapon. He clenched the Winchester's butt under his arm and pulled the lever with one hand. He fired without using the sights, only pointing forward. His aim lost effectiveness, but the .44 caliber rounds were still fearsome. In addition, the horse ran rampant through the camp, pushing the men and knocking down the tents at its unbridled pace. Hunt hardly needed to guide it. The animal was an innate warrior.

The men's screams of terror, mixed with some instructions that no one followed, were drowned out by the thunderous noise of the firing of revolvers and rifles. Hunt kept moving, wreaking havoc in the camp. The more trained enemies had barricaded themselves behind large boxes with supplies and from there tried to knock down the swift horseman. But the horse made their task impossible. It galloped to its maximum capacity and jumped from one place to another, never stopping. The shots disppeared in the air or went where the horse was no longer there. Hunt was exultant on the saddle, his body full of adrenaline rushing through his veins like blood on fire.

Then he saw Moon Goldeneagle. In his haste to attack the camp and in the midst of this devastation, he had completely forgotten the woman. She was now looking at him from the other end of the redoubt. She was standing outside her tent, legs apart planted firmly on the ground and arms akimbo. From a distance, the captain could not determine the expression on the woman's face, but her eyes shone like lava about to erupt. Hunt knew he had to worry about her, but the constant gunfire from the bandits prevented him from approaching the tent.

He threw the second rifle to the ground and drew one of the peacemakers. Its range was less than that of a rifle, but the handgun was much more maneuverable with one hand. Hunt led the horse with his left hand and fired comfortably with his right. His enemies fell one by one. The horse understood that the greatest threat was behind the crates of supplies. It let out a furious neigh and rushed toward the last stronghold of the bandits. Hunt gripped the saddle tightly. He leaned his body forward and prepared for the onslaught.

The charge of the pinto ended with a powerful jump over the boxes. The men threw themselves to the ground when they saw the animal coming at them. The horse fell on the other side and immediately turned to face the bandits. Hunt was ready. He raised his revolver and unleashed a deadly burst on his enemies. The men's bodies were twisted by the impact of the rounds. When the cylinder was empty, Hunt dropped the revolver, drew his last gun with his left hand, and fired with it.

He was not as skilled as when using his right hand, but at close range he managed to catch up with the last men still standing. For a moment the abrupt silence became as heavy as the roar of the gunfire that had filled the air a few moments before. The captain's ears buzzed like a thousand bees fleeing from a honeycomb. He was covered in dust and sweat. In the stillness, he noticed that some enemy bullets had grazed him in various parts of his body. His wounds were burning, and his clothes were charred by gunpowder.

The gallop of another horse made him turn suddenly in his saddle. Moon was racing on her horse, a revolver stretched out in front of her. Now he could clearly see the expression of hatred and fury that twitched the woman's face. Hunt raised his own revolver and charged his mount into the last enemy. Maybe there was no one else left, but she was the only one who mattered. If he did not succeed in defeating her, the attack on the camp and the defeat of the bandits would have been of no use.

They charged against each other, like two ancient medieval knights facing each other in a joust. Hunt's horse snorted through his nose and lowered his head to run in a hurry, showing no sign of fear. The captain leaned forward and held the pistol pointed at his opponent. Moon immediately fired a quick burst from her revolver. Hunt heard the whistle of bullets whizzing past his head. As he approached the woman, he dropped his body to the side and hung by the horse's back. Only then did he return fire, protected by his own mount. The opponents crossed paths in a tiny instant, both riding at full speed. None of them had hurt the other one.

Hunt turned his horse with a sharp tug of the reins and immediately dove in the opposite direction to make another pass against Moon. The woman was also coming back. The pounding of the hooves on the ground made the earth rumble and drowned out the other noises of the ruined camp. At that time there was only Hunt and his fearsome rival. Both emptied the cylinders of their weapons before meeting face to face for a split second, as the horses sped past each other.

Moon let out a furious shriek and looked at him with twitching features. He didn't even manage to react. His horse had already carried him away, riding wildly. The captain had exhausted all his ammunition, but he wasn't going to give up. The horse turned once more and again the animal responded with a precise and quick gesture. But this time Moon hadn't returned to face him. Hunt observed that the other horse got into the trees and disappeared in the distance. The woman had chosen to flee. It was obvious that she was carrying the medallion with her. For a moment, Hunt wondered where

Hyam Noone was, but decided that the artifact was the most important thing at the moment.

His partner would understand. As he spurred the horse to go after the woman, he glanced around the camp and promised himself that he would return at once for his wounded friend. Then he also entered the trees and looked for the tracks that the fugitive left in her path. Soon he heard the furious gallop of the other horse and the screams with which the woman spurred the horse.

"You won't be able to run away, Moon!" Hunt shouted.

The woman half-turned on her mount to determine the position of her pursuer, but she did not slow down her escape. On the contrary, she whipped the horse's back with the reins and loudly shouted an order for the animal to use all its strength. Hunt hurried his own horse and let himself be guided through the dark forest. The lower branches of the trees beat against his chest, and the wind buzzed in his ears.

Further on the forest ended. Hunt crossed the edge of the trees and went out into open ground. He saw Moon riding ahead toward the edge of the cliff. She was trapped! He laughed like a madman and went in pursuit. The woman's horse did not slow down or veer off course. A wrinkle of surprise formed on the captain's forehead. What did that woman want? An instant later, the horse disappeared over the edge of the mountain. Not even a neigh was heard. Hunt reached the edge and his own mount stopped in its tracks. Hunt held on tightly to the horse so as not to be thrown into the void.

He jumped out and looked over the precipice. The drop to the edge of the canyon was more than ten meters. Despite the darkness, it was evident that there was nothing at the bottom. Hunt looked up the cliff wall but saw no tracks. A shiver ran through his entire body. Somehow, the woman and her horse had vanished into thin air. Hunt stood there for a few minutes, unable to believe what had happened. Then he remembered his friend and immediately returned in search of him.

He stopped in the middle of the camp and dismounted. The tents were destroyed, and their contents scattered around them. Some had even burned when the logs on the campfire were thrown into the fray. There were bodies lying everywhere, mostly motionless. Only a few of them seemed to be still alive. They barely moved a hand or emitted muffled moans. The ruins of the redoubt presented a horrifying panorama. Hunt shuddered to think that most of the devastation had been caused by him, but then he told himself that these men had deserved it.

"Hyam? Hyam Noone!"

He didn't see his partner anywhere. Hunt feared the worst. Perhaps Noone had succumbed to his wounds and the bandits had simply thrown his body into a ditch or riverbed. He realized that he had arrived too late. A sudden pain crushed his heart. The prophecy of the Indian elder had failed.

"Peter? It's you?"

The voice sounded weak and pitiful. The captain shouted calling the agent.

"Peter... here."

Moon's tent, of course. Hunt ran to the tent the woman had occupied. It was the only one that was still intact. Inside, Hyan Noone lay on some blankets. He was dressed in rags and bathed in sweat. Even without touching him, Hunt realized that the Secret Service agent was burning with fever.

"You're back," Noone stammered. "You came back for me."

"No man is left behind," said Hunt.

It was the creed of every soldier. Hunt carried Noone on his shoulders and took him to the horse. He hung him across the animal's back and then he jumped into the saddle. Immediately, the brave pinto horse galloped, as if it felt the need to carry the wounded man back to the natives' village soon. Hunt rode through gritted teeth, mentally hurrying his mount. Noone had fainted, but his body was still shaking.

In the middle of the forest the two native scouts suddenly appeared. They said nothing, but stood on either side of Hunt, and his horse seemed to go even faster. The three horsemen galloped relentlessly, through woods, fording streams, and through narrow valleys. Night gave way to day. The cold turned into an increasingly intense heat, but the three men didn't even notice the change in temperature. The horses galloped like overcome with an infernal impulse. After several hours of incessant and exhausting running, the horses entered the hidden canyon. Finally, Hunt caught sight of the great house. He breathed a sigh of relief.

"The gods are claiming him," said the old man when he examined Noone. "We must claim him back."

Between several natives, they placed the agent on a newly erected altar in the center of the town square. The old man stripped him completely naked and washed him with a water impregnated with wild flowers. Some women helped treat the gunshot wound in the agent's back and cover it with a smelly poultice. Young men lit a fire at the feet of the wounded man from which a thick and aromatic smoke quickly emanated, covering the body, and forming a dense cloud around him. Then everyone left.

Hunt watched the whole ritual at the foot of the altar. He should take Noone to a hospital, he thought, but this will have to do for now. At least his partner was still alive. The old man called to him from on high.

"When the gods come for him, you must

fight them, captain."

Hunt gaped at the old man. Fight against gods? What was the man talking about? Hunt sat on his legs on one side of the body, just as the old man had done on the other. His mind was a whirlwind of thoughts, but he realized that he could not trouble the old man with his questions. The old man had bowed his head and was intoning a kind of prayer in his ancestral language. Hunt also bowed his head and maintained a respectful silence. He wished he had been a believer so that he could at least pray to some god.

The altar was enveloped in the thick smoke of the bonfire. The smell of herbs and hot air were becoming unbearable. Hunt felt dizzy, but he forced himself to resist. Noone was pale and sweaty. The old man kept muttering his litany with an increasingly intense rhythm and voice. Hunt felt a severe headache creep over him.

"They're coming, captain! Prepare yourself!" cried the old man, interrupting his prayer.

Hunt could see nothing through the smoke. But then he felt... something. He turned and tried to see through the dense fog. He was sure that something had touched him. He slapped blindly in front of him, but there was nothing there.

"Hold him, captain! They're taking him!"

Noone's lying body was in strong spasms. Suddenly Hunt saw a shadow envelop his friend. It was a kind of translucent shape that seemed to dance on his body. Hunt lunged at Noone and held him under his own weight. The agent was on fire. Hunt felt his own skin burn on contact with his partner. But even so, he did not let him go.

"Stay away from him, you damned ones!" He cried out in despair.

He didn't know why or who he was yelling at, but he felt the need to do it. Noone was stirring so hard that he threatened to throw him away at any moment. Hunt held his position as hard as he could, shouting imprecations at those ethereal gods who were struggling to take his partner's soul.

Now the old man was intoning his litany at the top of his lungs. Hunt glanced at him askance and saw that the translucent shapes circled around the old man as if they wanted to knock him down. But the wise man stood firm and continued with his prayer, raising his hands to push away those immortal creatures. For his part, Hunt lost track of time. Noone's skin burned to the touch, and his body stirred as if it were about to explode. But Hunt closed his eyes and told himself that if they wanted his friend, they would have to finish him off first.

These creatures fluttered over the altar like crows from hell. Hunt felt them brush against him and pierce his skin, filling him with bile and fateful thoughts. He screamed to scare them away and fought against them, without worrying about his sore skin or his dry throat. The old man's chants could scarcely be heard under the shrieks of the creatures. The smoke was getting darker and darker, and Hunt began coughing. His strength was weakening. He thought that he would not be able to withstand the onslaught of the creatures for much longer.

"Don't let him go, captain!" cried the old man. His voice was far away. "Don't let him go!"

Hunt made his last effort when he felt Noone's body begin to rise, carrying him as well. He kept his feet with all his strength on the ground and clung to his partner's body as a castaway would to the only board that floated next to him. He gave a scream of fury and dread as he felt the ethereal beings swoop down on him. His own body felt on fire and his head ached as if he had been kicked. But at no time did he let go his friend's body.

Suddenly, it was all over. Noone lay limp on the altar and the smoke cleared. In the sunlight that lit up the town square, there was no sign of the translucent creatures that had tried to take Noone. Hunt dropped to the ground, exhausted. He looked at his hands and saw that his skin was full of burns. His throat stung and his eyes were glazed over. He got up heavily and examined the Secret Service agent. Noone slept breathing rhythmically. He was no longer shaking, and his skin had a normal temperature.

"We've done it," Hunt said, his voice raspy.

No one answered him. He jumped up and circled Noone's body. The old man had fallen on the other side. He was lying on the ground and not moving. Hunt helped him up. The man's face, which already looked very old as a result of his age, was now stained, and furrowed with scars. The eyes had turned white and milky. Hunt waved a hand in front of the old man, but he did not perceive the gesture. Hunt shuddered. The old man had gone blind.

"A victory against the gods comes at a high cost," murmured the old man.

"We must go to a hospital." Hunt spoke agitatedly. "I'll take you and Noone."

"The white man's medicine can't do anything with me. But it can help your friend, captain."

The young warriors went up to the altar and took the old man on their shoulders. They turned immediately and headed for the main *kiva* of the village. One of the young men, the same one who had served as Hunt's guide the night before, approached Hunt. With one finger, he pointed at a pair of horses waiting on the side of the square.

"Those will take you to the nearest town, captain." At Hunt's expression, the young native added, "Don't worry, they know the way by heart."

The natives of the village gathered around the decrepit old man and carried him in a procession to the ceremonial hall. Hunt pushed his way through the crowd and managed to take the weakened old man's hand. He thanked him and wished him well. The poor man did not react. No one in the village paid attention to the captain. He saw them walk away and finally returned to the fainting Noone and took him in his arms.

In the saddlebags of the horses were clothes and supplies. Hunt left his friend by the saddles and waited for him to recover. When Noone was more awake, Hunt motioned for him to get dressed and then they both rode on the animals. The Secret Service agent was recovering quickly. He opened his eyes wide and looked around the great house. At the same time, the mounts were set in motion.

"My God, Peter!" Noone exclaimed. His voice reflected that he was still perplexed and disoriented. "Where are we? What the hell happened?"

"We have several hours ahead of us, my friend. I'll tell you all along the way."

Noone took one last look at the village and then shook his head. It was evident that he could not believe that he had awakened in this place. He looked at Hunt and he smiled.

"It's good to have you back, Hyam."
"And the bandits?"
"Forget about them. They will no longer be a problem."
"Moon?"

Hunt pondered for a moment. The woman would be indeed a problem. A big problem. As soon as they were back in the woods, leaving the horses to find their way on their own, Hunt told Noone what had happened since they had parted at the edge of the river. The American agent did not stop cursing until they had the railway tracks in sight.

13. WALDORF-ASTORIA

A comfortable, spacious cab painted yellow took Hunt to a Romanesque-style building in Manhattan's West Village. After his return to the imposing city, the captain no longer found it as attractive as before his departure. Now it seemed to him like a gigantic gray labyrinth, whose buildings leaned dangerously over those who sought a way out, threatening to fall at any moment on the hapless explorers. Undoubtedly, the wide and natural landscape of New Mexico caused that effect of claustrophobia within the city, so crowded and with its streets full of vehicles.

The return trip had felt like an eternity. Both men were tired and worn out after all the dangers they had faced in the mountains. Although he had only been in New Mexico for a few days, it seemed to Hunt that several months had elapsed since he had left New York aboard the 20th Century Limited. Traveling through a large part of that vast country, back and forth, was exhausting. Hunt didn't even have the book and magazine he had bought to read with him. Noone had been quiet for much of the trip, and Hunt would have liked to have some reading to distract himself.

Once they were in town, the Secret Service agent told Hunt he would call him and then disappeared into the crowd that filled the railroad station. Hunt resented the abrupt farewell, but he realized that Noone was still in shock. No doubt the agent would have a lot of personal matters to sort out. It was a week before Hunt got his call. At least Sir John Connelly had already recovered from his wounds and together with the captain they continued their investigations into the Anasazi treasure and the mystical powers of the medallion. The head of Department X asked his investigator to tell him several times the full story of his adventures in New Mexico. After repeating the story constantly for a couple of days, Hunt felt fed up.

With not much to do, one afternoon he simply left the Biltmore and started walking. It was a pleasant spring day. After walking a couple of streets he reached the famous Fifth Avenue and headed north there, walking unhurriedly. He watched the passers-by, the windows of the luxurious shops, and the dozens of different models of cars driving on the road. After about twenty minutes, he reached the southeast corner of Central Park. Hundreds of families enjoyed the outdoors on the extensive grass zones. Numerous visitors walked the paths that went through the thick vegetation of the wooded areas.

He took one of the trails and soon reached the edge of the Pond, one of the park's artificial lakes. It was built below sea level, so the noise of the city was quite attenuated there. Hunt thought that it was a very nice place, great for relaxing. The following days he made the same walk and went up the adjoining promontory, where he could see a large number of birds. On the other side of the promontory, a thick schist bridge spanned the Pond. Hunt paused there for a few moments to decide what he would do for the next few days.

He had not heard from Daniele Monreale. The mafia boss had remained in the shadows for those days. His name did not appear in the newspapers associated with any criminal act either. Hunt assumed that Monreale was engrossed in his plans to use the medallion that Moon Goldeneagle had brought him. If he was already in a position to use the 'beacon', as he called it, he could soon unleash his new powers against his enemies, or against the entire city, if that was what he wanted. Hunt had read about the wars between mafia gangs and knew that one of the most powerful factions was that of the King of Little Italy.

If Noone didn't get in touch soon, Hunt would have to talk to Sir John to make a decision. Either they would take some action against Monreale on their own account to prevent him from using the medallion, or they would be better off returning to London. They were still considered guests of the American Geographical Society, but after Robert Lester's death interest in the find in New Mexico had waned considerably. The outlook was not promising. Hunt told himself that perhaps his days in New York were already coming to an end.

Until Hyam Noone called Hunt at the hotel and left him a message. He was waiting for him the next morning at an address in the West Village. Noone had set up a base of operations on the ground floor of the building. Upon getting out of the taxi, Hunt found several offices occupied by young men, dressed in shirt sleeves, sitting in front of dozens of files, maps, and photographs. They all looked very busy. On the walls hung cork panels with sheets of paper, graphics and drawings pinned down.

"What is all this?" Hunt asked Noone when the agent came out to meet him.

Noonet was clearly recovered from his injuries. He looked good and walked with a confident step. He wore an impeccable bespoke suit in his usual black color. The shirt was starched, and the knit silk tie, also black, shone in the light of the lamps.

"This is New York's new anti-mafia task force," Noone replied, with a satisfied smile. "Its only missiion: to put an end to Daniele Monreale's criminal empire."

"Wow, it looks like your report on the situation in New Mexico was read at length in Washington," Hunt remarked, admiring, seeing that the Secret Service had set up the entire operation in less than a week.

"The truth is that I had to spend hours on the phone and collect a lot of favors," Noone said. "But here we are. Come, my friend."

The agent led the captain to his own office. It had only a desk and a couple of chairs, but from the window there was a beautiful view of the street that led to the Hudson River, located only a block to the west.

"Are you recovered yet, my friend?"

"Absolutely, Peter. Totally! Someday I'll have to thank that old Indian. I don't know what he did, but he worked wonders."

Hunt had told Noone of the battle he and the old man had fought against the gods of death, disputing the body of the badly wounded agent. However, Noone had not been entirely convinced that there was a supernatural element to his recovery. During the return train ride, the agent had not mentioned the subject again. Surely, it was a lot of information to process in such a short time. Hunt left him alone and let his friend process what happened in due course.

Noone lit a Lucky and motioned for Hunt to sit on the other side of the desk.

"Together with my boys we have managed to gather a lot of information about Monreale," he reported. "That bastard controls an empire dedicated to all kinds of crimes. His base of operations is here in the city, but he has connections to the Chicago Outfit and to the old guard, back in Sicily."

"You're working fast, huh?"

"I can't lose time, Peter. I got experienced investigators transferred from my own service, the Bureau of Investigation, the Department of Justice, the Bureau of Prohibition, and several other federal agencies. Each one contributed its own files on organized crime."

"Do they know about the medallion?" Hunt asked.

The face of the American darkened.

"I can't face that man alone, Peter. We both know the power he has. But neither can I reveal the true nature of his wickedness. I guess my men... they wouldn't believe it." Noone shrugged. "To them, Monreale is a dangerous currency counterfeiter who plans to affect the country's economy."

"Cause enough for the Secret Service to launch an investigation against him, right?"

"That's right. But that same trick also works

against me."

Hunt raised an eyebrow.

"I can't go head-on against him," Noone explained. "To the outside world, this is a formal federal government investigation against Monreale. That means I have to build a case, file charges with a district attorney, get warrants from a judge—a damn sea of bureaucracy!"

Suddenly, Hunt laughed.

"I was already wondering why you had invited me to come." Noone just smiled with a knowing smile. "You need someone who can act outside the rules, right?"

"I assumed you were still interested in getting your hands on that bastard. Besides, you are aware of the true nature of the case."

Hunt leaned toward Noone across the desk.

"I will not leave the United States until I see Monreale and his mafia clan destroyed."

Noone nodded solemnly. Then he shook hands with his partner.

"Welcome to the team, Captain Hunt."

"A pleasure, Agent Noone. So, what should I do?"

"Oh, something very simple. You just have to go to a party."

It would have been easy to go unnoticed at a banquet with more than seven hundred guests, but Peter Hunt managed to get noticed. A long time later, as he recalled the events of his first visit to New York City, he concluded that he had been lucky to get out of that ballroom alive. But when he arrived at the entrance of the Waldorf-Astoria Hotel, dressed in his bespoke dinner jacket, he could not know how the evening would unfold. He simply stood in the long line of attendees who were still making their entrance and mentally prepared himself for any eventuality.

The ballroom was as lavish as Noone had described. Dozens of tables comfortably occupied an area of twenty by thirty meters that also housed a musical orchestra, hundreds of guests, and a small army of waiters. Still, there was enough space to socialize, move from group to group, and even dance in front of the stage occupied by the musicians. The hall was three stories high and decorated in an ornate Louis XIV style, including a huge fresco on its ceiling. The noise of music and the voices of the attendees flooded the atmosphere. Bottles of champagne were uncorked at every moment, filling hundreds of glasses, as if Prohibition did not exist in that corner of America.

As Noone had informed him, the most important figures of the Italian-American community gathered at the party, both those who were on one side of the law and those who were on the other. Although Hunt was not familiar with their faces or names, he had no trouble at least distinguishing the different groups that made up the heterogeneous crowd.

The politicians were the most graceful, they wore a chiseled smile on their faces, and they shook hands with anyone who crossed their path. The artists dressed like bohemians and surrounded themselves with a large entourage of sycophants. And the mobsters wore flashy clothes, gold accessories and strutted as if they owned the place.

Hunt grabbed a glass of champagne and paced for several minutes through the crowd, trying to find the host of the party. He saw many murderous-faced men, surrounded by vivacious women and shadowy bodyguards, but there was no sign of Daniele Monreale. After pacing the room several times, Hunt decided that he would have better luck observing the room from above. On the two upper levels of the hall there were boxes that overlooked the hall, allowing the enclosure to also serve as a theatre.

As the orchestra played tunes from the Gershwin brothers' musicals, Hunt slipped through a half-open door on the side of the room. From there he ascended the staircase that led to the two levels of the inner boxes. When he reached the first level, he saw that there was someone in one of the boxes. He came a few steps closer and discovered that it was a woman. She was alone, standing in the shade of one of the columns that flanked the balcony. The light projected from below allowed only her profile to be seen, but it was enough to capture an undeniable beauty. The nose, straight and thin, projected gracefully from a face framed by dark and wavy hair. Hunt took another couple of steps toward her until she sensed his presence and turned to him.

"Excuse me. I didn't want to disturb you."

She peered into the light. She was a really beautiful young woman. She was dressed in a simple but elegant dress. Hunt estimated that she was about twenty-five years old.

"The party is downstairs," the young woman reminded him.

Hunt smiled at her.

"Too many people. And too much noise." He held out a hand. "Captain Peter Hunt."

She shook his hand after a brief hesitation.

"Lucia Monreale."

Hunt did his best to remain impassive.

"Beautiful name. After your mother?"

"No. My father is a fan of opera..."

"*Lucia di Lammermoor*? A little tragic for a little girl, don't you think?"

The girl laughed.

"It was that, or Aida. I guess I came out on top."

"I think so."

"You're English, aren't you, Captain Hunt? How do you know my father?

'Oh, we met when he tried to kill me at Mount Sinai Hospital', Hunt thought. Instead, he said:

"I'm afraid I don't really know him. I'm here just for business."

"Like everyone else," the girl murmured.

She turned to the box. For a moment she looked over the splendid party that was taking place in the ballroom. Hunt stood next to her and took the opportunity to look for the host in the crowd.

"It seems that your father abandoned his guests."

"He must be in another room, with his *soldati*... er, his partners. My father never misses an opportunity to do business."

Hunt noticed an obvious resentment in the young woman's voice. Could he use it to his advantage? Perhaps he had found an unexpected ally in his mission. However, he had to be very careful. Would she be willing to betray her own father? It was not an easy favor to ask. After all, this young woman was the daughter of a ruthless mobster. For the moment, he decided that he should get to know her a little more.

"You don't seem very comfortable with the party either, Miss Monreale."

"Too many people. And too much noise." She smiled broadly. "And call me Lucia."

"Maybe we could go somewhere else... quieter," Hunt suggested.

He noticed that the young woman's eyes narrowed for a moment, in a gesture of annoyance. Damn! He had been very daring. But then the same eyes shone with excitement.

"If it were any other girl, I would gladly accept your invitation, captain. But I am the host's daughter, and the furthest I can get away from the room is this box."

"I understand it perfectly, Lucia. I apologize for bothering you."

Hunt made a gesture to leave, but she turned to him and looked at him expectantly.

"You don't need to leave. But if you're going to stay, you could be helpful."

She said it with a smile on her lips. Hunt nodded, relieved. He was back in the race.

"I am at your service."

"Do you know the foxtrot in England? I hope so because this is my favorite piece."

The orchestra had begun to play a dance music. Hunt grabbed Lucia by the waist and took her hand. She put her free arm on his shoulder. They immediately began to dance, moving slowly in the tight space of the box. Below, dozens of couples danced in the packed hall. Once Hunt got used to the rhythm of the music, he was able to carry the steps more fluidly. The girl easily followed him. It was evident that she knew that dance perfectly. They danced in silence, letting themselves be guided by the orchestra, until the piece concluded.

Lucia was radiant. Her chest rose and fell seductively to the rhythm of her agitated breathing. Hunt kissed her hand.

"I hope I did well," he said.

"I think you could get a place in the *Ziegfeld Follies*, captain."

Hunt had hardly heard of the musical revue, but he figured it must be a compliment. Perhaps it was time to try again another approach to the beautiful daughter of his enemy. Since they couldn't leave the party venue, he could at least take her to the hall to drink a glass of champagne together. However, he did not manage to make his invitation. The young woman's face darkened as she gestured toward the ballroom.

"Here comes my father. And he brings that woman," Lucia muttered.

Hunt followed the young woman's gaze. Daniele Monreale had entered the ballroom through a door next to the orchestra's stage. He was followed by a small group of men who tried to monopolize his attention by elbowing and pushing each other. But the mafioso advanced unperturbed towards his guests, like a true king. Holding his arm, Moon Goldeneagle shone like the true queen of the place. Hunt's heart raced.

"I suppose you are not friends," Hunt remarked.

A gleam of fury appeared in Lucia's eyes.

"Of course not! That woman is a witch."

For a moment, Hunt didn't know whether to take the girl's words metaphorically or literally. From his recent experience with Moon, he told himself that both alternatives could well be applied. Lucia turned and took him by the hand.

"I could use a glass of champagne," she said, as if she had read his mind. "Will you join me?"

"It will be a pleasure."

They descended the stairs and entered the crowd. The orchestra played a melody with a frenetic rhythm, led by trumpets and trombones. Dozens of couples danced enthusiastically on the floor in front of the stage. Hunt kept his head down and mingled with the other guests. Suddenly, Lucia turned around with two glasses full of bubbly liquor in her hands. He handed Hunt a glass and drank his own at once. The captain looked at her with an amused expression.

"Wow, you were thirsty!"

"I think this party has become interesting!" Lucia exclaimed.

"Here's to that," Hunt said.

"Come, Peter, let's find a table."

They did not manage to advance more than a few meters before Lucia Monreale stopped suddenly. Hunt nearly collided with her. He looked over the young woman's shoulder and his enthusiasm immediately evaporated. Moon Goldeneagle blocked their way, watching them with her arms crossed and a sardonic smile on her face.

"What a pleasant surprise, Captain Hunt! I didn't expect to see you again so soon."

"Well, here I am, my dear."

"You couldn't stay away from me, could you?" She added, in a mischievous tone.

Lucia Monreale blushed as she alternated her gaze between the two.

"Do you know each other?"

Moon walked past her and grabbed Hunt's arm. He tried to pull away, but the woman was faster.

"I didn't know you liked little girls," she whispered in his ear. "If you prefer a real woman, come with me."

Hunt politely but firmly pushed her away with one hand. Moon was forced to let go of his arm.

"I'm sorry, but Miss Monreale and I already have plans."

Lucia was still confused, but she took the opportunity and grabbed the captain's arm.

"I'm afraid Lucia won't be able to make plans tonight," said a thunderous voice behind her.

The moment Hunt feared had arrived. He would have preferred this meeting to be on his own terms, but Lucia's appearance had thrown all his plans overboard. He took a breath and turned slowly, as if he had barely noticed the newcomer.

"You are the hostess of the party, my daughter," said Daniele Monreale, almost without concealing his tone of reproach. "You can't abandon your guests."

"They are your guests, *papà. Ed è la tua festa.*"

Monreale took his daughter by the arm. She hid the pain of the squeeze. Hunt felt his blood boil. He barely refrained himself to avoid a scandal.

"Aren't you going to introduce me to your friend, *cara*?"

"Captain Peter Hunt, let me introduce you to my father, *signor* Daniele Monreale."

The mobster flashed a wide, fake Cheshire cat smile as he held out his hand to his enemy. Hunt squeezed it tightly.

"Don't we know each other, captain? I think I have a blurry... memory. As if I had ever seen you before."

Hunt remembered Monreale pointing his gun at his face, amid the gunpowder smoke that filled the hallway of Mount Sinai Hospital. Once again, it was the mobster who had the upper hand.

"I doubt we know each other," Hunt said, raising his voice. "I don't usually frequent... these circles."

"But you have come to my humble celebration anyway." Monreale didn't seem to be offended by the comment. "Come on, my friend. A friend of my daughter's is also a friend of mine."

A man stood next to Monreale. Hunt recognized him from the photographs of the police files that Noone had shown him earlier that afternoon. Franco Gagliano, the deputy head of the mafia clan. As dangerous and ruthless as his boss. Two other sinister-looking men stood behind Hunt. He was surrounded. Monreale started walking. The group moved around him. Immediately, Lucia hung on the captain's arm and walked beside him. Hunt felt her tremble.

They left the ballroom through a corridor that led them to the back of the hotel. They walked past the large, noisy kitchen of the establishment, the huge laundry room and the employees' dressing rooms. No one spoke. Finally, Monreale opened swinging doors and motioned for the group to follow him inside. Hunt discovered that they were in a long, high exercise room. It was provided with parallel bars, pommel horses, horizontal and vertical ladders, rings, and ropes. He had a bad feeling about it.

"Do you train, Captain Hunt?" Monreale asked as he looked at the implements.

"I play sports when I have time," Hunt said, unsure of the meaning of the question.

"Yes, it seemed that way to me." Monreale walked over to Hunt and watched him closely, assessing him. "Interested in some exercise, Captain?"

"Now?!"

Hunt gestured to his dinner jacket. Then he looked at the others. Moon smiled cryptically. Gagliano muttered with his two soldiers. Lucia had turned pale.

"Bah, the party is getting boring," said the mafioso. "Well, my friend?"

Hunt estimated his chances. Obviously that staging was some kind of trap, but he couldn't decipher Monreale's plans. What would Moon have said to Monreale about him? If the mafioso intended to kill him, why bother so much?

"I don't think we're dressed for the occasion." Hunt smiled. "But we could meet to play golf or something else you like."

"I prefer contact sports," Monreale said. His tone of voice had become serious. "For that I need an opponent who is worthy. Are you, captain?"

So it was a challenge. Monreale wanted to prove what Hunt was made of. And obviously I intended to beat him, in whatever I had prepared.

"If all this is to make me confess that I came uninvited," said Hunt, laughing, "I plead guilty."

"Half the *stronzi* out there came uninvited," laughed Monreale. "Well, Captain Hunt? It seems that you are shying away from me."

Hunt shrugged.

"Of course not, Dan. I can call you Dan, right?"

Monreale clenched his jaws but managed to smile.

"That's what my friends call me. *Dan the man*. As I told you, a friend of my daughter's is my friend too."

"Then I accept, Dan."

"Splendid! Franco, go get the box I have in the car."

Gagliano ran out to carry out his boss's order. As he returned, no one moved from his place or said anything. Tension hung in the air like a viscous substance. Out of the corner of his eye, Hunt saw that Lucia looked like she was about to faint. Moon, on the other hand, looked excited. That woman was completely crazy. Monreale took off his dinner jacket and crossed his arms as he waited.

After a few minutes, the deputy clan chief returned with a long, flat box. He put it down on a pommel horse and stepped back. Monreale opened the lid of the box. He motioned for Hunt to come over and look at its contents. Inside were two gleaming short swords that must have measured in total about sixty centimeters long. Each blade was fifty centimeters long and five centimeters wide. The handles were made of carved wood.

"Do you know what they are?" The mafioso asked, while looking fascinated at the weapons.

"They're Roman swords, aren't they?"

Monreale nodded.

"They were called *gladius*. They were carried by the soldiers of the legions and also by gladiators, who took their name from the sword." Monreale stroked the blade of one of the weapons. "They are authentic. They were found in an excavation in Sicily a few years ago. I acquired them and sent them to be restored by an artisan."

Monreale carefully picked up one of the *gladii* and handed it to Hunt by the hilt. The captain recalled seeing a vivid painting by the French artist Gérôme, in which one gladiator crushed another with his foot in the middle of the arena, while the audience roared in euphoria. In the front row of the stands, bloodthirsty vestals raised their fists with thumbs down. He felt a chill run through his entire body.

"You're joking, aren't you?"

"Oh, come, captain! It will only be a small practice. After all, we are not in the Roman Colosseum."

The two clan soldiers stood behind Hunt. He understood that he had no choice but to follow this dangerous game if he wanted to gain some time. He picked up the sword and weighed it in his hand, waving the blade back and forth. The weapon weighed less than a kilo. It was light and very maneuverable. Hunt also took off his jacket and stood in the center of the room, where there was a free space to train. Monreale ran to meet him immediately.

The metals of the blades clashed with a loud *clang!* that echoed throughout the exercise room. Lucia was visibly startled. Moon panted like a cat in heat. Monreale's henchmen smiled in amusement. Hunt raised his sword and stopped another blow from his opponent. Short *gladii* were not suitable for fencing. They were designed to slash and cut the enemy. However, it was supposed to be a small practice. Or so Monreale had said. Hunt watched him for a moment among the crisscrossed blades. The mobster had his eyes wide open and gave a devilish smile.

The blows of the swords followed one another without respite. Monreale lunged forward, pushing his *gladius* to stab. Hunt blocked attacks as best he could, dodging his opponent and deflecting thrusts with his weapon. Hunt had read somewhere that Roman soldiers attacked in this way, piercing their enemies with the broad, sturdy blade. In hand-to-hand combat, it was a difficult technique to counter. Now he understood why. The light, short sword cut through the air with ease, aided by the thrust and weight of the attacker himself.

Monreale's pushes became more insistent. Hunt understood that the man wasn't really practicing but was trying to really hurt him. Or maybe he was thinking of killing him. Hunt kept watching the mafia boss's thugs out of the corner of his eye, wondering if they would intervene in the event that he managed to defeat Monreale. A question that did not seem so simple. It was evident that this man practiced regularly with the *gladius*. He probably saw himself as some kind of reincarnated legionnaire. Or as a heroic gladiator.

Hunt decided to test Monreale's true intentions. While still moving with each attack, he also began to throw his own thrusts. Although he set out to limit the thrust he gave to his attacks. He did not wish to hurt his opponent.

"Well, well! We go on the offensive, huh, captain?"

Both men were sweating profusely and breathing heavily. Hunt was already learning how to handle the sword. He threw several thrusts in a row, using his own body to push the attacks. This time it was Monreale's turn to back down. The mobster laughed and counterattacked. He chased Hunt around the room, still swinging his sword and stabbing. The shrill noise of the metal clashing cut through the air with high notes.

Suddenly, Hunt managed to duck and threw a violent thrust into Monreale's belly. In a split second he understood that it was a mortal blow and deflected his attack a few millimeters. The sharp blade cut through the shirt cleanly and grazed the mobster's skin. Monreale gave a scream of surprise and stopped abruptly.

"I'm sorry, my friend," said Hunt, snorting I let myself be carried away by emotion.

Monreale felt the wound. Seeing that it was superficial, he smiled.

"First blood, huh? I guess we're raising the bet."

Before he had finished speaking, he had

launched himself again at Hunt. The captain saw the look of fury that dominated Monreale's face. This time he would try to kill him. His stabs were accompanied by screams and gasps. His eyes shone like two fiery rubies. Hunt fought back with all his energy, though he felt like he was already beginning to wear thin. The sword no longer felt so light, and the sweat from his hand had made the hilt slippery.

For several minutes the combatants chased each other around the room and clashed their swords, without giving quarter. Hunt took a few shallow cuts but managed to keep his furious opponent at bay. Monreale breathed through his nose like a fighting bull, ready to launch his final attack at any moment. Hunt knew he couldn't kill him in front of his own men, but he couldn't let the fight drag on too long, either. He had to find a way to end the match as soon as possible. And definitively.

Then he saw that behind Monreale stood one of the pommel horses. Hunt took a deep breath and lunged with all his might, stabbing again and again, advancing with his feet as if it were a deadly dance. Monreale was also exhausted. He had no choice but to stop the attacks with his own blade. Hunt screamed for encouragement and kept stabbing over and over again. The tip of his *gladius* reached closer and closer to his opponent's body. If he wasn't careful, he would go through him cleanly.

He continued to attack like a madman until Monreale collided with the pommel heart on his back. Hunt rested his free hand against the mobster's body and pushed him over the top of the sports equipment. Monreale somersaulted in the air and landed spectacularly on the other side. Lucia squealed. Gagliano and his henchmen ran to their boss's aid. Hunt jumped over the pommel horse and threw himself on Monreale, who was on his back on the floor. The *gladius* stopped millimeters from the mafioso's face. The other mobsters drew their pistols and pointed them at the captain.

"Will you yield?" Hunt asked.

The henchmen cocked their weapons loudly.

"It's enough!" Lucia Monreale shouted.

She made her way through the men until he reached the two combatants. She pushed the sword away with her hand and helped his father up. Hunt dropped the *gladius* and raised his hands to the mobsters. Then he looked at Monreale and smiled at him.

"*Ave Imperator, morituri te salutant,*" he said, bowing.

Monreale looked at him with contempt and anger but said nothing. Lucia stood between them.

"The party is over," said the young woman.

Her face was red and streaked with tears.

"Thank you for the splendid evening, my friend," said Hunt, in a restrained tone. "I really enjoyed your... little practice."

14. PUBLIC LIBRARY

He slept until noon. He only woke up when the sun's rays managed to sneak through the edges of the thick curtains and one of them hit him squarely in the face. He sat up slowly and sat for a while on the mattress. His body was sore, and his skin was furrowed with cuts, some more superficial than others. The night before, during the fight with Monreale, adrenaline had kept the pain at bay. He didn't even notice that the gladius' sharp blade had cut his skin on his limbs and torso. In any case, he told himself, the worst part had been taken by the mafioso. He would probably wear the scar on his side for life.

He ordered a succulent, and belated, breakfast of scrambled eggs, coffee, and toast. Then he climbed into the bathtub that he had filled with cold water. His body felt the effect of the low temperature and reacted immediately. A rush of energy ran from head to toe, rekindling him. He forced himself to remain totally submerged for more than five minutes, with only his nose sticking out of the surface to breathe. When he got out of the water, he rubbed his body with the towel until his skin was red. Finally, he dressed in a dark gray suit, a light blue shirt, and a black knit silk tie.

The breakfast was waiting for him on a table by the window. As he watched the city's heavy traffic in the distance, filling its long, wide avenues, he ate a dozen egg-filled toasts and drank several cups of coffee. At some point in the day he would have to report the facts of his violent night to Hyam Noone, but first he wanted to speak to Sir John Connelly. After the attempt on their lives, the head of the department had decided to remain in the consulate. He even suggested to Hunt that he also move to the diplomatic building, but the captain insisted on continuing at the hotel. He felt that from there he would have more freedom of movement, although it was also riskier for his safety.

He looked at the corner of the room where Allison Macgregor had fallen. There was no trace of the shooting. Biltmore personnel had cleaned and repaired the room during the captain's journey to New Mexico. He wondered if the girl would be okay in Montana, or wherever her parents had taken her. Either way, she was safe, far from the clutches of the Monreale clan. This isn't over, Allie, Hunt thought. At least last night

I dealt the bastard a blow. A small cut on the side of the torso, but a blow, after all. Soon there would be another fight, another round, as they said in boxing. And this time the captain would be wearing his gloves.

There was a knock on the door. A bellboy handed him a handwritten note: "This afternoon at three. Public library, main entrance. Connelly." Hunt smiled. Sir John was back in action.

At the scheduled time, he walked to the imposing 120-meter-long Beaux-Arts building, which housed the main headquarters of the New York Public Library. It was located on Fifth Avenue and 42nd Street, just three blocks from his hotel. He ascended the marble staircase, flanked by two stone lions, which led him to a pavilion located under a portico supported by six Corinthian columns. Hunt was surprised by how crowded the place was. Hundreds of people were entering and leaving the building. In the crowd it took him a long time to locate Sir John, who was standing by one of the niches on the side of the portico. Inside the concavity was a statue standing above a water fountain.

Sir John leaned on a cane. For the first time, Hunt noticed that his boss had aged quite a bit since the attack. He was weaker, although he still had a haughty and elegant bearing.

"It seems that your party last night ended badly," commented the head of Department X, with a wry smile.

Hunt looked at his freshly pressed suit. Then he raised an eyebrow.

"It's your face, Peter, not your suit."

Hunt smiled. He had looked in the mirror before leaving the hotel, convinced that he looked respectable. But he knew he couldn't fool his boss. The shadows under his eyes and the sunken cheeks betrayed that he had not rested the night before. In addition, he had some quite visible bruises on one of his temples and neck.

"At least I met an interesting girl," Hunt said.

"And she left you like that? Wow, she must be *very* interesting!"

Hunt shook his head as they entered the building. Sir John led him directly into a small reading room in an inconspicuous corner of the building. The walls were covered with carved wooden panels. There was a table with six chairs in the center of the room. Three green-shaded lamps, arranged on the table, provided the only illumination in the room.

"While you were partying," said Sir John, "I was talking to the president of the American Geographical Society. The new president, I mean."

There was a moment of awkward silence as they both remembered the man who had invited them to New York. Professor Robert Lester, the society's former president, had been murdered in front of them just outside the organization's headquarters in Washington Heights.

"Well, as I was saying," Sir John cleared his throat, "I talked to the president to get access to certain archives that the library has in its American history division. It is a valuable collection related to the history of the Anasazi and their relationship with the Spanish conquistadors."

Upon returning from New Mexico, Hunt had met with his boss on a couple of occasions to continue his inquiries into the medallion. Sir John had managed to collect some books that had taken him to the premises of the British Consulate, but they both knew that they would be insufficient. They needed much more information if they were to know in detail the powers of the medallion and thus be able to stop Monreale.

"This very morning the library staff gathered several volumes and documents and prepared this room for us to work on," Sir John continued. "So, let's get to work."

A young and smiling woman, who said her name was Alice, entered the room and told them that she would bring them all the material they needed. As a couple of administrative assistants dragged a cart full of documents to the reading table, Alice insisted that she was at their beck and call and left, but not before giving them another radiant smile. Hunt wondered if it had been some invitation to another kind of availability, but Sir John immediately cleared his throat and pointed to the books with a dry gesture. Nothing escaped the old professor.

"What exactly are we looking for?" Hunt asked, somewhat disheartened, seeing the huge pile of books that had formed on the table.

"The history of the medallion. According to the documents I have been able to see, there are several mentions of the artifact over the years. Of course, in all the books it is mentioned as lost, since no one related it to the Salamanca expedition."

"Are there also mentions of the powers granted by the medallion?" Hunt asked.

Sir John nodded.

"Several explorers looked for it after Salamanca. Not only conquistadors. There were also Mexicans, European adventurers, and even some settlers from the Wild West."

Sir John read quickly as he took notes in his notebook. Hunt took the books the professor pointed out to him to look for the references Sir John mentioned. Soon the time passed, and it began to get dark. For Hunt, being buried among the volumes was not as exciting as searching for the lost treasure in the field, but he was still absorbed by the stories and tales of other men who, like him, ventured into what was now the state of New Mexico, in search of that mystical medallion that had disappeared at the time of the Conquest.

After the Mexico War of Independence, and

during the brief reign of Agustín I, a Mexican expedition had departed from Albuquerque, entering the territory of the Pueblo Indians in an attempt to discover the mythical city of Cibola. The texts that Hunt read mentioned Francisco de Coronado, but not Rodrigo de Salamanca. Apparently, the mountains had completely swallowed up the second Spanish expedition. As in previous attempts, the Mexican expedition returned empty-handed. However, in the chronicle of the trip, a military officer in the imperial army made a note that caught Hunt's attention.

"Listen to this," he said to Sir John: "'Yesterday we came to one of the Indian villages under a great crag. The village was in ruins and uninhabited, but you could feel the souls lying under the rocks. The horses and laborers retreated in fright, but the sergeant ordered us to approach the place. By the Mother of God, that was purgatory! Then a very old Indian appeared, as if he had come out of the stones. He told us to leave. He did not raise his voice, but the sergeant obeyed him immediately. We moved away from that damned place and swore never to return'."

Sir John took the book with great interest and briefly studied it.

"It is the transcription of the original chronicle in Spanish. How I wish I had that soldier's manuscript!"

"I think it's the town where we were with

Noone and Professor Grant," said Hunt. "Under the cliff at the end of the canyon."

"Yes, it is possible. Let's look for a geographical reference or the name of some expeditionary. That will lead us to other stories."

For another hour they were immersed themselves in books. Hunt was now more anxious about the discovery he had made. He felt a special feeling of having visited the same place as those soldiers. However, he had counted on the puzzle box and the turquoise spheres that marked the way to the lost treasure. He wondered what would have happened if those Mexican explorers had also found the remains of the Salamanca expedition and the mighty medallion... Perhaps Mexico would still be an empire!

This time it was the head of Department X who found another reference to the lost treasure of Cibola:

"There's something interesting here, Peter. Nothing less than in a pulp magazine of adventures of the Old West dating 1890. He held up a very rustic bound booklet for the captain to see. Then he read: "'The group was formed with the most diverse people. There were not only battle-hardened gunmen, but also Indian guides, women, and children. Apparently the story of the treasure had attracted them all from beyond the New Mexico Territory. The people even mentioned a medallion capable of controlling the minds of enemies. The reporters of Santa Fe published...' Wait a minute!"

Sir John rose from his seat and looked out the door. He made some kind of gesture and soon the librarian Alice appeared.

"Are you still here, my dear?" Hunt commented.

Outside it was already dark.

"The library closes at ten o'clock at night," she explained. "Besides, my boss asked me to stay as long as you needed me."

"Just one last request, and we won't bother you anymore," said Sir John. "Among the documents you have about the Anasazi and New Mexico, are there newspapers or photographs?"

"I guess. I'll go check and be right back."

"Poor girl," said the captain. "As compensation, we could invite her to dinner."

"We still have a lot of work ahead of us, Peter. Maybe we'll eat a snack later."

Hunt mumbled something as he pretended to read a thick volume of history. Alice returned a few minutes later with a thick folder full of old newspapers and yellowed photographs. She smiled politely and left.

Sir John unfolded the newspapers and found some copies of *The Santa Fe New Mexican* from the 1890s. While looking for a story about a group of adventurers who had participated in an expedition to native territory, Hunt began to review the photographs. Most were worn out over time, but the images could still be clearly seen. There were portraits of politicians and businessmen, railroad inaugurations and town foundations.

After a lot of searching, he came across a photo of a group of people riding in wagons, about to leave on a trip. It seemed to him that it might be the expeditionary party mentioned in the pulp magazine, because in the image there were several armed men, elegantly dressed women, natives on horseback, and men dressed in suits with notebooks in their hands. Those must have been the reporters who had come to cover the trip. Perhaps one of them had written the story. After staring at the photograph for several minutes, Hunt felt a rush of adrenaline coursing through his body.

"It can't be," he murmured.

"What's the matter?" Sir John looked up from the newspapers.

Hunt handed him the photograph and put a finger on one of the people portrayed.

"Do you know who that woman is?" Sir John asked.

Hunt nodded absently.

"I don't just know. I have seen her up close. It's Moon Goldeneagle."

The discovery produced an electric shock in both researchers. Sir John frantically searched for references to this woman in the various texts at his disposal. Hunt, for his part, could not take his eyes off the image. Although she was dressed in Old West fashion, Moon looked exactly like how he had known her and seen her again the night before. A striking woman in her thirties, with jet black hair and features of untamed native beauty. However, the photograph was thirty-five years old. For her part, Moon had not aged a single day.

"Here are some mentions of a 'mysterious Indian woman' who accompanied the group," said Sir John. "But it says nothing about her origin or the reasons why she was among the party."

"Maybe she was one of the native guides on the expedition," Hunt said.

"It's possible. But neither the magazine nor the newspapers delve into the matter."

"I could take the photograph to Noone so he can try to find out more about the woman," the captain said. "Certainly, he has as much interest as I do in catching her."

Sir John checked the time in his pocket watch.

"Alice must be gone by now. I will leave a note informing her that we borrowed the photograph. First thing tomorrow you go to see your American friend. I think we have an important clue here about the mystery of the treasure."

Early the next day, Hunt headed back to the anti-mafia task force's office in the West Village.

He had the photograph with him. For the first time since his return to New York, he was in good spirits and confident that they could stop the plans of Monreale and his mysterious accomplice. Hunt had no doubt that Moon and the mobster were lovers. That woman knew how to seduce men and use them for her own ends. He even wondered if the whole operation wasn't actually the woman's idea. Perhaps it was Monreale who was the accomplice and not the other way around.

He got out of the taxi in front of the federal building and headed towards the entrance. Before reaching the stairway, a voice called his name. Surprised, he turned around immediately. The old man who had rescued him from the clutches of the woman, in the Sangre de Cristo Mountains, stood there with a serious expression. Hunt didn't know what impressed him the most. Whether to see him there suddenly, dressed in a simple suit and tie, or the thick sunglasses that completely hid his blind eyes.

The old man's face was streaked with wrinkles even deeper than Hunt remembered. Incredibly, he looked older than he had a few weeks ago.

"How did you know it was me?" Hunt asked in a surprised tone.

"I don't need my eyes to see."

"Was you waiting for me?"

The old man nodded with an almost imperceptible gesture.

"Come with me, Captain Hunt."

"Are we not going to enter?"

The old man shook his head. Then he turned and started walking with a sure step. They walked silently down the street that led to the bank of the Hudson River. The old man led Hunt to some trees. There was no one around. Hunt guessed that somehow the old man knew they were safe from prying ears there.

"Soon the witch will unleash her full power," said the old man, in a cold tone that chilled the blood. "Now that she has the medallion, and access to the conquistador's resources, there will be nothing that can stop her."

"The witch? The conquistador? You mean Moon and Monreale, right? Who is that woman?"

Hunt pulled the photograph from his jacket pocket but stopped when he remembered that the old man couldn't see it. However, the old man nodded.

"I think you already know that, captain."

"I only know that she is older than she lookss. And that her powers are linked to the medallion."

"She's an Anasazi witch. She was a healer at first, but then she began worshipping the dark gods and gained all the power for herself. Instead of healing, she killed and destroyed. Her tribe drove her out, but she took revenge on them and eliminated them. It took the power of all the healers united to take away her gifts."

"The witch was banished, but she was still powerful. Before losing her fight, she created the medallion and transferred her mind control spells there. However, being deprived of her abilities, she was never able to manipulate the artifact again. Since then, she can only use others to wield the artifact."

"When did all this happen?" Hunt asked, though he sensed the answer.

"In the time of the white man, more than four hundred years ago."

Hunt felt an invisible force shake him. The old man seemed to read his mind.

"The witch used the power she had left to stay young and beautiful. She knew that in this way the men would do whatever she asked of them."

"She drove Salamanca to Cibola, didn't she?"

"She managed to seduce several conquistadors before him, but that man was more ambitious and ruthless than the others. When the expedition arrived at the village where the witch lived under a hidden identity, she led him to her cabin and there she gave him all the pleasures he desired. Salamanca found the treasure, killed the inhabitants of Cibola, and fled with the gold on the back of his horses. He was supposed to return to the village with the treasure, but instead he immediately returned to his own lands."

"The healers of all the tribes were attentive to the witch's movements. When we learned that the conquistador was fleeing with the treasure, we dispatched our warriors to stop the invaders. After some skirmishes, the final fight took place in one of our villages, under a cliff."

Hunt nodded. He already knew part of the story.

"Salamanca fell under the attack of your warriors. But he wore the medallion, and everything was hidden under the ruins of the village."

"That was our mistake," said the old man, in a sorrowful tone. "We thought the witch would give up her treasure. But over the centuries she has always found ambitious men who are seduced by her promises... and by her body."

Hunt looked down. He, too, knew the pleasures of that fiery body first-hand. How close had he come to succumbing to the charms of that immortal witch? The old man put a hand on his shoulder.

"Don't get upset, captain. It is very difficult for a mere mortal to resist the spell of the dark gods."

"At least I managed to escape alive from the clutches of that woman."

"A fate that few have had. Most of the men who set out to fulfill the witch's destiny lose their lives in the attempt."

"The Mexican military expedition, the Old West group..."

"There are many more, captain. Other parties that disappeared without a trace in the mountains, swept by the wind, swallowed by the rocks."

"But now Monreale seems to have achieved what no one has achieved before."

"The white man is getting more and more ingenious," said the old man. "And more dangerous. The witch realized that she had to come east, to the big city, in search of a more suitable candidate. And she found that foreign criminal, willing to do anything to achieve his goals. Just like her."

"What can we do?"

"We can no longer do anything. The time of the Anasazi is over."

The old man's face was stony, but tears fell from under his sunglasses.

"Now is your chance, captain. The gods have chosen you to face the witch."

"It's an arduous task, wise man." Hunt felt a strong shudder run through his body. "I will gladly assume it."

To Hunt's surprise, the old man shook his head.

"It might as well be your doom, captain. But it is a sacrifice that humanity deserves."

Hunt had never been afraid to face his own death. In the Great War he had known danger up close, and since working for Department X, he had been nearly killed so many times that he had lost count. However, the words and voice tone of that old man left him cold. He felt as if death itself had come to look for him. However, that native healer was right. Death was an acceptable sacrifice if it would stop Moon and Monreale.

"I am willing, wise man. And I think you know that."

For the first time, the old man made a grimace that looked like a smile.

"After four hundred years, I finally have someone to replace me. The gods allowed me to live as long as the witch also lived, but the constant struggles have taken a toll me."

He put a hand under his shirt and took off a medallion that hung around his neck. Hunt found the artifact eerily similar to the one the witch had created.

"A medallion for evil, a medallion for good. Use it wisely, Captain Hunt."

The old man handed the artifact to Hunt. When he let it go, his body shuddered, and it looked like he was going to fall. Hunt held him by one arm.

"Come, wear it on," the old man insisted. "You should carry it with you all the time."

Hunt hung the chain around his neck and held the medallion in his hands. For a few moments he watched it as if hypnotized under the sun's rays. The solitary turquoise in the center of the medallion seemed to glow brightly. After several minutes, he managed to come to his senses.

"It's beautiful," murmured Hunt. "I feel like I..."

He found that the old man was no longer with him. He looked around, but the native sage was nowhere to be seen. Hunt realized that the man had gone to rest in the eternal lands of his people.

The medallion hung heavily around his neck, but it was not a physical weight, but the full force of the powers that the elders had deposited in the artifact. Still, he felt revitalized. He walked at a brisk pace back to the federal building. He found Hyam Noone working alongside his agents in a room full of documents. The Secret Service agent came out to meet him as soon as he saw him.

"Peter, my God! I thought you were hurt, or dead! What happened at the Waldorf? I heard rumors that Monreale had been absent from the party for a long time. When he returned, he looked quite upset. They say there was a fight. From your face I would say it's true."

Noone kept talking. Hunt tried to silence him with a gesture, but the American agent was frantic. Hunt realized that he should have gone to talk to him the day before, but the discoveries they had made with Sir John Connelly had kept him busy all afternoon.

"Listen, Hyam..."

"I think something is going to happen soon, Peter. I have people watching the Monreale headquarters in Bowery and I have been reported that there was a lot of movement in the place."

"Forget about it, Hyam. There is something even more important."

The captain's gaze was so intense that the agent immediately fell silent. His friend looked even more worried than he was.

"What's the matter?"

"It's Moon. It's always been Moon."

"Always? What do you mean?"

"She's behind the whole thing, Hyam. Monreale is just a puppet."

"How do you know?"

Hunt touched his medallion over his shirt. He decided not to reveal to the agent that he was carrying it.

"I can only tell you that I know for sure. Moon is going to unleash her full power on this city with the help of his puppet Monreale."

"My god! How can we stop her, Peter? That woman... well, she is not just any woman."

If you only knew, Hunt thought. Suddenly, he realized what he had to do. He had a destiny to fulfill."

"I am the keeper now, my friend," he said solemnly. "I must stop the witch."

He put a hand on Noone's shoulder to comfort him. However, the agent gaped at him.

Clearly, the captain's words were beyond his comprehension.

15.
MANHATTAN BRIDGE

He stormed into the lobby of the Biltmore Hotel. The events were happening very quickly and the end seemed closer and closer. An open confrontation against Monreale was already a reality. Hyam Noone had decided to unleash the full force of the law against the mafia clan. However, there were several operational and legal aspects to fix before he could act. Mafia networks were widespread in city and state public agencies. Several bureaucratic barriers would have to be broken down and, at the same time, the corrupt officials who were at the service of the mafioso would have to be fought.

Hunt told himself that Moon Goldeneagle's plan was perversely admirable. A powerful mob boss was the best ally she could have had in her four hundred years of searching for the medallion of power. Not only was the man smart and ruthless, but he also had an army of henchmen at his disposal and millions of dollars to fund the operation. A confrontation of the public forces against that clan would be a real war. Hunt feared that the streets would be filled with blood, but there seemed to be no alternative.

He walked through the lobby straight to the elevators, but before he could board one of the cabins, someone grabbed his arm and spun him sharply. He was about to put his hand under his jacket to grab his revolver, but Lucia Monreale's distorted and pale face dissuaded him just in time.

"My God, Lucia! What's the matter?"

"Peter, my father—he's going to do something horrible!"

The young woman trembled from head to toe. Hunt noticed that she was disheveled and without makeup, as if she had hurried out of her house. Or maybe she was even running away from someone.

"You must calm down first, my dear. Come, let's sit down somewhere."

He led her to the hotel's tea room. They sat down at a table in a corner, away from prying eyes. Hunt would have liked to drink a good measure of Glenlivet at that moment. And the young woman could have done with a glass of sherry, but Prohibition was strictly observed in public establishments. And they didn't have time to look for any of those *speakeasies* that seemed to abound in the city. They had to content themselves with two cups of steaming Earl Grey tea.

"Very well, my dear," said Hunt after Lucia had drunk half her cup. "Now tell me what happens."

"My father and that woman—Oh, she's a witch, Peter!"

"I think so," murmured the captain.

"Lately, my father has been acting very strangely. I know it's the influence of that horrible woman. She was away for several days and since her return the matter is getting worse and worse."

"What do you mean by a 'strangely'? Considering the activities your father does, they may not be so 'strange' after all."

The young woman looked at him with a gesture of annoyance.

"I know my father is a mobster, Peter, if you mean that."

He nodded seriously. Tears came to the poor girl's face.

"I'm fed up, Peter. You don't know what it's like! He presents himself as a businessman, organizes these charity events, but at the same time orders all kinds of crimes. When one of his associates disappears, he tells me that he went on a trip, but then adds that he will never come back. I'm not an incredulous child!"

After throwing that string, Lucia burst into tears. Hunt handed her a handkerchief. She wiped away her tears. After a few moments she managed to compose herself.

"I'm afraid my father has gone mad, Peter."

Hunt was sure he was, but he waited patiently for the girl herself to explain it.

"He has a place in the basement, far away from his offices, where he performs some kind of rituals. Something like black magic. The woman taught them to him."

Hunt had been in Monreale's private *kiva*. He nodded without saying anything yet.

"Moon handed him a medallion that he wears all the time." Hunt stiffened at the sound of this. "I thought it was just an amulet, but apparently it's some mystical artifact. I saw my father staring at the medallion, whispering to him. That thing is consuming him, Peter."

"Why did the woman give it to him? Does it have a purpose?"

"They talk about some kind of power. I heard the woman say that now she could reach the whole city with her power."

Hunt stretched out a hand and placed it on the young woman's arm.

"Did she say how she would do it? Reach the entire city?"

"They mentioned some antennas. I think my father's men have been installing them on the buildings in the city."

Involuntarily, Hunt squeezed the girl's arm.

"Please, Lucia. You must tell me all the details you remember."

"My father acquired an electrical repair company a few months ago. He uses it to install those antennas in Manhattan's skyscrapers."

"Does he plan to use those antennas soon?"

She nodded.

"I couldn't take it any longer, and I came at once to see you, Peter. I'm desperate!"

Lucia had stopped the sword fighting in the exercise room the other night. She had then accompanied Hunt to get a taxi, thus preventing his father's men from attacking him by surprise. Before saying goodbye, Hunt had told her that he was staying at the Biltmore and that she should not hesitate to look for him if she needed him. That night he had gained a very valuable ally in his fight against Monreale. His own daughter!

Damn, Hunt thought. Noone should hear this right away.

"Listen, my dear. Are you willing to go to the authorities?"

Lucia looked down. Hunt understood that it was difficult for her to betray her father. He hoped that her sense of duty would prevail in this mental struggle. After a few moments, Lucia looked him in the eye again. Then she nodded solemnly.

"We'll go see a friend," he said. "He is an agent

of the government."

"Will he arrest my father?"

"The government has been investigating him for a long time, Lucia. You said it yourself. He has committed very serious crimes."

Yes, I understand."

They got up to leave. Hunt sensed danger at that moment. His survival instincts always alerted him to the presence of some mortal danger. He looked through the hotel lobby and discovered a couple of men near the entrance who were watching them surreptitiously. However, it was evident that they were waiting for them and that they intended to block the exit if they tried to flee.

"Your father's men may have followed you here."

"What?!"

"They're near the entrance," he whispered. "Don't look at them! We must find another way out."

"I have my car parked outside. I don't usually drive, but I wanted to get here early to warn you of what was going on."

"Good girl! Now the important thing is to get to the car."

They walked away from the lobby in the direction of the restaurant. Hunt recalled that the establishment had its own exit to the street. He mentally prayed that there would be no more mobsters roaming the hotel. As he passed in front of a wall mirror, he saw that the men were following them. He took Lucia's arm and quickened his steps. When they arrived at the restaurant room, a waiter approached them to serve them. Hunt pulled out a wad of bills and placed them in front of his face.

"Do you see those guys over there? I'm afraid my fiancée's father has hired detectives to get rid of me. It would be a great help if you could delay them for a few moments."

The waiter immediately put the bills away. Then he winked at the captain.

"Don't worry, my friend."

As the waiter intercepted the gangsters and urged them to occupy a table with great fanfare, Hunt and Lucia ran. They went out into the street and immediately began to surround the building in search of Lucia's car.

"There it is!" She said.

She pointed to a slender open-top two-seater sports car painted bright yellow. It was a gleaming Marmon Speedster. 'A gift from my father for my last birthday', Lucia explained as they jumped into the car. Hunt took the driver's seat and started the engine immediately. He pressed the accelerator to the full and set off aimlessly. He was only trying to put distance between them and their pursuers.

The streets of midtown Manhattan were filled with motor cars, buses, and streetcars. At all intersections, dozens of passers-by crossed at the same time, stopping the traffic of vehicles. Hunt made several laps down side streets, veering at the last minute, with no clear sense, trying to confuse anyone who might be following them. The small car was responding well, but it couldn't reach a high speed in the heavy traffic.

"Where shall we go?" Lucia asked.

Her eyes were wide open and a rictus of fear on her lips.

"My friend Hyam has his offices in the West Village," said Hunt. "We will be safe there."

He told the girl the location of the place where they were going. She suggested taking Seventh Avenue in the direction of southern Manhattan. He followed her instructions, but before taking the avenue he discovered that their pursuers were following them.

"Are you sure?" Lucia asked, with a shriek.

"There's a Hudson sedan with three guys on board that follows the same route as us. We crossed paths with them just now, but now they are coming after us," he explained. "I managed to spot your father's two thugs. The third party must be the driver. I'll try to lose them," he added.

He turned onto the avenue and floored it. The speedy sports car rocketed through the other cars, which responded with furious honks of their horns. Hunt managed to dodge several cars, but after a few streets he was again immersed in the city's traffic.

"This is impossible!" The captain complained as he tried to make his way through the other vehicles. "This way we will never lose them."

He checked the rearview mirror. The black Hudson was still behind the Marmon, about twenty meters away. Hunt cursed to himself. At the next corner he turned the steering wheel hard to take the side street. Although the traffic there was less dense, the narrow street prevented progress very quickly. The mafiosi's car did not take long to take the same road.

"Damn it! It's not hard to follow a bright yellow car in the middle of these traffic jams," Hunt complained.

"I'm sorry, Peter! I didn't want to involve you in my problems," Lucia whined.

Looking straight ahead, Hunt reached out and stroked her chin.

"Actually, I involved you in mine, my dear."

In the midst of the chase, he explained to the astonished young woman his investigation on the Anasazi treasure and the confrontations he had had with his father to find the medallion. He left out only the most lurid details of his encounter with Moon Goldeneagle at the camp, in the middle of the Sangre de Cristo mountain range.

"Are you a kind of private detective?" She asked after hearing his story.

Hunt shook his head.

"Believe it or not, I work for a museum."

After several random turns, they found themselves in a residential district populated by terraced houses with stairways at the entrances and pleasant apartment buildings. The streets were flanked by well-trimmed plane trees. Lucia explained that it was the Chelsea district.

"Later we could continue down Ninth Avenue to the south," she said. "From there we will arrive at the West Village."

The Hudson sedan gave them no respite. Hunt drove the Marmon as fast as the streets would allow, but he couldn't get the other car to disappear from his rearview mirror.

"I must get rid of those guys before I get to the federal building," Hunt muttered. "I don't want to put them on alert about the Secret Service investigation."

But fate seemed to mock him. Just then, a second car turned a corner ahead and darted straight into the yellow sports car. From a distance, Hunt saw that it was a Ford sedan with three other mobsters on board. Then he realized why he had not been able to give their pursuers a run. All along they had been using two cars, no doubt signaling from one to the other to track down the fugitives. In addition, these men knew the city well and had the advantage over the English. Hunt threw several mental obscenities and cursed his overconfidence.

They were now trapped between the two vehicles. The Ford sedan dove straight into them from the front. One of the men opened the back door, leaned outside, and stood on the running board of the car. Hunt saw that he was holding on to the body with one hand, while in the other he was brandishing a Thompson submachine gun.

"Bloody hell!"

Hunt spun the Marmon sharply in the middle of the street. The burst of the automatic weapon mixed with the screech of the brakes. Several pigeons took flight from nearby trees. Passers-by walking on the sidewalk began to run in terror. Hunt managed to completely change direction and immediately launched himself in the opposite way. A second burst of gunfire swept through the air over the fugitives' heads. Lucia screamed in terror.

The Hudson was now coming towards them. At the last second, Hunt swerved to dodge it. The sports car climbed onto the sidewalk, brushed past a couple of trees, and jumped back onto the road. Hunt managed to regain control and threw the car down the middle of the street, at full speed. In the rearview mirror he saw that both pursuers were making a U-turn to continue the chase.

"We must get out of these narrow and crowded streets," said the captain. Beside him, Lucia was pale and teary-faced. "Come on, my dear! Guide me!"

Lucia was slow to react. She wiped her tears

with the back of her hand and looked around to get her bearings.

"Seventh Avenue is there." She pointed a finger forward. "That's where we can go faster."

Hunt took the route she had indicated. He had gone around so many times that he felt totally lost.

"Are we still heading south?" He asked.

"Now, yes. But then we must turn west to go to the federal building."

The captain shook his head.

"We must get rid of those cars, but we won't make it in the middle of the city," he explained, still turning the steering wheel in his desperate flight. "Your car has greater speed and is more maneuverable, but we will only have those advantages on some highway."

"Then we must get out of Manhattan," she agreed. "Maybe we could try Brooklyn."

"Perfect. Once we lose your father's minions, I'll call my friend Hyam from some pay phone."

At the mention of Monreale, Lucia shrank in her seat and cried again. Hunt put an arm around her shoulder and pulled her to him. For a few minutes they continued in silence, dodging cars and crossing the tram tracks to avoid the slow cars that moved down the middle of the avenue. Lucia had her eyes closed. Hunt thought she had fallen asleep, but suddenly she straightened up and motioned for him to turn left onto Canal Street.

The two mafia cars were racing fast along the small sports car. Hunt gripped the steering wheel so tightly that his knuckles turned white. They had traveled half of Manhattan, and he still couldn't get away from those gangsters. If he didn't leave them behind soon, he would have to face them with gunfire. He knew it would be a suicidal fight. He was only armed with his trusty Webley Mk VI six-shot revolver, while his enemies carried machine guns and pistols.

When they reached Chinatown, the advance became more and more difficult. The street was lined with street vendors and carts with food stopped by the curb. Hundreds of pedestrians walked along the road. The place was an open-air market. Hunt slowed down just enough so as not to run over anyone. He honked his horn furiously to get people to move away. The men who chased him were less subtle. They simply pulled their machine guns out of the windows and fired several bursts into the air. Immediately chaos took over the neighborhood.

Dozens of people were running in all directions. The owners of the carts were trying to save their goods. The women screamed in dozens of Chinese dialects. Hunt zigzagged to avoid the crowd, but there were still too many people on the street. In the end he had to stop the car with a sudden braking. Further back, he felt the other cars also come to a screeching halt, amid the shriek of their brakes. Without hesitation, Hunt drew his revolver and ordered the girl to switch positions.

"When I tell you," he said, "start the car right away."

Without waiting for any answer, he turned and took cover behind the back of the seat. He rested the gun on the edge of the backrest and waited for the mobsters to show up. Four men had got out from both cars and were advancing through the crowd towards the Marmon. Hunt kept his hand steady and waited for a clear line of fire. He could not risk injuring any passerby.

The gangsters pushed people away. Some people rebuked them in their languages, but most were just trying to get to safety. After a moment, Hunt had one of the mobsters in his sights. He fired immediately. The man fell backwards and rolled on the ground. His companions crouched down and immediately raised their weapons.

"Let's go, Lucia!" shouted the captain. "Now!"

The young woman sped up the car in the midst of a burst of shots. The tires skidded on the pavement from the sudden acceleration. The bullets pierced the rear of the bodywork, producing a small metallic symphony. Hunt fired at another of the men, but this time missed. Finally the car clung to the pavement and was thrown off. The sudden movement of the car destabilized Hunt and caused him to lose his shooting position. The mobsters swept the street with bullets once again, but the Marmon was no longer there. Between curses, the guys ran back to their own cars.

A street sign indicated the intersection of Canal Street and Bowery. Hunt realized that they were on the edge of Little Italy, the kingdom of Daniele Monreale. He smiled with a cruel expression. How appropriate it would be to defeat him on his own ground. It was a comforting thought. To do this, he had to first stop the mafiosi who were following him. He peered in the rearview mirror and saw that both cars were getting closer and closer to his.

"What is that?" He asked Lucia.

They were heading towards an imposing Beaux-Arts triumphal arch flanked by two colonnades.

"It's the access to the Manhattan Bridge. On the other side is Brooklyn. There we can lose my father's men."

"All right. As soon as we cross the bridge, I'll take the wheel."

Lucia looked at him with an amused grimace.

"My father gave me the car, Peter, but I chose it."

With studied movements, she shifted gears and launched the sports car like a fireball towards the entrance of the bridge. She dodged several cars with ease and entered the midday traffic. Hunt watched her with fascination. Lucia

Monreale was a box full of surprises.

However, the mobsters who work for her father did not give up easily. A chorus of honking horns told the captain that the chasing cars had also sped toward the bridge. Hunt looked at the steel cables that supported the suspension bridge. They passed in rapid succession in front of his eyes, causing a hypnotic and sedative effect. Maybe that cleared his brain because an idea formed in his mind.

"Slow down and let one of the cars approach," he said to the girl.

She looked at him as if he had gone mad.

"We must get rid of one of them!" he insisted. "Otherwise, they will always have the upper hand!"

After passing through the first suspension tower, Lucia slowed down the Marmon. Immediately the two cars that were chasing them narrowed the distance with their prey. Hunt watched them in the rearview mirror.

"Close the distance with the Hudson," he said to the girl.

The sedan was approaching from the right side of the Marmon.

The barrels of the machine guns were already peeking out of the windows of both cars. Hunt could see that the gangsters were smiling like maniacs. No doubt they believed that they were close to capturing the fugitives. Lucia maneuvered deftly, bringing the rear of the sports car closer to the front of the Hudson. Then Hunt turned in his seat, raised his revolver, which he had ready in his lap, and fired two accurate shots at the driver of the vehicle. The windshield shattered, but Hunt didn't wait to see the outcome of his attempt. The Thompson submachine gun sticking out of the rear left window opened fire immediately.

Hunt clung to his seat to dodge the furious burst that swept the air over the car. Almost immediately he felt the Hudson's impact against the rear of the Marmon.

"Keep it firm!" He shouted to the girl.

The driver of the sedan had died instantly. Hunt's two shots blew out his brains. As he fell forward, the inert body spun the steering wheel uncontrollably. As a result of the proximity to the sports car, both vehicles collided immediately. But Lucia still maintained control of her sports car. Inertia then launched the Hudson in the opposite direction. Launched at full speed, the sedan lurched against the side barrier of the bridge. The impact lifted it up and caused it to hit a pair of suspension cables, which held firm. The Hudson made one last turn in the air, passed between the following cables, and plunged into the void.

Hunt watched in fascination as the car disappeared over the edge of the bridge. He thought he heard the screams of terror of the mafiosi on board, but in an instant the car sank into the river, forty meters below, and there was silence again. One less, he thought relieved.

The Ford sedan was on top of them. Lucia screamed as the car hit them from behind. The Marmon lurched loudly, but the girl managed to control the direction. Hunt leaned out of the seat and risked his final two shots. The windshield shattered, but the captain could not see if he had guessed correctly. A burst of bullets responded from the Ford and then the sedan rammed them again.

"Floor it, Lucia!"

It all happened at the same time. The girl stepped on the accelerator and the Marmon responded immediately. The Ford wasn't as fast, but it was heavier. It managed to hit the sports car from the side just as it began to accelerate. The impact destabilized the Marmon. Its rear wheels lost contact with the pavement. Immediately the car rose into the air and was about to rollover. In an open car, it was a fatal accident. Lucia reacted at the last moment and saved the lives of the two occupants. She turned the steering wheel in the opposite direction and took his feet off the pedals. The wheels brushed the pavement and moved freely on the ground. If she had tried to brake, the car would have spun like a spinning top.

Its own momentum launched the Marmon against the side barrier of the bridge. In a moment of terror, Hunt imagined himself flying as the Hudson had done a few moments before, straight into the icy waters of the East River. But the car only stopped, amid the horrible noise of the twisted irons, and was crushed against the barrier. Hunt's head was spinning. His vision was blurred, and his shoulder was sore, and he had hit the back of the seat. He felt paralyzed all that area of the body. The twinge of pain reached all the way to his back and neck.

"Lucia... are you okay?"

The young woman did not answer. Hunt turned his head with difficulty. Lucia was leaning over the steering wheel, inert. The captain stretched out the arm he could still move and felt the girl's face. She emitted a faint groan. Hunt felt no blood. Maybe it was just a concussion.

"Dear." He felt his own voice as if it came from a faraway place. "We must get out of the car."

He heard speeding footsteps heading toward the wreckage of the car. For a moment he fantasized about the idea that some motorists had stopped to help the victims. But a second later he saw two sinister-looking men leaning over the cabin of the sports car. The broad brims of their hats hid their faces, but Hunt knew they were Monreale's henchmen. Between them they grabbed Lucia by the armpits and pulled her out of the car.

"Damn you!" Hunt muttered.

He tried to struggle with them but found that half of his body was motionless. One of the mobsters hung the girl from his shoulder and walked away with her. The other thug grabbed Hunt tightly and pulled him, but he couldn't lift him up. In the midst of his growing drowsiness, Hunt realized that he was trapped in the wreckage of the Marmon.

"I can't get him free, Vito!" The mafioso shouted at his partner.

Vito was next to the Ford, a few meters away.

"Then kill him, Luca!"

"But the boss said—"

"You can't leave him alive, damn it!" Vito insisted.

The sound of sirens flooded the bridge.

"Hurry up, Luca. The police are coming!"

The mobster named Luca put his hand inside his jacket, but he did not manage to pull out his pistol. The Ford stopped next to him with a screech of the tires.

"I'm getting out of here, Nico!" Vito shouted from the driver's seat.

The wail of sirens was louder and louder. Luca realized that he had to choose between killing the stranger or escaping with his life. He looked at Hunt with a disgruntled expression, but in the end his survival instinct prevailed. He yanked open the door of the Ford and threw himself headlong into the car, which sped away.

Hunt breathed a sigh of relief before

fainting.

16. BRITISH CONSULATE

He opened his eyes and saw Hyam Noone standing above him, watching him with a sly smile. Behind the agent he saw some white walls. He discovered that his body was resting on a soft bed.

"You always manage to get some rest, huh, buddy?" The American joked.

"Where am I?" Hunt asked, though it was obvious.

"At Bellevue Hospital. The police brought you yesterday and..."

"Yesterday?!"

He sat up abruptly on the bed. He felt a little dizzy, but he closed his eyes and in a few moments he felt better. He put a hand with a desperate gesture to his neck, but when he felt the medallion hanging in its place, he calmed down. Then he pulled back the sheets and looked for his clothes.

"Monreale has Lucia, Hyam."

"Isn't it his daughter?"

"Her father's thugs nearly killed her on the bridge. They shot and crashed the car without caring that she was on board with me."

"Tell me about it! What a chase! You drove through half of Manhattan, a shootout in Chinatown, the accident on the bridge..." Noone handed his clothes to the captain. As Hunt dressed, he added, "I think we have enough evidence to go after Monreale. I spoke to a federal judge last night and it is likely that we will get an arrest warrant today."

Noone explained that Hunt would have to testify before the district attorney as a witness. But he was confident that they could delay the hearing for a few days until he felt recovered.

"This matter is going to be over much sooner, Hyam. Lucia told me that her father will be acting very soon."

He told his friend about the plan to install the antennas on the tallest buildings in the city. Noon's jaw dropped. The scope of Monreale's plan exceeded his biggest projections.

"Finish dressing, Peter. I'll go get a phone to call my office. I'll get the boys to investigate this matter."

He returned a few minutes later. Hunt was meeting a doctor who reluctantly discharged him. Noone showed the doctor his badge and informed him that the British citizen was part of a top priority federal investigation. The doctor signed the papers and left as if those men had the plague. Noone laughed. He took Hunt into the parking lot, where a large black sedan with the engine running was waiting.

"Where are we going?"

"I met your boss, Sir John Connelly. He is quite a character."

"He came to visit me?"

"Of course. He spent most of the night in the hospital, organizing everything."

"What do you mean?"

"Your belongings were taken from the Biltmore to the British Consulate. From now on you will stay there and have an armed escort, courtesy of Uncle Sam."

"Armed escort? Come on, Hyam, you know I don't need..."

The agent interrupted him with a gesture.

"It wasn't my idea, mate. Sir John woke up very important people last night. From now on, you and he are official visits of the United States government."

Hunt leaned back in his seat and smiled. Sir John was renowned for his level of contacts and organizational skills. It was likely that his complaints had gone directly to the White House. Daniele Monreale did not suspect it, but he had made a powerful enemy. For the first time in a long time, Hunt was confident that they could thwart the plans of the mobster and his witch. But first they had to do something about Lucia. Would Monreale be so heartless as to hurt his own daughter? Of course, his henchmen didn't care if the girl was hurt, but Hunt consoled himself by the assumption that the clan chief would act differently.

The car dropped them off in front of the British Consulate General, opposite Battery Park. Sir John Connelly immediately went out to meet them with the consul, Sir Harry Armstrong. The diplomat, an enthusiastic middle-aged Irishman, told them that all the consulate's resources were at their service. After escorting them to a first-floor lounge, he left them alone. In a gesture unusual for him, Sir John then gave his investigator a hug.

"I'm glad you've recovered, boy!"

"Thank you very much, Sir John. It was nothing very serious. I am more concerned about what has happened to Lucia Monreale."

"We've got surveillance on the apartment on Lafayette Street and the offices in Bowery," Noone said. "Later I will meet with my men to find out if there is any news of the young woman."

They all sat in comfortable wing chairs.

"In the meantime, there's something I must tell you," said Hunt.

He pulled the medallion from under his shirt and removed it from his neck. Sir John and Noone came to admire the beautiful piece.

"It's very similar to the other medallion," said Sir John. "How did you get it?"

Hunt explained to them the sudden appearance of the old Anasazi man and what he had revealed to him about the witch and her powers. The other two men listened to the story absorbed.

"I'm supposed to face the witch now," Hunt said when he had finished. "This medallion will protect me from the power that Monreale can use with his own artifact."

"Hmmm, dual medallions," said Sir John. "Very interesting. That means that although both artifacts are opposites, they actually complement and depend on each other."

"Like Chinese yin and yang?" Hunt asked.

He had been in Shanghai for some time on behalf of Department X. During his stay he learned a lot about the local customs and beliefs. Sir John nodded.

"Exactly. Do you say that the old man vanished?" Hunt nodded. "So he must also have a dualism with the witch. While she represents evil, the old man represented good. Now he passed that symbolism on to you, Peter."

Noone shuddered.

"Heavy burden, my friend."

Hunt nodded solemnly.

"I still can't believe it, you know?" Noone scratched his chin. "That Moon is more than four hundred years old..."

"Witchcraft is a very common phenomenon in many cultures, Agent Noone," explained the head of Department X. "As well as spells and magic."

"I thought they were more like superstitions."

"The old customs have led to that, without a doubt. What for modern man has a rational or scientific explanation, for ancient peoples was a miracle, or a supernatural event."

"Now I understand why they burned the witches," Noone said.

Sir John shook his head.

"The witchcraft trials in sixteenth-century Europe originated from a religious issue. Christianity at the time regarded witchcraft as heresy and apostasy, but the witch hunt was also related to a theme of propaganda, political persecutions, and personal disputes. The same thing happened here in America during the Salem trials, which occurred in Massachusetts in 1692."

"But were those witches real?"

"Of course not," said Sir John. "Real witches, I mean women who acquire supernatural powers through spells and enchantments, usually live in isolation and require many years of learning to obtain their powers."

"The elder Anasazi told me that Moon was ultimately banished from her tribe," Hunt added. "The healers of the tribe, along with other witches, had to use their own spells to counteract the powers of the woman."

"Moon was probably a practitioner of necromancy," Sir John reasoned. "The kind of witchcraft that used the spirits of the dead to gain spells and thus more power."

"God!" Noone whispered. "Now I really could use a drink."

Sir John cleared his throat.

"Well, remember that we are in a diplomatic compound, protected by British sovereignty."

"I see where you're going," the agent smiled.

"As American law does not apply here, my friend the consul keeps a reserve of his best Scotch whisky. Peter, would you do the favor?"

Following a gesture from the professor, Hunt approached a sideboard from which he extracted a decanter filled with the amber liquor and three crystal glasses. Noone drank his in one gulp.

"Well, this is very good."

"Glenlivet," Hunt remarked after drinking from his glass. "Unmistakable."

"Very well, Sir John," said Noone, after refilling his glass. "I think the time has come to go on a witch hunt, don't you think?"

The three men drank for the success of their enterprise. When they emptied their glasses, Sir John stared at the other two younger men.

"Gentlemen, we must prepare for our final battle."

"Ask me what you need, Sir John," said

Noone. "In the West Village headquarters I have gathered about twenty men heavily armed."

The former history professor smiled benevolently as he shook his head.

"I'm afraid that's not the point, Agent Noone. To defeat the witch, we will have to use her methods. Not ours."

The consulate building had an enclosed backyard in view of the street. Sir John had asked the consul to clear it and forbid all officials to approach it during that night. At midnight, the three men gathered in the middle of the courtyard, where previously the head of Department X had set up a bonfire in the exact center of the space. The full moon shone brightly high in the dark sky, bathing the courtyard in an intense whitish light. Hunt helped his boss light the fire, and then the professor threw dried herbs into the flames. Thick black smoke flooded the courtyard, filling the air with a strong sweet smell.

"I hope I have all the elements for the ritual," said Sir John. He had a thick book in his hands and at his feet he had left bowls with colored pigments. "All right, Peter. Take off your shirt, please."

Hunt stripped from the waist up. The cool night wind made him shiver. The smoke from the herbs was transforming into a thick mist that covered the entire courtyard. The heavy scent penetrated through his nostrils, and he felt it spread quickly through his body. A sense of peace came over him. It felt as if his body was floating, rising from the courtyard into the endless night sky.

He thought he heard Sir John's distant voice, but he did not understand what he was saying. He used a mysterious and harsh language. However, he knew that his words were directed at him. Suddenly, something happened inside him. A sudden, but slight transformation. Suddenly he perfectly understood the meaning of the litany:

"… in our ancestors. You are us, and we are you. The strength and wisdom of the people is within you and wherever you go, we will go with you. The dark forces will not be able to touch you while you are with us. The spirits of good protect the chosen warrior. The gods have appointed you and you must fulfil your duty. The witch will succumb to your power!"

Sir John looked up from the book and looked at Hunt. He hoped to have pronounced the spell correctly, written in the guttural and mysterious language of the Anasazi. He had been practicing for several days, ever since his investigator returned from New Mexico, but he didn't think he would really have to resort to the incantations of the ancient text. He had spent hours studying the English transliteration, practicing the mystical texts, and checking all the elements necessary to complete the ritual.

Hunt stood still on the other side of the fire. His body was bathed in sweat, enveloped in the thick smoke of mystical herbs. In spite of the cloud that covered the courtyard, Sir John saw that the captain's eyes were open, though it was evident that they could see nothing. Hunt was in a deep state of trance, induced by the hallucinogens that the herbs gave off when they were burned.

"Agent Noone, take those bowls." Noone did as he was asked. "You must make these drawings on Peter's torso and face while I continue with the spell."

Sir John showed the agent an image from the book that showed the ritual painting of an Anasazi mystic warrior.

"The result must be identical," said Sir John. "With the same strokes and colors."

Noone stared at the image, memorizing it in his mind. After a few moments he nodded. Then Sir John sang his litany again in the language that only Hunt could understand. Noone stood next to his partner. He plunged the fingers of both hands into two bowls, staining them with paint. Then he began to trace thick marks on the chest of the motionless captain, who seemed oblivious to the presence of his friend. Noone painstakingly recreated the drawings in the image of the book, painting long and thick lines of red, blue, and green colors.

It was as if Hunt wasn't there. His body stood

firm, but he didn't seem to hear or see anything that was going on around him. To Noone's ears, the litany that Sir John sang sounded like squawks, but a twinkle in Hunt's eyes indicated that he did understand the strange message. Noone continued to paint the ritual drawings, but he had to move away from the flames, which were becoming more and more alive. The smoke irritated his eyes and he felt dizzy, but he forced himself to continue spreading those pigments on his partner's torso and face.

At last the drawings were complete. Noone stepped aside and admired his work. The dense, dark fog completely enveloped the captain, but the drawings shone on his body. The moonlight reflected off the drawings through the dense smoke of the campfire. Suddenly, the American agent understood that the colored stripes were increasing in brightness. He looked up and found that the moon was just above the courtyard. Its light was so intense that it almost seemed like daylight.

A strong wind blew and abruptly dissipated the cloud of smoke. Sir John's singing reached its maximum intensity. The medallion hanging from Hunt's neck began to glow. With a swift gesture, the captain took the device and raised it above his head. The turquoise shone for a moment and then the moonlight concentrated on the stone. The whole courtyard was dark, except for the bright white beam that linked the medallion with the distant natural satellite.

For several moments, the turquoise seemed to drain the moonlight, increasing its brightness until it became a small star in the middle of the courtyard. Sir John and Noone had to look away, but Hunt held the medallion aloft, undeterred. Finally, the light accumulated on the small stone burst into a blinding white cloud that expanded throughout the courtyard and then climbed back towards the moon, illuminating the entire sky in its path. A strong gust of wind accompanied the explosion. It made the men's clothes wave and shook their bodies, almost knocking them down.

When the energy wave died down, the courtyard went dark. The fire had been extinguished, and only a few small wisps of smoke emanated from the burnt logs. The air was cold and parched. Hunt was lying on his back on the ground.

"Noone, help me take him to his room," said Sir John.

"Is him ok?"

The head of Department X crouched over his investigator and examined his vital signs.

"He just fainted."

"Look at the medallion, Sir John."

The metal of the artifact looked gleaming, and the turquoise shone with its own light, as if it were a miniature moon.

"We did it," commented the professor. He looked up at the agent and nodded. "The medallion now concentrates the power of the moon. Peter is now ready to face the witch."

Hunt woke up the next morning. He had no memory of what happened during the ritual, but he felt a strange energy that ran through his body as if it were a discharge of electricity. He jumped up, washed up and dressed, and joined his boss in the hall where they had been served breakfast. He devoured several plates of eggs with bacon and drank almost a liter of coffee. Sir John watched him with a mixture of curiosity and surprise.

"Whatever it was, it made me as good as new," Hunt smiled.

His boss had told him everything that had happened in the courtyard during the night. Hunt touched the medallion and felt it vibrate slightly on contact. The turquoise stone shone brightly with its own light. Hunt felt himself burning with desire to go and confront the witch at that very moment.

Hyan Noone arrived at the consulate shortly after. He was accompanied by two stocky men with a weathered appearance. It did not escape Hunt that they were both dressed in black, just like the Secret Service agent. None of them spoke and they just saluted with a bow of their heads.

"These are your bodyguards," Noone said, pointing a finger at them.

"Do they have a name?"

"Not really," laughed the American.

Both men were indistinct, although one of them was taller than the other. Hunt observed them for a moment and decided to call them Phobos and Deimos, after the satellites of the planet Mars. If Monreale had his own 'moon', he would be like the god Ares and would have 'fear' (*phobos*) and 'terror' (*deimos*) on his side.

Noone sat down next to Hunt and lit one of his Luckys.

"I have news for you." Sir John was sitting across the table. "We've been tracking down that electrical repair company that Lucia mentioned. Apparently, its trucks recently visited several skyscrapers to install radio antennas on rooftops. Somehow, Monreale obtained permits from the mayor's office and from the homeowner associations of private buildings."

"Do you have a list of the buildings?" Hunt asked.

Noone nodded. He took out a folded sheet of paper and handed it to his partner. Hunt unfolded it and whistled under his breath. There were more than twenty names and addresses written down. He was already familiar with the map of Manhattan and discovered that the buildings covered most of the central and southern part of the island, where the tallest structures were concentrated.

"When do you think they will put in motion their plan?"

"Tonight. Our watchmen have detected

unusual movements in the Bowery's lair. Something big is cooking in there."

"Perhaps you should attack Monreale's headquarters before he gets moving," Sir John suggested.

Noone shook his head.

"Even if I got a search warrant, I wouldn't be able to prove more than minor offenses." He exhaled the smoke from his cigarette forcefully. "I must catch him red-handed. Something that I can take directly to a federal prosecutor."

The head of Department X nodded.

"You're right, Agent Noone. Sometimes I forget that your legal procedures are different from ours."

Noone looked at both men seriously.

"You are right, Sir John. For this reason, I am thinking of creating a unit that investigates these matters on an ongoing basis. Something like your own Department X. A small division of the Secret Service that deals with the occult and paranormal phenomena."

The two Englishmen watched him with interest.

"I already have a huge file on Monreale's mystical activities. And I have heard of other investigations related to paranormal phenomena that have been filed with different federal agencies. There are certainly a lot of lost files out there full of valuable information."

"If I can bring all these files together, classify

them and analyze them, I think I will be able to convince the government to establish some agency, or a unit, in charge of these matters."

"You'll have to convince them first that this is all real, Agent Noone," said Sir John. "Believe me, it will not be an easy task. Rational people find it difficult to believe in these phenomena, even if they have them right under their noses."

"I suppose you're right," the American reflected. "Maybe I should contact a museum, like you."

"Our Government is fully aware of the existence of the department," confided Sir John. "But in this way it is easier for them to deny any connection with our affairs, in case something goes wrong."

Noone thought about all this for a few moments. Hunt patted him on the back.

"So you'll have your own Department X, huh?"

"Hmm, I prefer a more discreet name. You know, something that doesn't arouse suspicion about the nature of the files that I plan to gather."

"And what will you call them? X-files?"

Noone lit another cigarette. He looked at Hunt with a resigned expression.

"Very funny, Peter. Very funny."

17. WOOLWORTH BUILDING

Armed men ran through the corridors getting their equipment ready. Like Hyam Noone, they wore shirt sleeves or only their waistcoats, over which leather holsters had been hung. Several of them carried machine guns and shotguns, in addition to their handguns. The offices were flooded with tobacco smoke. The venue smelled of sweat and tension. Everyone knew that they wouldn't carry out any ordinary raid that night. This time they would go to war.

Noone looked at the huge map of Manhattan that took up an entire wall of his conference room. He had stuck pins in all the places that corresponded to the buildings where Monreale's electric company had installed the mysterious radio antennas. Half of the island was furrowed with pins.

"Damn, there's a lot of ground to cover!" He complained.

"Doesn't this distribution of the antennas tell you anything?"

Hunt was further back, staring at the map with half-closed eyes. For several minutes he had been trying to look for a pattern on the map, a design that would indicate the distribution of the antennas. He was sure that it could not be something chosen at random. The mind control ritual required several perfectly executed stages. He was sure that the location of these devices had some specific purpose.

"Maybe he chose the tallest buildings in the city," Noone said. "To cover as much field as possible with the transmission of the spell."

"I think so," Hunt agreed. "But this area of Manhattan is full of buildings. Why did he install antennas in some and not in others?"

"A specific distance to some point," Noone ventured. "Or maybe it only had a limited number of antennas."

Hunt shook his head, not taking his eyes off the map.

"Monreal has been preparing his plan for years. And in Moon's case, several centuries. I don't think they leave anything to chance. Nor are they going to limit their operation due to the lack of some element."

Hunt and Noone had arrived at the headquarters of the anti-mafia task force shortly after sunset. They were sure that the execution of Monreale's plan would be that night, but they still did not know where the mafia boss himself would be stationed. Or if he would be accompanied by his witch. There were dozens of people to guard and the enemy's operation covered a large part of the island of Manhattan. The feeling of imminence was unbearable. The agents under Noone's command were prepared and could hardly wait to go into action.

"One minute!" Hunt exclaimed. "Do you have a spool of thread or something similar on hand?"

Noone slowly turned to look at him.

"Thread? But what the heck..."

Hunt's gaze was still fixed on the map. The American agent broke off. After a brief hesitation, he asked:

"Would a skein of wool do? Our secretary is knitting all the time and I think she keeps several skeins on her desk."

Noone returned at once with a skein of red wool which he handed to Hunt. The captain knotted the end of the thread on a pin and then joined it with the next, without cutting it. With the wool he drew a diagram on the map, carrying the thread from one pin to the next, as if it were a curious loom. On each pin he would turn it around to hook the thread and then tighten it until it passed over the next, always trying to form a figure on the map.

After a few moments all the pins were

joined by the thread of the wool. Hunt cut off what was left of the skein and walked away to watch the result from a distance. Noone whistled in surprise. The drawing on the map formed a perfect five-pointed star that seemed to be embroidered between the pins.

"What's there?" Hunt asked.

At the exact center of the star, several threads converged, forming a thick knot in the core of the drawing. Noone approached the map and read the names of the streets that delimited that city block. He knew immediately what was in that lot.

"It's the Woolworth Building. On Broadway, across from City Hall Park."

"Of course!" Hunt exclaimed. "The tallest building in the world!"

A caravan of vehicles headed into Lower Manhattan shortly after. The armed agents were in two army trucks that Noone had obtained thanks to his contacts. He, for his part, was driving a government car that led the march. Hunt sat next to him. The two bodyguards, Phobos and Deimos, were in the back seat. It was already close to midnight and traffic on the streets had decreased considerably. The caravan was advancing at a good speed, but without attracting too much attention.

In the car no one was talking. Noone was focused on driving, while Hunt mentally went over everything he knew about Monreale's medallion and the mind control spell. In the back, the bodyguards checked their pistols in the midst of a concert of metallic clicks. The tall building they were heading for became visible shortly after. The golden pyramid that crowned the tower shone in the moonlight. Hunt felt a rush of adrenaline through his body.

Upon arriving at City Hall Park, Noone turned into a side street and headed toward the opposite side of the park from Broadway. He drove past the City Hall building and stopped the car ahead, next to the New York County Courthouse. He parked by the curb and stuck his arm out of the window to signal the trucks to stand behind his vehicle.

"We'll have to make the final approach on foot," Noone told his teammates. "If there are men stationed in the tower of the building, they will see the vehicles from afar."

"And goodbye to the element of surprise," murmured Hunt.

He drew his revolver and cocked it.

The twenty men of the anti-mafia force gathered in a wooded space located between the town hall and the courthouse. For a few moments, only the clanging sound of the slides of the guns and magazines being checked for the last time could be heard. The men watched their chief with their faces tightly together, barely visible under the brim of their hats. The air was charged with the electricity that caused anxiety.

As Noone prepared to give instructions for the assault, a scream from across the park startled them all.

Hunt and Noone ran through the trees, toward Broadway. A car had stopped on the side of the park. Two men were descending, dragging a woman. She was the one who had screamed. Hunt stopped suddenly and raised his revolver.

"It's Lucia!"

The two thugs took the girl by her arms and lifted her up. Then they crossed the street at a brisk pace. Lucia struggled and screamed again, but her captors ignored her. Noone put his hand on Hunt's revolver and forcibly lowered it.

"If you shoot, you'll alert the entire Monreale contingent."

"Damn it, Hyam! I must get her out of there!"

"We'll do it when we storm the place."

Hunt gave him a withering look.

"Let me try, Hyam. If I don't succeed, you can launch your entire squad."

Noone saw that his partner was determined to attempt the rescue. He already knew him well and he knew that he could not stop him.

"All right." He sighed and tried to smile. "Can you do it without making too much fuss?"

Hunt gave a dry laugh.

"If I don't come back in five minutes... unleash hell!"

He crossed Broadway with a carefree step, trying not to attract the attention of the lookouts who were undoubtedly stationed at the top of the tower. He didn't dare to look up, but he was sure that he was being watched. The huge building rose to a height of two hundred and forty meters. Being so close to its façade, the summit was lost to sight. He reached the opposite sidewalk and pricked up his ears. He thought he heard hurried footsteps on one side of the building. He headed there and turned down the side street. The structure occupied the entire block.

He spotted the two thugs and Lucia about twenty meters ahead. It seemed to him that they had stopped by a service door in the corner of the building. He quickened his pace, holding the revolver to the side of his body. His hat was well pulled on and with the brim down. The men did not notice his presence until he was about five meters away from them. They watched him suspiciously, but they were not uneasy.

"Could you help me?" Hunt asked. He tried to hide his English accent and changed his tone of voice. "I think I'm lost."

"Get out of here!" One of them snapped, making a gesture with his thumb.

"I just need you to show me the subway station more..."

"Get out!"

One of them waved the pistol he was carrying. Hunt stopped.

"Hey, I'm just asking..."

"Peter?"

Damn! Lucia had recognized him. One of the guys was still holding her arm. He turned her around and stuck her face to the girl's.

"Do you know this man?"

The man with the gun approached Hunt. The captain raised his revolver and shot the thug in the middle of the forehead. The bully made a gesture of surprise a second before dying. His limp body fell backwards, but before he touched the ground, Hunt had already turned toward the other man. He stood behind Lucia and used her as a shield. Hunt cursed his cowardice.

"Let her go and I won't kill you!" Hunt exclaimed.

He kept the Webley pointed at the front, but he didn't have a line of fire. Lucia obstructed all his view. The thug was holding the girl firmly with one hand, while trying to open the door with the other behind his back. Hunt heard the jingle of the key hitting the metal lock. Lucia struggled, but her captor threw her arm back and made her moan in pain.

"If you hurt her...," Hunt threatened.

The thug managed to get the key into the lock and opened the door with a loud creak from the hinges. He took a step back, keeping the girl always in front of him, like a human shield. Hunt also advanced. He told himself that if they managed to enter the building he would lose the advantage over the thug. He did not know the interior distribution and did not know how many of Monreale's men could be inside.

Lucia and her captor crossed the threshold with their backs turned. Hunt muttered a curse and wondered if he would be able to shoot. His index finger gently pulled the trigger, but his mind made him hesitate. The interior of the building was dark, and the girl was still struggling to get rid of her captor.

"Help!" The mobster shouted. "I'm Mario!"

Immediately footsteps were heard running inside the building. Monreale's men came to help their comrade. Around the same time, Hunt also heard someone running down the street. He glanced over his shoulder and saw Phobos and Deimos running with their pistols pointed forward. Hunt feared the worst.

"Lucia, to the floor!"

The young woman screamed inconsolably and began to stir in despair. Her captor tried to control her, but it was impossible for him to hold her with one hand. Both fell to the floor. Three gangsters appeared by the doorway and began shooting immediately. Hunt dove headfirst to the ground. Further back, the two bodyguards returned fire. A burst of bullets swarmed on the street. Hunt rolled away from the shooting and fired in turn, but he had lost sight of the mobsters.

"Watch out for the girl!" He warned his own men.

The noise of the gunfire was deafening. The flashes lit the threshold of the door in both directions. Hunt crawled across the ground toward his men. At that moment, Phobos, the taller of the two, was thrown backwards. Deimos roared in fury and shot his way inside. Hunt got up and ran after him. The door led to a large service hall where goods and supplies brought by the suppliers of the building tenants were received. At that hour it was dark and deserted, except for the three bodies that lay bloodied in the middle of the room.

Deimos had fallen by the door. He was sitting with his back against the wall and was also bleeding from several gunshot wounds.

"At least I managed to shoot them down," he murmured as Hunt crouched down beside him.

"And the girl?"

"I think a guy took her there."

With a weak gesture he pointed towards a corridor.

"Help will come soon," Hunt said.

Wished he knew the bodyguard's name, but he couldn't stand there talking to him. He just patted him gently on the shoulder and ran down the hallway.

The interior of the building was very vast and cavernous. Hunt ran through a wide central gallery but saw no sign of the girl. He remembered that the building had a U-shaped base that rose up the first thirty floors. Then the tower continued, for thirty more floors, on the façade facing Broadway. He assumed that Lucia would be taken to the top of the structure, which involved taking an elevator located at the front. He headed there and finally reached the immense central hall.

It was rather a cruciform arcade in which two double-height passages intersected with the vaulted ceiling. Hunt stopped to listen just below the central dome. He thought he heard a noise coming from outside, but everything inside was silent. Probably Lucia and her captor were already on their way to the tower. He looked for the elevators and mentally prayed that Noone had already begun his assault on the building.

* * *

Hyam Noone had given the order. The shooting on the side street of the building cut through the silent night with a roar. The agent had no choice but to send Hunt's two bodyguards behind the captain. He knew immediately that they had been ambushed or had simply had to shoot at Monreale's henchmen. As the bursts thundered around the structure, on the other side of the street Noone turned to his men, who remained sheltered under the trees of the park. With a gesture he motioned for them to move forward.

"Gentlemen, remember our orders," he

lectured them for a second before launching into the attack. "Eliminate Monreale and the woman who's his partner. Only capture alive if there is no risk in arrest. Rescue Captain Hunt and his friend Lucia alive. The young woman is a valuable witness."

The men nodded or cleared their throats to show they understood. Noone raised his pistol and cocked it.

"Watch out for snipers in the tower. Go! Go! Go!"

The detachment of the anti-mafia force crossed Broadway on the run. They had almost reached the opposite sidewalk when the first shots fell from the height. None of the men wasted time trying to return fire. They simply quickened their paces and sought cover next to the wall of the same building. The snipers, who were on the roofs of the base's two wings, managed to kill three law enforcement officers. Their deadly rifles were fired accurately at targets advancing directly toward them.

The men fell in the middle of the street, fulminated. The shooters reloaded their guns, but at over a hundred meters high, it was impossible to shoot straight down at a right angle. In addition to the distance, the architectural ornaments of the façade interrupted the firing line of the men on the roofs. They abandoned their precision rifles and ran to meet their comrades to find a place to defend their position.

Noone was carrying a Colt 1911 pistol. He fired toward the entrance of the building as he ran across the street. The front doors were ajar. From inside, the gangsters returned fire. One of the federal agents stopped in the middle of the street, dropped one knee on the ground, and raised his rifle. With absolute coolness, he fired accurately at the defenders of the entrance, shooting down two of them before throwing himself away to avoid the enemy bursts.

The members of the squad regrouped next to the façade of the building. The noise of the shooting had ceased, but the air was heavy with the smell of gunpowder. In the distance it could be heard the wail of police car sirens. Noone had sent a courtesy notice to the local police department, but his real message was clear: stay away. This is a federal operation. Noone knew that the police were full of mob informants, so he had sent the message just minutes before leaving for the Woolworth Building.

"You two," he called a couple of agents. "Throw a smoke bomb in there."

One of the two officers advanced to the door with his body pressed against the wall. He inserted his pistol through the crack in the door and fired blindly inside. His partner ran forward, activated the heavy smoke bomb, and threw it inside with all his might. Soon there was silence in the hall. The officers stationed in the street waited with their weapons raised, their muscles tense and their faces twitching, until smoke began to escape through the cracks in the doors.

"Open those doors!" Noone ordered.

The main entrance was under a huge arch three stories high. In the center was a revolving door, which remained locked. On either side were normal doors that were ajar. The agents approached the latter in two groups and pushed them by force to make their way. The lobby was shrouded in smoke from the bomb. Noone ordered his men to wait a few moments for the air outside to clear the stale environment. He looked up and wondered what Peter Hunt was up to. Hold on, my friend, he thought. We're coming for you.

* * *

The elevator car stopped on the 53rd floor, the last habitable level of the building. Hunt cautiously stepped out into the hallway; his revolver raised. Noises came from the upper levels. He ran through the corridors in a hurry, trying to find his way around. Finally he found a door, at the end of a corridor, marked with an arrow pointing diagonally upwards. He crossed it and ran up a narrow staircase that ascended on the interior of the building walls.

The crown of the building was pyramidal in shape and its floors were intended for the maintenance of the elevators and the systems of the structure. Even though it was night, the interior was quite hot. Hunt climbed two levels and reached the end of the crown. From there began another pyramid, smaller, with an octagonal base and topped by a spire. The noise grew clearer, and Hunt realized that it was several voices talking agitatedly.

"Peter!"

Lucia was further down the narrow corridor. Her captor was pulling her with difficulty. Obviously the guy was already exhausted from having to drag the girl from the ground floor. Hunt stretched out her arm with the Webley in front, but this time it was Lucia who managed to break free. The gangster decided to forget about her and confront the captain. That was his mistake. Without hesitation, Hunt shot him between the eyebrows. The man stumbled while still trying to pull his gun from under his jacket. Then he fell to his knees and finally fell face down to the ground.

"Peter!" Lucia exclaimed again.

Hunt looked at her smiling.

"Do not be afraid. Everything..."

He felt, more than he saw, a shadow appearing next to him. He realized too late that Lucia had tried to warn him of this sudden appearance. Before he could move, Hunt felt a small, hard object pressed against the base of his neck.

"Say hello to my little friend," whispered Moon Goldeneagle.

With the derringer tightly pressed against his neck, the woman ordered Hunt to continue forward.

"You don't want to miss the show," said the witch.

On the 58th floor was an outdoor observation deck that surrounded the entire golden pyramid. The view of the city was spectacular. Hundreds of buildings were silhouetted against the darkness, bathed in moonlight shining high in the clear sky. Millions of lights lit in offices, apartments, and in the streets twinkled as if they formed a small galaxy in the sky. Despite his situation, Hunt could not help but marvel at the sight. It really was like being on top of the world.

Daniele Monreale was standing next to a radio antenna that his lieutenant Franco Gagliano was adjusting according to his boss's instructions. There was a strong breeze that shook the thin steel rods. Gagliano tightened the wires that held the antenna and finally it stopped moving. Moon handed Hunt's Webley Mk VI to the mobster. He examined it for a moment and then put it under his jacket. Only then did he turn to face his enemy. He wore the Anasazi medallion hung over his jacket. The artifact glowed ominously.

"Good evening, Captain Hunt. I was waiting

for you."

"I was also looking forward to this meeting." Hunt took a step forward and put a hand to his ear. "Do you hear that noise, Monreale? Federal agents are storming the building. The whole place is surrounded."

"I have men stationed on all the floors, captain. Agent Noone will have to overcome quite a few barriers before he gets here."

"You're trapped, Monreale!"

The mobster shook his head.

"I just need my men to delay your friends, Hunt."

"They'll get through anyway," Hunt insisted.

"By then, it will be too late," Monreale said. "Come on, Hunt, your front-row seat is reserved."

He gestured to Gagliano. The lieutenant pointed his pistol at Hunt. Moon pushed the derringer aside and put it back in her clothes. Lucia stood next to the captain. She was pale and trembling. Hunt snugly reached for her hand and squeezed it. Monreale approached the girl and looked at her with a cold gaze.

"My daughter, you will have to learn to choose your friends." Then he raised both arms and let out a devilish laugh. "Let's begin!"

The captives were left in the care of Gagliano, who kept them at bay with his weapon. Monreale and Moon stood next to the railing that delimited the observation platform, below the radio antenna. The witch began to chant a spell in the ancient Anasazi language. Immediately, the medallion hanging from the mafioso's neck intensified its brilliance. Hunt remembered the ritual Sir John had practiced on him in the consulate courtyard. He understood that both ceremonies had the same function. Now it was the witch who intended to attract the power of the moon to Monreale.

"Oh, Peter, I'm afraid!" Lucia exclaimed. "My father has gone mad!"

"He'll not get away with it," he muttered.

Moon was performing the ritual passes with her arms and legs. She seemed to perform a silent dance in front of Monreale, who was merely holding the medallion aloft. The enchantment increased in intensity. The witch's harsh, dry voice rose above the platform and seemed to flood the air around the building. Moon sang her chant faster and faster, and her spins around the mobster made her a blurred figure. Wisps of smoke emanated from her clothes, as if she had been transformed into a human bonfire.

Then Hunt realized that this was true. That witch was no longer human. She was kept alive only by her necromancy and by the blood of the hundreds, or perhaps thousands, of men and women she had killed in her four hundred years of life. Four centuries driven by her wild desire to recover the medallion and obtain its impure power. As the witch's ritual reached a paroxysm, Hunt felt his own life energy renewed, as if it were an antidote to the diabolical spectacle unfolding before his eyes.

A beam of light descended from the moon directly to Monreale's medallion. Lucia uttered an exclamation of horror, which was drowned out by the witch's ecstatic howl. For a moment, Monreale was plunged into a stream of blinding white light. Then the medallion drained all the cloud of light, until the turquoise in the center shone like a small sun.

Then it was Monreale who uttered some ritual words and, at the same time, grasped the base of the antenna with both hands. A discharge of whitish energy ascended the rods, cracked like lightning on the observation deck, and then projected itself in a vibrant, sonorous discharge across the sky. Lucia and Gagliano looked away, but Hunt watched open-mouthed as the volley spread across the city. The rooftops of several buildings glowed in the distance as their own antennas picked up the discharge like lightning rods.

From each repeater antenna, another discharge spread which, together with the main discharge, formed a network of white rays that illuminated the night. The air vibrated strongly and gave off an intense smell of sulfur. The energy of the medallion spread swiftly across the sky and covered the entire view wherever one looked. For a moment, it seemed as if night had turned to day. The sky was shining, clearly illuminating all the buildings, skyscrapers, streets, and parks of Manhattan. Hunt couldn't stop looking at the horizon. Monreale had succeeded. He had cast his spell on the entire city.

Finally, the light went out and the night regained its darkness. The lights of the city were still on, but there was something different in the atmosphere. It took Hunt a while to notice, but then he discovered that the whole city was in an unnatural silence. It was as if he had suddenly gone deaf, but he knew that was not what it was about. The island of Manhattan had fallen under Monreale's influence and had simply stopped. Completely.

Hunt glanced blankly at Lucia and found that the young woman was motionless and staring. A sense of horror ran through her body. Then he discovered that Gagliano was also under the mental control of his boss. The lieutenant was looking at the horizon without really seeing anything. He had also lowered his gun unconsciously. Only Hunt had escaped the witch's spell thanks to his own medallion. He thanked the elder Ansazi and told himself that he would fulfill his mission.

The time had come to act.

18. TOP OF THE WORLD

Hunt threw himself like a panther on Monreale. Only five meters separated him from his prey. His arms, stretched out and with his hands hooked, were his only weapons. He aimed directly at his enemy's neck, ready to squeeze and never let go, even in spite of his own life. The fraction of a second he spent in the air, thrown like an arrow, seemed like an eternity. He saw the mobster standing by the railing, staring at the skyline with ecstatic expression, knowing that he had the entire city under his control. Monreale had not even noticed his attacker. The impact would be deadly...

Moon Goldeneagle roared and leaped like a wild beast, intercepting Hunt in midair. Her alarm instincts had four hundred years of training. Hunt felt the two bodies collide and drift off target. He rolled across the floor with the woman on top of him. Before she fell, she already had him by the wrists and was turning and showing her teeth like a lioness. Hunt tried to shake her off, but the witch had unleashed all her ancestral strength.

Monreale watched them as they struggled on the floor. He didn't seem to be angry, but rather had a surprised expression on his face.

"This man should be under my control!" He cried. "What happened, Moon?"

She didn't answer him. She was trying to scratch Hunt, who in turn intended to place her under him to crush her with his own body.

"Stop, Hunt! Obey!"

Monreale was increasingly concerned about the failure of his spell on the captain. He had millions of people under his mind control at the time, located kilometers away. How could a single man have escaped him, who was standing beside him? The mobster took the medallion with both hands and held it forward to the captain.

"I order you to obey me!" He shouted frantically.

"Help me, you fool!" Moon muttered.

Hunt was managing to impose his greatest strength. In a hand-to-hand fight, the witch was nothing more than a woman of delicate build. The captain managed to roll with her and stood on top of her. He forced the woman down and kept her close to the floor. She threw bites and scratches at him, but this time it was he who grabbed her by the wrists.

Still struggling with the witch, Hunt glanced sideways at Lucia and Gagliano. Both were motionless and with their eyes lost, under the dominion of Monreale. Soon the mobster would realize that he could order his lieutenant to attack Hunt. He, for his part, needed the girl's help. He carried all his weight against Moon and with one hand rummaged through the witch's clothes. After a few agonizing seconds, he felt the derringer with his fingertips. He clutched the small weapon and pressed the barrels against the woman's body.

"Waste... time," she whispered.

Hunt pulled the trigger, and there was a slight detonation. Moon laughed like crazy. Then the captain realized that the witch was immune to deadly attacks. The surprise distracted him, and she took the opportunity to push him to the side. Hunt wasted no time in continuing to fight with the witch. He jumped up, ran towards Gagliano, and fired the remaining three shots of the derringer in the chest. The lieutenant came to his senses for a moment. He put his hands to the wound and stepped back in his agony. He crashed backwards into the railing. His body swayed for an instant on the edge and then fell into the void, with a terrifying cry of terror.

But Hunt had already forgotten about the gangster. With a quick gesture, he removed his own medallion from his neck and immediately hung it on Lucia.

"Wake up," he said in a firm tone.

The young woman blinked several times and looked at Hunt in surprise.

"Peter? What has happened..."

"I must stop your father," he interrupted her. "You deal with Moon."

The witch was rising from the floor. Lucia saw her and smiled.

"It will be a pleasure!"

Monreale had observed with a gesture of amazement the whole scene that occurred on the platform. He was so focused on his mind control spell that he had forgotten what was happening in front of his very eyes. In a matter of moments, luck was turning against him. Franco Gagliano had died without being able to help him and his own daughter had turned against him. He watched her fight Moon and for a moment couldn't decide who she wanted to win. Then he saw Hunt coming towards him and had to mind his own business.

He instinctively raised his medallion to the captain. He couldn't convince himself that his power didn't work with that man. He focused his thoughts on his attacker and mentally ordered him to stop. To his amazement, he saw that Hunt wavered in his attack. The captain himself was surprised by his reaction. He had felt a voice in his mind giving him orders in a peremptory tone. Then he remembered that he was no longer wearing his protective medallion. However, he still felt in his body the energy that the ritual practiced by Sir John had given him. He cleared his mind and threw himself at Monreale.

The voice assaulted him again, but he managed to get around it and forced himself to continue. Suddenly, he found himself struggling with the mobster. The two were entwined in a furious hold. Hunt fumbled his hands for his enemy's medallion, the voice continuing to pierce his brain. His strength diminished every moment and he felt that the pressure of his arms was loosening. Monreale was struggling, but more than his physical strength, he was focused on using his mind control. Hunt realized that he would soon fall under his influence.

Then his fingers touched the familiar outline of his Webley Mk VI revolver. He remembered that Moon had given it to Monreale after taking it away. With his last ounce of will, he clenched his fist around the butt of the gun.

'Get away from me!' commanded the mobster's mental voice.

With no energy to resist, Hunt let go of Monreale and took several steps back. Far away, he heard a female voice calling him insistently. Why was that voice so familiar to him? But then he stopped hearing it and his mind was flooded by Monreale's voice. What was it that it was saying?

'Throw yourself over the railing'. 'Obey,

captain. Throw yourself over the railing'.

Hunt went to the edge of the platform to carry out the order. He grabbed the railing with one hand, but he couldn't grasp it with the other because he had something on it. For a moment he looked at the revolver with a blank eye, not knowing how he had gotten there. The female voice burst back into his brain.

"Wake up, Peter. Dammit!"

Without knowing it, Lucia Monreale was using the power of the other medallion. The medallion of good. Somehow, it was still tied to Hunt. For a moment, reason returned to his mind, and he remembered why he was carrying his revolver in his hand. He turned to the mobster, who was staring at him with the medallion raised towards him. The medallion of evil. There was the key, his tired brain told him. He stretched out his arm and aimed at the medallion. He only had one chance. He took a breath and cleared his mind. Then he fired. The medallion was shattered. Monreale was thrown backwards. The mind control was suddenly erased.

Hunt turned to look for the girl. He saw her roll on the ground, fighting Moon. Lucia did not stop shouting:

"Wake up, Peter, damn it!"

The women were struggling at the other end of the platform.

"Lucia, listen to me!" he shouted in turn. "Use

the medallion!"

The ancient Anasazi artifact hung around the girl's neck, halfway between her and the witch. Lucia realized that Moon avoided touching it at all costs. In a desperate gesture, Lucia let go of the woman and grasped the medallion with both hands. She then leaned her entire body against the witch and pressed the artifact to her chest. The effect was horrifying. Moon gave a terrifying shriek that spread through the air. Her body began to convulse, and her clothes gave off smoke. Terrified, Lucia turned away from her.

The true identity of the witch was abruptly revealed. Her skin peeled and her body shrank. Her beauty and youth vanished in spasms and shrill shrieks. Old age and decadence took hold of her. Her face withered and wrinkled until it was full of sores. The bones of the hands were exposed and in the end all the skin fell apart, leaving a skull with deep empty sockets exposed. The smoke enveloped what was left of the body, which stopped shaking. Finally, only a twisted and mummified skeleton lay on the floor.

Lucia ran to hug Hunt. They stood there for a few moments, catching their breath and comforting each other. Hunt was happy to feel the young woman's soft, warm body pressed against his. But there was also something else that relieved him. The city had recovered its usual rhythm. From the street, two hundred and forty meters below, came the noise of night traffic, a few honks, and the wail of police sirens.

"The spell was undone. We did it, Lucia."

"And my father?"

"I think he was hit by the bullet that destroyed the medallion."

They turned to the other end of the platform. Hunt discovered the shattered remains of the medallion, but there was no trace of Monreale. The captain cursed under his breath.

"Peter, what's that?"

Hunt turned and followed Lucia's gaze. On the other side of the building, partially obstructed by the pyramid and the spire of the tower, a huge white sphere could be seen floating up to the building. Hunt realized, with his jaw dropped, that a hot air balloon was streaking across the night sky at the height of the building's top level. When he managed to recover from the surprise, he threw himself into the pyramid. The staircase that connected to the lower floors ended in a small circular vestibule located in the center of the pyramid. The observation deck surrounded the entire exterior of the pyramid and there were two entrances on both sides of the vestibule.

Monreale had come out the other side and was gesturing his arms to the balloon crew. A rope ladder hung from the basket, where two men controlled the aircraft. Monreale looked over his shoulder and saw Hunt running toward him. The balloon was almost on top of the pyramid. The mobster climbed on the railing of the platform, gained momentum by bending his knees, and threw himself towards the ladder that passed several meters above the void.

For a second, Hunt thought Monreale wouldn't make it. But he managed to stretch out a hand and grabbed the last rung of the ladder. Then he grabbed the rope with his other hand and swayed away in the air, hanging more than two hundred meters high. Hunt had to admit that it was an impressive maneuver. Then Monreale managed to assert himself with his body and began the ascent up the ladder. Hunt cast a curse. He wasn't going to let the man escape, even though he couldn't use his evil powers anymore.

He pointed his revolver at the balloon. Lucia arrived next to him.

"I'm sorry, my dear, but I must stop him."

The girl's eyes filled with tears.

"Do it. He is no longer my father."

Hunt had read several reports on the operation of hot air balloons. During the Great War, Britain had used them extensively in the European theater to detect enemy troop movements and direct artillery fire. For that reason, he knew that the cloth bag was filled with hydrogen, a highly flammable gas, which was generated in a burner placed on the basket. With his arm fully extended, he used the sight of the revolver and aimed at the device.

The balloon depended on the wind to move, allowing itself to be carried by the currents at a greater or lesser height. For this reason, one of the crew members opened the gas valve for the aircraft to ascend and take advantage of the wind to move away from the building. A small flame appeared above the burner. It was all Hunt needed. He fired several times at the slowly receding balloon. In the distance, he could hear Monreale giving terrified instructions to the crew. His third shot hit the burner.

The explosion lit up the night. The noise of the gas exploding released a shock wave that heated the air around the consuming aircraft. Hunt felt a warm breeze pass over the building's pyramid. The cloth bag warped and went up in flames. Several of the cables that held the basket burned and left it hanging on one side only. One of the men fell into the void with a shuddering scream. Hunt didn't know if it was Monreale, but it didn't matter. A second explosion consumed all that was left of the balloon and sent a fireball flying to the ground.

Hunt buried Lucia's face in his chest so that she wouldn't even look. Then he took her in his arms and carried her to the stairs. Several federal agents, led by Hyam Noone, burst into the lobby.

"Hell, Peter, that was close," Noone said. "For several minutes I felt... empty."

"Monreale managed to cast his spell. For a

moment, he had all of Manhattan under his control."

Noone opened his eyes in surprise, but then laughed.

"Don't tell the mayor. He'll want to know how Monreale did it."

Hunt laughed too. He was finally relieved.

"I'm afraid my report will be quite long, Hyam. What happened up here was... *intense*."

"Don't worry, Peter. There will be time for reports. Now worry about the girl."

Hunt nodded. He took Lucia by the hand and led her downstairs.

* * *

Hunt awoke from a restless sleep. He was sweaty and disoriented. He glanced around the room and remembered that he was now staying in the bridal suite at the Biltmore Hotel. It was a nice gift from Uncle Sam.

"Peter, what's going on?"

Lucia Monreale stretched out a hand towards him, half asleep. Hunt patted the back of her hand.

"It was just a bad dream. Keep sleeping, my dear."

She woke up completely. She sat up on the bed and clung to him.

"Do you still have those dreams? It's all over, my dear."

A week had passed since the events on the rooftop of the Woolworth Building. The Bureau of Investigation had conducted several raids to take down the Monreale clan. The American Geographical Society was in charge of investigating the whole matter related to the rituals and artifacts of the Anasazi. The hot air balloon explosion was attributed to an electric shock that ignited the hydrogen. The press never learned of the involvement of British Captain Peter Hunt or about the existence of a Department X in the British Museum.

However, Hunt was having some strange dreams in which he saw himself in the desert, surrounded by Native Americans who practiced rituals to ward off the witch and curse her fateful medallion. He wondered if those visions were soon going away. Or sometime. He got out of bed and washed up and got dressed.

"Where are you going?" Lucia asked.

"I'll meet Sir John in the café downstairs. Tomorrow he returns to England, and we must finalize some details."

"You won't go with him, will you?"

"Of course not, my dear. I earned a well-deserved vacation." He walked over to the bed and kissed her passionately on the lips. "Tonight we're going to dinner somewhere nice."

"Then I'll get ready while you're with your boss."

She jumped out of bed and ran naked to

the bathroom. Hunt forced himself to go to his appointment.

Sir John Connelly was waiting for him at a quiet table in the corner. Always cautious, thought the captain.

"The Government of the United States has closed the Monreale case," explained the head of Department X. "That never officially existed, by the way."

"I guess Hyam must be very busy tying up all the loose ends."

"It seems so," agreed Sir John. "I haven't heard from him for several days."

"Hmmm, neither do I. Silencing the balloon crash must not have been easy," Hunt said. "By the way, did you know how the hell that aircraft got to the tower?"

Sir John nodded.

"Monreale had arranged for the balloon to pick him up in the pyramid after the ritual. He intended to fly over the city to observe the success of the spell, but eventually used it to escape."

Hunt looked at his boss. The scope of the mafioso's operation did not cease to amaze him.

"We must thank the Anasazi elder," said Hunt. "Without his help, we wouldn't have been able to defeat the witch."

They drank their cups of coffee in silence for a few moments, pondering how close the mobster had come to dominating the entire island of Manhattan and its inhabitants. Sir John caught the meditative gaze of his investigator.

"Do you still have those dreams, Peter? In which you fight Moon in the past?"

Hunt nodded.

"I was doing research at AGS headquarters," Sir John explained. "I believe that the medallion given to you by the old man created a mystical bond with the ancient Anasazi people. It was the only possible way for you to resist the power of the other artifact."

The captain reached into his pocket and took out the medallion that the old man had given him.

"Then it's time for this to return to its rightful owners."

"I will see to it that the Society gives it to the inhabitants of that village in the mountains," said Sir John, putting away the medallion. "If they manage to find them."

Hunt smiled.

"They will let themselves be seen if necessary."

Sir John rose to go. Hunt escorted him to the hotel lobby.

"Well, Peter, don't be long before you get back to London. We have a lot of work ahead of us."

"I promise it will only be a few weeks."

"I imagine that Miss Monreale is worth them. Give her my regards, Peter."

"See you soon at the Museum, Sir John. Have

a good trip!"

In the afternoon, Lucia and Hunt came down from the suite in full dress to go to dinner. The girl looked radiant in her silk dress. Hunt wore his freshly ironed dinner jacket. The doorman called them a taxi. Upon boarding, the captain gave an address to the West Village. As they set off, Lucia looked at him with a questioning gesture.

"I thought we would go to dinner..."

"Indeed. But there's something I need to do first. It will be just a small detour."

The hired car dropped them off in front of the federal building. Hunt asked Lucia to wait for him on the sidewalk and he went to the headquarters of the anti-mafia force. With a growing sense of anxiety, though not surprise, Hunt arrived at the offices occupied by the squad led by Hyam Noone. The facilities were empty. There were only a few pieces of furniture left, so anonymous that it was impossible to deduce from them who had occupied those rooms. Or if someone had really been there recently.

Hunt didn't bother to walk around the entire venue. Somehow, he already knew what he was going to find. Or, rather, that he would not find anything. He went outside and asked Lucia to accompany him to the post office on the next block.

"What's the matter, Peter? Why did we come to this place?"

"On a hunch, I suppose."

At the post office he entered a telephone booth and asked to speak to the operator.

"Get me the local Secret Service office, please."

He heard the peal of lines and pegs. The operator returned in a few moments.

"Sorry, sir. The Secret Service has no office in New York. I can connect you to headquarters in Washington if you wish."

"All right."

He deposited the coins into the slot for the amount of the long-distance call. Then he waited patiently to be communicated. The Secret Service receptionist took the call. Her voice sounded muffled.

"Good afternoon. I want to speak to Special Agent Hyam Noone, please."

"One minute. Stay on line."

A couple of minutes passed before he heard a voice again. It was the same woman.

"I'm sorry, there's no agent with that name."

"Are you sure?" This time, he spelled out his friend's name.

"We have no one with that name, sir. No one."

Hunt hung up the phone and stayed in the booth for a moment. By spelling out the name for the operator, he had discovered the deception. Hyam Noone: *I am no one.* The special agent did not exist. Whoever that man had been, he was not called that. Hunt stepped out of the booth and realized that Noone, or whatever his name was, had most likely not even been a Secret Service agent. His sudden presence at the treasure site, his high-level contacts in the government, the formation of his private squadron, suggested another kind of organization. Something much more secret.

Yes, it was obvious. Noone himself had hinted at it to Hunt and Sir John that night at the consulate. He didn't plan to create that paranormal affairs office... The unit already existed! No doubt the United States Government had been collecting and studying these X-files for quite some time. Noone had misled them all. Hunt felt betrayed, but at the same time he told himself that he should have sensed it. He shook his head and went to meet Lucia. He was sure that his path would soon cross paths with the man in black again.

"You had me worried, Peter," the girl said as he took her arm. "Are you ok?"

"Yes. Now, yes. I'm just saying goodbye to an old friend."

"Noone?"

"No, no one."

She raised an eyebrow in question, but it was he who asked:

"Ready for dinner?"

"I'm starving, Peter Hunt."

"Me too. Do you know that place, Cotton

Club?"

"In Harlem? I've always wanted to go, but my father never allowed me to. He told me it was too sordid for me."

They looked at each other for a second and laughed. Hunt hugged her and held up a hand toward the street.

"Taxi!"

THE END

Printed in Great Britain
by Amazon